ROMAN RESCUE

MICHELLE GILLIAM

Cover Art by
Jonathan Laing

WBD

This book is a work of fiction. The names, characters, places and incidents are either the product of the author's imagination or have been used fictitiously and not to be construed as real. Any resemblance to actual persons, living or dead, events or locales is entirely coincidental.

ALL RIGHTS RESERVED. This book contains material protected under International and Federal Copyright Laws and Treaties. Any unauthorized reprint or use of this material is prohibited. No part of this book may be reproduced or transmitted in any form or by any means, electronic or mechanical, including photocopying, recording, or by any information storage and retrieval system without express written permission from the author / publisher.

Copyright © 2016 by Michelle Gilliam

Thank you for buying an authorized edition of this book and for complying with Copyright laws by not reproducing, scanning, or distributing any part of it in any form without permission from the author. You are supporting writers everywhere to continue to enlighten, entertain, and imbue the imaginations of everyone, everywhere.

Library of Congress Cataloging-in-Publication Data
Gilliam, Michelle
Roman Rescue/Michelle Gilliam
ISBN-13: 978-0692695296

Dedication

To my family, some who have passed on the gift of storytelling, and those who had to put up with the rest of us. To my sons, they already know, never give up on your dreams. I love you so much.

Chapter 1
Roman Tongues

When I walked into FCO, Fiumicino *(Leonardo da Vinci Aeroporto)* from the landing tarp, I squared my shoulders and tried not to look like I'd never done this before. Italian words filled the monitors with flights to European cities: *Parigi, Madrid,* and *Francoforte* as accents blared overhead. My carry-on luggage rolled behind me as I followed the English words in white and Italian words in orange past the baggage claim (*ritiro bagagli*) and all the way to the exit (*uscita*).

I tried to phone my brother, but a message barked through the speaker to say my phone was out of service. Now, what? I'd left so fast, I forgot to get international service on my phone.

I hunted for a pay phone. Using gestures instead of my butchered Italian, a uniformed woman behind a counter directed me to the closest phone after selling me a calling card. I navigated the endless numbers I had to dial before I heard my brother on the other end. For the third time today, I questioned again why on earth was I in Italy. I could still feel the airplane's turbulence in my stomach as I waited for my brother's voice.

"Hey, Paul, what's up?"

"Maggie? You're in Italy?"

"How did you know …?" My voice trailed off as I wondered why I ask stupid questions.

"You're calling from a Roman number. Maggie, I can't believe you did it. Shit. I told you not to come."

"Don't be mad. It'll be okay. I'm taking a taxi and will be at Pinar in half an hour. Could you let me in? Well, if it's still cool with your friends."

He sighed so deep I could almost feel it through the phone. "I'll meet you there."

"Thanks. See you soon."

I raced through the crowd with purpose, finding the word *Tranporti*. I walked toward the words *Il Taxi* without hesitation, almost running, as if escaping. I opened the back door of an empty white car as a scruff-faced man took my suitcase.

"San Lorenzo," I said.

He nodded. *"Va bene."* His eyes cut through the rear view mirror at me.

I tried not to judge every scowl-faced man with suspicion, but being alone, I realized Fear had made the trip with me. Of course he would. He had been there since my parent's divorce, protecting me. Since I was a little girl, I could sense him, but after my dad met my step-mom, I could see him. He kept me safe from my stepmom's rage, my dad's co-dependence, and my mom's stupor.

I collapsed into the seat of the exhaust-filled taxi as it began to move, relieved to breathe fresh air through the open windows. The cabbie took the scribbled address Paul had given me from his less-than-sober night in Texas. I hoped his best friend, Luke, and wife, Kayla liked surprises.

I closed my eyes and thought of how all this had started with one phone call from my mom. I hadn't talked to her in five months, and that conversation was shorter than three puffs on a cigarette. She wanted me to come to Texas, dangling Paul's trip home to the States like chocolate to a girl with PMS. I loved my brother, and since my father's death, he was everything to me. She knew I wouldn't say no.

The trip to Dallas to meet her new husband proved to be awkward. It was Paul who surprised me, though. My strong, independent Marine brother needed his baby sister? I couldn't resist.

I assured him I could help, but being in Rome revealed my doubt. How was I going to convince an Italian girl I'd never met to let Paul be a part of their unborn child's life? Was it even Paul's? I knew I had promised more than I should, but Paul's negative attitude wasn't something I could ignore.

I stared out the window. Green palmettos and palm trees manicured the area. If not for the foreign writings on buildings and street signs, I would have thought the plane had taken me to the wrong place. It felt like South Carolina. Home. Where I grew up, where I lived when Mom and Dad were married, and where I had just finished my first year of college.

The green fields stretched out on both sides of the highway to the horizon. Tall poles lined the road, not with lights but flags. I only recognized the Italian red, green, and white one. We entered Rome and buildings came into view, some old brick versions and some newer with green windows, but no skyscrapers. By my map, we wouldn't be entering the heart of Rome. I didn't know what I'd expected, but spread out and tropical wasn't it.

The taxi stopped. "San Lorenzo," the driver called out. "Forty-five," he said in English.

I handed him my credit card and double-checked the receipt he gave me. It confirmed forty-five euros, not dollars.

On the fifth floor of the apartment building, waiting for Paul, while sitting on my suitcase, I reached up to the conch pearl around my neck. With a deep breath, lifting it to my lips, I felt the weight of it, holding all the things my father had said to me. It reminded me I was strong. It told me I could do this.

Maybe thirty minutes later, Paul came off the elevator with a long face. His skinny frame stood lean, and his ears protruded more from a new haircut.

"Hey, big brother." I cocked my head to the side and gave him my pouty smile to deter his anger.

Paul laughed in disbelief. "You *are* here. Actually here."

I stood and hugged him. "Yep."

He squeezed me hard, and by his smile, I knew I'd done the right thing.

"I haven't asked Luke or Kayla. I guess it'll be okay," Paul said while unlocking the door. "They're both working. I'll make a call and give them a heads-up."

"Thanks. I mean it. Thanks for not being mad at me." I rolled my luggage in and set my bag on the couch.

"Mad at you? No. But, happy with you? Hell no." Paul stayed by the door. "You just came over here? Does Mom know?"

"No." I held up two fingers from each hand in air quotes. "And you aren't going to tell her either," using his same words back to him from the night in Texas when he told me about Eleana's pregnancy.

"Funny. That's a nice one. You just left without telling anyone?"

"Shawn knows. I told him before he got on the plane back to Columbia."

Paul nodded.

"Right after we broke up."

"Why did you bring the guy all the way to Texas to meet your mom and then break up with him? He's a nice guy."

"It's a long story. But, more than anything, I want to help you with

Eleana."

"I'm not sure you can. She won't even see me. We'll talk about it later. Right now, I've got to get to work. I'll be back when I get off."

We hugged goodbye.

It infuriated me that she wouldn't see him. Who did she think she was? Get pregnant by a Marine and then walk away with his genetic property? I looked toward the window and took a deep sigh.

I looked around the apartment, deciding to be optimistic. Somewhere inside my doubt, deeper down, I believed I could help.

I became familiar with the bright apartment of white walls and honey wood floors. Royal blue couches and curtains framed the room. Glass tables balanced the floating staircase in the center of the apartment. Wire-basket desk drawers and open bookshelves made it a modern space in an old building. I loved it. I walked over to the butcher-block kitchen table and peered out the window, taking in a deep breath at the sight of the sun coming through and hitting the stainless steel pots. Fuchsia bougainvillea climbed the buildings. Palm trees and a swing set in a park of groomed grass made it resemble Miami. My eyes sifted the familiarity and newness. I'm supposed to be here. I knew it in the air and the rhythm of everything around me.

Beyond the park, taller pink and red buildings created a backdrop. I had an incredible urge to go for a walk and explore this beautiful city. Sleeping all morning on the plane had filled me with excitement and energy to blow off. I left my luggage with a scribbled note and set off with the key Paul gave me.

People walked by, staring. There weren't many blondes. It wasn't like being dropped into Mexico City, but there were stares just the same. The dark-haired and dark-eyed Italians dressed like magazine models. Where were they headed? My faded jeans and tennis shoes stood out worse than my hair. I would have to dress up more in Italy—maybe even buy some of the pretty little sandals everyone wore with their flowing sundresses.

After a block, I heard bells striking eight o'clock. The sun dipped behind the roofs, throwing off orange rays. Kayla worked the night shift as a nursing assistant, and Luke worked at the embassy with Paul, so I settled in to be alone during my first night in Italy. I went in search of some good Italian food. I browsed through windows, noticing the streets were lined with shops selling antique art and vintage clothing next to cozy *cafés*.

I stopped into a vintage record store and browsed the 45 vinyl records and found Elvis. I scrolled through the titles "Hound Dog" and "All

Shook Up," but I pulled "Love Me Tender" out of the divider. I could imagine the deep voice of my father singing it. So animated, so compassionate. He would sing it to me with a wooden-spoon microphone. Then, without fail, a faster rock song would play afterward, and he would fly into "Burning Love," singing it to my step-mom, complete with Elvis gyrations and air strumming an invisible guitar.

I strolled further down until I found a pizza place and dove in for a slice of basil, mozzarella, and sausage. I ordered a Coke, but it came at room temperature, so I changed it to water instead. But, pizza and water weren't the right combinations. Maybe I tasted the tomatoes more, or the sauce's bright red color made it look too eerie. Again, I blamed it on Fear whispering warnings of stares from unsmiling eyes. Wasn't Rome the city of romance? Then why did I see figures in the shadows, taxi drivers with guns, and blood in the pizza sauce?

On the way home, I tried to ignore the shadowed alleys and drivers staring me down as they passed by. I double-checked that my debit card hadn't fallen out of my bra. It was still there, safe from thieves.

The night air, fruity and moist, smelled unlike the air back home. I walked, taking deep breaths with my nose to the sky. Going through the park, a breeze whipped by, causing me to imagine the world before cars, a time when the Roman statues were real. I could see it. I could see me in it, wearing a long tunic. What did Dr. Francisco call it in English class? A *stola*, yes. I would look good in a *stola*, gold chains strapped around me. I imagined the horse dung in the streets and stopped romanticizing. I wouldn't call it pessimism but realism. Life had taught me not to believe in the wonderful, magical, or romantic. Not that I hadn't tried.

I pulled the key out of my bra and entered the apartment. I glanced around for a television and spotted the floating stairs. At the top of the stairs was Kayla's and Luke's bedroom, tidy and simple with a triple-tier shelving of masculine books: *Shooter*, *Abraham Lincoln*, and various spy novels. I also found a TV. I smiled and threw myself into a chair after emptying the clothes from it.

That is where Luke found me, asleep in his bedroom chair. His wide shoulders and his body blocked out the light. It alarmed me. Only a dark sketch of him stood there, looking down at me.

"According to this note, you must be Maggie."

"Please, tell me your name is Luke, so I won't have to kill you," I managed to get out while stretching my arms and rubbing my eyes, barely awake—barely thinking—but not afraid.

"Yep, you're Maggie. I've heard of your quipped tongue."

I sighed. "Great, my reputation has preceded me all the way to Italy. At nineteen, I'm not sure that's a good thing."

"Nineteen, just a baby."

That riled me. When I should have asked to stay on his couch, I couldn't. I stood. "I'm not a baby." I squinted at his dark silhouette and tried to look him straight in the eyes. I stood on my tippy-toes, but his eyes were still inches away, taller and higher, out of my reach. "Well, damn, are you six-four, or what?"

"Maybe six-three," he said with pride.

I composed myself after a thick swallow. "Must be hard to be that tall."

"Sometimes." His insecurity showed. His voice wavered or his shoulders dropped; it was so subtle and so quick. I don't know, I could just tell.

I took the clothes from the bed and put them back on the chair.

"You don't have to mess with that."

"I moved them; I'll return them. What time is it?"

"Twelve-thirty."

I took a deep breath, walked over to the top of the stairs, and looked back. That's when I noticed Luke's face: soft reddish-tan complexion and pool-water blue eyes. I paused, wordless for too long. "Paul said he'd be here in the morning."

"Yeah, that's what he told me, too. I got the impression he didn't know you were coming."

"Not exactly. We talked about it but didn't follow through with all the details." I descended the stairs and ended up in the kitchen.

Luke followed me down. "And yet, here you are. Pretty sharp for a teenager."

I swallowed my pride and kept my thoughts to myself about his digs at my age. "Do you mind if I stay here tonight until I can talk to Paul in the morning?"

"Not at all. Maggie, you're more than welcome to stay here your whole visit. The hotels can get expensive and that place Paul calls home—"

"Yeah, I've heard. Rather nasty."

He snapped his eyes closed and shook his head. "You have no idea."

"Thanks. I appreciate the offer. Check with Kayla first. I don't want to be a bur—"

"Never. I mean … you could never be a burden. She'll love it."

"You don't know me yet. You might change your mind."

A huge smile covered his face, almost breaking into a laugh. "Yeah, you're right. I might."

I stifled a nervous laugh. A suppressed smile emerged instead.

He turned toward the sink and hid a yawn.

I turned away, burning his face in my mind. "Thinking of crashing myself. Sheets down here?"

"I'll get them for you."

I followed Luke, looking him up and down. It annoyed me that his shirt clung to his chest and at times fell flat against ridges in his abdomen. His politeness irritated me—or the way his smile dangled from his mouth, or the light that reflected in his eye. I didn't know. Maybe I missed Shawn. Maybe I missed him so much that I projected him onto everyone I met. I tried to imagine Luke as a brother and behave like a sister.

He handed me sheets and a light blanket.

"Thanks." I grabbed them and turned to convert the couch into a bed.

He threw me a pillow from five feet away. "Get some sleep. Sun comes pretty early around here. It'll feel like midnight."

"Okay. Thanks, Luke—for letting me crash."

"Anything for my boy. He's family, so you are, too."

I smiled. They were a lot closer than I knew.

I fell asleep fast and didn't stir until I heard the lock jiggle and then open. I rolled over with my back to Kayla. I did not want to meet her yet. I imagined her crawling into bed next to Luke. It might be hard to stay here. Taking my mind off Luke, I thought of Shawn.

Where would he be if he were here right now? He would want us to have our privacy. He would insist on being close to me and would sleep on the shag rug, so he could reach up and hold my hand. None of that would happen now. He lay in his own bed in Columbia, South Carolina, wondering why I broke up with him. But, he wouldn't think too long about it. He would dive into his internship and work long hours to forget me. He had always been good at blocking pain from his life. In the past, he walked away and never looked back. I would be no different. He wasn't the kind of guy who had to know why. The complete opposite, I dove into pain while looking back and always wondered why.

After another forty-five minutes, I heard the coffee drip. My body or my brain had decided I'd had enough sleep, and this bright apartment demanded I get up and live. I stretched, relaxing my tensed shoulders. I sat up to find Luke's bare back and a pair of long pajama pants tied loose, hanging low around his waist. Being from Orlando, his skin must have basted in the sun all his life. How could a blond be so tan? He turned around, and I dropped my eyes.

"You drink coffee yet?" Luke asked. His word *yet* hung like a bar I had to grow tall enough to reach.

Chapter 2
Tell Me More

"I'm in college. We live by it." I sat up and went to the kitchen to pour a cup.

"Good. There's cereal in that cabinet, too."

"Coffee is enough, thanks."

He walked over to the computer in a cubby that separated the kitchen from the dining room. His eyes were puffy and he squinted more today. I left the kitchen to give him privacy and sat on the couch. I stretched my fingers around the warm hand-painted cup and watched him in my peripheral vision.

"What's on your agenda today?" I asked.

"Paul texted. He's already on his way."

"Oh ... yeah. My phone isn't working. I guess I better look into it."

Luke laughed. "Do you have an international package?"

"No." How did he do it so well? Reduce me down to a teenager who knew nothing. I knew plenty, more than most my age.

"Well, there you have it."

Paul walked in as I folded the sheets from my couch bed. His disposition had softened since the night before, and he had fewer face creases.

"Hey, Luke," Paul said while he gave me a hug. "So, Sis. Why don't you call Mom and let her know you're here?"

"You've got to be kidding me."

Luke piped in from the computer, "She's full of surprises."

"Then we can tell her the good news." I held my hands in a cradle and pretended to rock a baby to add to my sarcasm. "I think she's busy enough figuring out how to get me to move back to Dallas and be a 'happy' little family with her new husband, Mark."

"He seemed like a nice enough guy," Paul said.

"He did. It's just too late. I'm grown, and it's too hard to block the vodka memories, ya know?"

"She was depressed for a lot of reasons, Maggie. She's been sober a year, and you still won't let it go?"

"Why is it the son lets it go too soon? Have you even talked to her about it?"

"I don't have to."

"Well, that's where we're different, Paul."

"Be careful. What excuse will you have left if you get that chance?"

Distracted, noticing Luke, who had just heard every word, I whispered, "This is no place to be having this conversation."

"Sorry, Maggie. Luke knows *almost* everything about me," Paul said.

"Hey, what are you holding back?" Luke asked Paul.

I turned to look over at Luke sitting at the computer with his chair facing us.

I switched the subject. "I'm here. So how can I help?"

"Help?" Luke asked.

"I'm going to talk to Eleana, make sure she knows Paul *will* be involved."

"Oh, yeah, that'll work." Luke rolled his eyes.

"Whatever," Paul said. "You're here. It can't hurt, one girl to another. Maybe she'll see I have a family, and there are more people who are involved in her decisions."

"When do I meet Eleana?" I asked.

"How on earth did you get the money to get here?" Paul asked, ignoring my question.

"With a little help from Mom, who was quite generous. First, there was a payoff to make the trip to Texas in the first place, I think, to cover what my summer job usually would. Then, she added a bonus for my birthday."

"Yeah, but she isn't going to like how you spent it," Paul said.

Luke leaned forward, staring me down like a parent, hanging on our every word. "So she'll meet with you?" I asked, trying again.

"Well, sort of. I told her we needed to talk, one last time. Maybe if you came—"

"Does she know I'll be there?"

"No. She wouldn't come if she knew."

"Wow. Maybe you need to fill me in on her."

Luke clicked the mouse and closed a window on the computer. "Oh, I can fill you in." He stood and walked toward us. When Luke approached and his face engaged, it made me want to hear every word he had to say. I sat to focus on his words.

"Well, sure. Luke might be impartial in giving you some perspective on Eleana."

"She's a lying bitch who cares only for herself."

"She's not all that. He's just looking out for me."

"Maggie, Paul can't see it. From the moment he met her in a pub one night, he disappeared and left us all there, not knowing what happened until the next day. They were together every day he had off, and the moment she ended up pregnant, she dumped him. That's a bitch in my book. I even heard from a bartender she's dating her ex-boyfriend. What a sweetheart."

"She said she isn't. So we don't know if that's true," Paul said.

"Paul, this is odd. What's her reason for breaking up?"

"She didn't want my pity. It was weird, like the pregnancy broke us up. Maybe it's someone else's and that's why she dumped me." Paul sat in the blue chair.

"Then why'd she tell you it's yours?" I asked.

"I don't know." Paul stared at the floor.

"When are we supposed to meet her?"

"Today at one-thirty, down the street at Ferraza."

"Okay, sounds good. Showers?"

"Just the one upstairs off our bedroom," Luke said.

I cleaned up first and then had some small talk with Paul about his job while Luke showered. When Luke came down the stairs, he suggested we go sightseeing while Kayla rested.

Once down the street from the park, I smelled fresh flowers and coffee. Graffiti covered the buildings we passed. Suffering airbrushed characters trying to tell the world something? I stared. I *wanted* to get it.

Paul and Luke walked ahead of me, glancing back every so often. They both had so much presence here. Luke stood out the most among the streets, his height, his blond hair, and even his muscles. Most Italians were less than six feet and not addicted to the gym.

After a few blocks, we came to a hole in the wall, big enough for a restaurant. In a small space of narrow pathways around clustered tables, the boys marched their way to sit down. They wove with little grace, and disrupted the empty chairs on the way there. A lady came over and stopped them, addressing them with Italian to sit closer to the front. Not able to interpret but understanding her ninety-percent nonverbal, I laughed.

The three of us talked strategy over *fettuccine*. Paul wanted us to proceed by asking for mercy, and Luke wanted us to "bust her ass." Entertained by the two opposite views, I laughed at their extremes to lighten the tension. But then, I asked what Kayla thought about all of this.

"She's a Southern girl who aims to please everyone, so when she sees conflict she can't fix, she avoids it," Luke said.

"What? She just doesn't talk about it?"

"Well, no. It just isn't the main point in her life. When we talk about it, she starts cleaning."

I squinted, picturing Luke's description. It was inconceivable. "Does that bother you?"

I surprised him. He looked at me as if I was nuts for a second. "Why in the hell would that bother me? Kayla can clean whenever she wants to."

I hit a chord, but he could sure be an ass. "Okay, then I can consider Kayla to be out of this plan of ours?"

"I think we made that clear," Luke said.

"Dude, lighten up. She's just trying to understand," Paul said.

"What do you think your sister can even accomplish here anyway?" Luke asked.

"Listen, I'm the first to tell you, I'm not thrilled with her being here." Paul eyed me for a second. "Sorry, Sis. But Luke, just like Maggie doesn't understand everything here yet, you don't know her. She's good at reading people, what they think and feel. She can talk to them, and for some strange reason, they tell her the truth. They tell her their secrets. We all know this can't turn into a legal battle. I don't have the money, and I wouldn't win in this country anyway."

I took a sip of water to hide being moved by my brother's words, but I knew this ability of mine he described didn't apply to men. I thought of Shawn and how unreadable his silence was to me. I interpreted every smile and touch into something more. My discomfort with Paul's compliment became obvious to Luke, and his attitude softened toward me. He almost looked afraid of me all of a sudden. Little did he know, he was safe.

"Well, let's get on with it then, utilizing all our secret weapons." Luke had a slight grin in his eyes.

After full strategy talks, agreeing on who would say what, I asked to borrow Paul's phone. We still had fifteen minutes to kill before we met with Eleana. I excused myself and walked outside for some privacy. Shawn picked up on his end, sounding dry and distant. My upbeat mood changed.

"Thanks for letting me know you're safe." His sarcasm wasn't funny.

"My phone doesn't work over here."

"How convenient."

"Really? You're going to do that?" Why couldn't boys just talk, spit out what they were thinking? Silence filled the distance between us. "Not much to say?" Only Shawn's breathing could be heard. "Well, I won't keep you then. I just wanted you to know I was here safe and sound."

"Thanks." He volunteered nothing. Conversation with Shawn had been difficult in person. Now, it was painful. I pushed him to get mad at me. Somehow, it made it easier to get over him if I knew he didn't want to talk to me.

"Maybe we'll talk about us when you get back," Shawn said.

"I'm not holding my breath. Some walls will never talk." I left no hope. How could I when I felt none? Our goodbye sounded final.

Paul came outside and approached me. "You ready? The café is down there."

I looked over at Luke, approaching. "Let's do this."

I buried my frustrations with Shawn.

We arrived at Café One before Eleana and ordered some lattés.

At one-thirty, we were sipping coffee, eyeing the *bomboloni*, Italian donuts.

At one forty-five, half our lattés were gone, and the other half room temperature with crumbs left on a plate.

At two, our faces were long. No one could say it.

Luke broke the mood of the people-watching Americans. "Well, that's just bullshit."

"Apparently, I need to know where she lives." My anger boiled over for multiple reasons.

"Now, Sis, we need to stay on her good side."

"Oh, we will."

Paul eyed me when my verbiage didn't match my snarling lips. We paid the bill and resumed a huddle outside the café door.

"Lead the way." Luke pointed down the sidewalk.

"Actually, I was thinking I'd go alone," I said.

"That's not a good idea. Just come back, and I'll get hold of her and set this up again," Paul said.

I wanted to find her for myself. I wanted to figure this out. A baby's face with American-Italian genes formed in my mind. I loved children. I couldn't let this happen to our family.

I made the excuse that I wanted to explore. *"Campo di' fiori*, a one-stop shopping area is only a few blocks away."

"I've got to get back," Paul said.

Get back to what? I didn't ask.

"You know, roaming these streets alone is not a good idea," Luke said.

I wanted to see all the beautiful art drawn on the buildings, the shops, street flowers, people on mopeds and motorcycles. I couldn't get enough. I wanted to walk every single street.

"It would be better if you took someone with you, Sis." They both followed in my direction.

"Wow," I squatted down next to a building and stared at a black and white sketch on the wall of a man squatting, mirroring my very position. He wore a 1920s suit and hat. Their street art could be in a museum. Maybe I could come back here and intern after I finished my art degree.

"By the way, that over-the-shoulder satchel is a good idea and all, but when the gypsies steal, you'll never feel a thing," Luke pointed out.

"Tell her about Kayla."

I stood to listen to their story, still glancing over at the detailed strokes that made the man on the wall appear so real.

"Had it tucked into her jacket this past winter. They stole her card and a hundred euros. I recommend no cash. Keep the check card–"

"Here, good enough?" I pulled out my check card from inside my bra.

Luke's eyebrows rose.

"Full of surprises, you said?" Paul said to Luke.

"I guess you're not as dumb as you look," Luke said.

"Hey," I protested, but the guys just laughed. I let it go. Those assumptions of a stupid blonde with no common sense were exactly what I had to fight in high school. Luke's first impression of me didn't faze me. "Show us where she lives, then you can run off," I told Paul.

We walked a few blocks over, and Paul showed us Eleana's place. We could see her pink-grapefruit apartment building sporting a string of clothes, towels, and a Winnie the Pooh hung up by his ears and drying on a line. Paul pointed to the second story, the third window from the left.

"Do you have a picture of her?"

"No, she has all of them. We only dated for two months, and I don't own a camera, except on my phone. Wait—she sent me one in an email once. Hold on." Paul stood, clicking away on his phone.

"Not exactly the nice part of town," Luke said.

"No, I guess not. Luke, do you know who her ex-boyfriend is?"

"No, but I can find out. Tonight we'll go out. Over here, little sis, you can drink," Luke said.

"Nah, I don't do much of that anymore."

"Everyone drinks." Luke squinted at me. "You have something against relaxing? You do strike me as the uptight type."

"I'm not a type, I promise you that."

"Right. All teenagers say that. I'll have you figured out by the end of the night."

"Do you make it your personal business to 'figure' people out?" I walked closer to him.

He raised an eyebrow. "College girl not had psychology yet? Men compartmentalize."

I cocked my head to the side. "I've had psychology, sociology, and abnormal psych, and I'm starting to think you fall into the latter."

Luke belly laughed. He turned around to scan the people walking on the street. "Just look for auburn hair."

"Sure, just pull aside all redheads and ask them their name." It sounded ridiculous.

My sarcasm hit him like a water balloon. "Now that would be hilarious."

I turned away and perused the streets myself. A redhead in Italy, how many could there be?

"I got it." Paul showed me his phone. A picture of almond brown eyes, big red lips, and pale skin stared back with a smile. Her hair was colored auburn, but her roots were dark along with her eyebrows. Men never knew these things—real from fake. I looked around at the faces on the street again. A black-haired girl with red streaks dressed in all black bent down to pick up a lighter, her hand shaking with an unlit cigarette. A natural, light-redhead girl, probably Irish, wore a headband and a forest green backpack. But, long auburn hair resembling Emma Stone was nowhere around.

"Okay. I got it. I'm going to just walk around and sightsee, hang out, and see what happens. You two can go back."

"I'll hang with you. I need to pick up a few things anyway," Luke said.

"That's a great idea. Thanks, Luke. Okay ..." Paul walked away after a glance at his watch.

"But—"

"I'll see you back at the flat," Paul yelled from across the street.

"That wasn't necessary. I was alone down here last night."

"Not this part of town, you weren't. Not at night. I would've never met you," Luke said.

"Ha, ha, funny. No need to be melodramatic."

"You might be good with people and reading them, but I'm good at danger, security. Let me do what I do best. Then you can do your thing."

I shook my head, realizing it would be no use to argue with him. He wouldn't leave. I didn't mind, deep down. Someone to talk to or bounce ideas off could help.

The streets were closed to autos and filled with beautiful Italian things. I bought a yellow sundress that draped off the shoulders and a leather purse with detailed stitching. We even bought bread, steak, and vegetables for dinner, fresh from the outdoor marketplace. Luke complimented the sundress and offered help with the food choices. He carried all the bags, and everywhere we went, he trailed behind me, watching. I felt safe with Luke. When I lingered too long, he never complained. The tension between us dissolved. Despite looking for Eleana, we were both relaxed.

He taught me to get store clerks to write down the amount owed to *see* the numbers, since their accents and names for numbers could cause discrepancies, usually in their favor. We always ended agreements over a purchase with an "Okay?"—the universal language of the world and known in fifty countries worldwide. I made the last part up, but I bet it's something like that.

Despite Luke's suggestion that a redheaded Italian would stand out, it proved a common color. The hair color industry had made its way to Italy a long time ago, and this country strutted red hair as much as its red flowers.

By five, we decided to take the food back to the flat and call it a day. When we arrived, Kayla welcomed me with beaming joy.

"Hi, it's so good to meet you," Kayla said in a high-pitched voice, grabbing me for a hug. Luke put the groceries down in the kitchen, his ear turned our way, listening for every inflection. With occasional glimpses in our direction, I could tell he watched every movement and exchange.

"Nice to meet you, too. I have heard so many great things about you."

"Oh, you're just so beautiful. Your skin is so clear. You'll have to tell me all your girl secrets later." She looked over her shoulder, then back at me. "When we're alone and all."

I smiled and agreed. She bounced around like a teenager full of enthusiasm and innocence. When she finally settled, I noticed a beautiful rock on her left hand. Wow. They were married? But Luke didn't wear one. Her voice snapped me out of my thoughts.

"You came here to help with this Eleana thing, but she didn't show up at lunch? Have any luck finding her?"

"No."

"But we got dinner," Luke added from the kitchen, confirming my suspicions of his eavesdropping.

"He's so good at doing that for me—insists most of the time. So, what'd y'all get?"

"Steak," I said as I walked over to help sort the bags.

"Squash and zucchini," Luke added, handing me the bag with my dress.

Paul walked in, and everyone greeted him.

Kayla helped empty the bags and said, "Oh, my favorite bread, too. Thanks, you're always so good to me." She kissed Luke on the cheek, and he tilted his jaw upward.

"All right, just tell me when we eat." Paul landed on the blue sofa, kicked off his shoes, and rested his head on his palms.

"Why did you have to leave today, loafer?" she said addressing Paul.

"I had errands to run. No big deal."

"You got out of paying and cooking?" I turned to Kayla, "How long have you all been letting him get away with this?"

"Oh, no. He pays for a lot around here. Don't let him fool you. Not to mention, Paul does all the dishes when he's here."

Paul nodded with pride.

Wow, Kayla had it made with two men doting over and working for her. I wanted to live here. I smiled to relay I understood.

I learned Kayla spoke freely, telling me most anything I asked. She grew up in North Carolina in a nuclear two-parent, two-child family. She met Luke in Norfolk when she went to Virginia Wesleyan. She did not finish school but dropped out to join Luke on deployment. I sat and wondered why.

Why did he feel the need to take her with him? Did he fear being alone, of dying, and no one missing him? Everything I learned about Kayla only made me wonder more about Luke. I discovered both his parents were dead, and he was an only child. Past that, I had no explanations. I hoped she would tell me more.

Chapter 3
Pub Crawls

After dinner, Luke explained where we needed to go to find the name of Eleana's ex-boyfriend. We changed clothes and hit the streets. Again, the sea of young people I saw the previous night were out and about hitting bars. We walked into an Irish pub, Fiddler's Elbow. It appeared to contain all the Irish within a fifty-mile radius. Redheads and blondes were the majority, but there were plenty of dark Italians trying to meet them. Luke led the way through the tight mass. People parted, letting him walk by, gawking. Kayla trailed behind him by the pull of his hand, like a caboose tossed around by the force of a big engine. Paul followed me, and the crowd closed in behind him.

Luke leaned in toward the bartender and ordered four drinks then stood back and checked out the room, while I noticed Paul looking for exits. When passed our beer, Kayla sipped her's and clicked her shoes together entertained by them. I laughed then gulped my own beer. I thought it would taste bad, but instead it went down like iced tea.

"What's so funny?" Kayla asked.

I squinted and shook my head. It would be impossible to explain amidst all the noise.

"You look good in that top," she spoke above the murmur and roar of the people, pointing to my satin, burnt-orange shirt, sexier than normal for me.

"Thanks." As it was customary to return a compliment, I looked down. "Your shoes are amazing. They even show up in the dark."

"That's probably why they're so popular."

"What do you think of Italy?"

"Oh, I love it."

"Could you stay here forever, or do you want to go back to the States?"

"I could. I would always want to visit home, but, yeah, I could live here and raise kids. It's just so beautiful, and I love the culture."

"I can see that." I looked over at Luke's probing gaze. "He's so intense, isn't he?"

"You have no idea." She talked with her hands. "He can't turn it off either."

"Turn it off?" I repeated, not sure if that's what she said and hoping she would elaborate.

"It has been drilled into him for so long—to look for danger."

"How long's he been in the military?" I asked with a sly inquisition into Luke's age.

"Seven years now, but he was taught long before that." She waved her hand like shooing a fly to show a passage of time.

"What do you mean?"

Her glare at the bar top contrasted to the bouncing music in the background. "His parents were murdered. You knew that, right?"

"Oh, shit. No, I didn't."

"Oh."

"How old was he?"

"Fifteen. His uncle—a Marine, too—finished raising him. He taught Luke self-defense and got him interested in weapons. It was only a matter of time before Luke would become a jarhead."

"I guess so."

I watched Luke peer over the foam in his beer. I drew a line across the room to the place his eyes stared. Some dark, greasy-headed man appeared to be yelling, insisting, and demanding to a short stocky man. Luke took it all in. I wondered if he read lips. I thought of all the things he'd had to learn to survive.

"Do they know who killed his parents?"

"He was told something different by the police, his uncle, and even his dad's company."

I wanted to know more, but the noise prevented any serious conversation.

Luke made his way back for another round of beers. I had finished only half of mine, so I guzzled the rest before the refills made their way to me. I passed the empty mugs back. Luke took my glass from Kayla then looked at me with approval by his smile, slowly nodding. I sassed him back with a smart-ass look, mocking his smile. His body shook with a laugh.

As the night progressed, Luke passed three more beers between us, and each time I mocked him with more and more exaggeration. Concentrating became difficult. I tried to focus on the noise, the beat of the music. My skin became hypersensitive to Kayla's bump into my arm and someone else trying to get out of a seat, hitting me with her purse.

"Excuse me." I passed by Kayla. "Excuse me." I tapped on Luke's back as he talked to the bartender. He turned and faced me. I staggered and got close to his ear so he could hear me. "Umm, please tell, umm ... who asking that guy, not ordering another. 'Cuz I don' tink I can walk outta here if I have one mure." What I thought and what I heard coming out of my mouth were two totally different things.

"Haha, you are quite the cheap drunk, little sis."

"Hey! I'm nut yur little sisss. I'm a gwoan ass wo-man!" I heard how ridiculous I sounded.

"Haha. I can see that. I was just talking to our friend here, so don't worry. I'll have you home soon, if I have to carry you myself."

"That'ss nut nessass ... saa ... sury." I waved my finger in the air. I wanted to leave, to stop talking.

"Okay. Just hold on to me and don't fall down."

I liked the idea of that. I grabbed his striped shirt and pulled down. Luke moved toward the door. He told Kayla and Paul by a hand signal that we were leaving.

My grip slipped, and my fingers fell down and grabbed something stronger, Luke's jeans. I had three fingers inside his jeans, holding onto him as hard as I could.

"That's it. Don't let go."

I stumbled out onto the pavement, and the noise, the crowd, and the dark were gone. A street lamp glared like a spotlight. I let go of his jeans as soon as the door shut behind me and I saw Kayla and Paul following.

"Okay, we need to get little sis here home."

"Hey. Stop callin' me that. I'm nut a shild, ya know."

"Ah, she's lit up. When did that happen?" Paul asked.

"We all had the same amount," Luke said.

"I feel pretty good," Kayla said with a big grin that made me want to laugh.

"Luke, she doesn't drink. Sis, you okay? You aren't gonna hurl or anything, are you?"

"I'm just sweepy." The same word I used as a child came out of my mouth. My eyes couldn't open beyond a squint. My feet side-stepped, and I reached out to hold onto something.

"It's okay, I got ya." Luke grabbed me.

"Ugh." I became dizzy, like on a roller coaster.

Luke hoisted me over his shoulders. I didn't protest, and my eyes fell closed. The bounce of walking made me open them again, and I saw Luke's underwear where his jeans gaped in the center curve of his back. "Shit!" I closed my eyes again. We walked until my eyes bulged.

"Here we are, little girl." My body lay against something soft.

I whispered, "Nut little ... girl."

Luke whispered back in my ear, "Oh, yes, you are," his breath hot on my neck.

I drifted into some kind of a dreamland, unable to recall even when I woke.

The next day my neck, face, and head hurt. I got up and went to the kitchen sink to drink a tall glass of water, then another. I found a note on the kitchen table.

For you, Sis. Hope your recovery is quick. —Luke.

The note sat under a bottle of ibuprofen. I took the note, crumpled it, and threw it in the garbage. I took four pills and fixed a bowl of Cheerios Treats that resembled Rice Krispies.

"You okay?" Paul asked from a blow-up mattress.

"Ugh, so-so. Just not sure what y'all see in beer? Especially if it makes your head hurt like this."

"It doesn't. We don't get that bad. You gotta know your limit."

"I guess mine's just a bit less than all of yours."

"It takes time to build it. You don't have to drink what we drink. Just do enough but not too much."

"So, why weren't you teaching me this when Luke served them to me all night?"

"He likes to make sure everyone is having a good time."

"To a certain point, it made just standing there doing nothing somewhat entertaining."

"Oh, one night drinking and you have it all figured out?" Paul laughed. "We drink to get through the boring parts."

"That's sad on so many levels, Paul. I just don't have the strength to laugh and debate them with you right now." I sat on the couch with folded legs and the bowl to my chin.

Paul laughed again, shaking his head.

After finishing my cereal, I lay back down. My eyes were closed, but my ears were wide open. Warmth flooded my neck and head, numbing me. I didn't want to move.

I dozed off a few minutes before I noticed more voices.

"How's our little girl?" Luke asked Paul.

"Fine. Got up and ate. She just needs more sleep." They whispered, but I could still hear them.

"Is she mad at me?"

"No. She's a big girl. She knows you didn't make her drink them." I wondered if my brother knew I was listening.

"She's hilarious. I hadn't seen someone that drunk in a long time."

"Hey, easy on her, Luke. Everyone in this country has been drinking since they were twelve, and you too, probably."

"I will. She just has this 'I'm tough' chip on her shoulder. I wanted to see her ... different."

"There's a lot about her you don't know yet. She has a soft heart to be so strong."

"No one's strong all the time, Paul."

"Well, all I can say is, I've never seen her weak."

"Maybe she should find out what her kryptonite is."

"Maybe."

At that point, I wanted to go box both their ears, but I had to continue the guise of sleep. I rolled over in anger so no one could see my face, and they stopped talking. I lay there thinking about Luke's comment. My weakness—why would he want to point it out? I didn't understand a person who would do that. I tried to make those around me stronger, not weaker.

A cell phone rang.

"Hello?" Paul said. "Hmm. Oh, no. I'm so sorry. I wondered what happened." Paul's footsteps turned into loud pacing on the wooden floor. "Are you okay?" He waited for an answer. "No. Why didn't you call me?" Paul continued to talk on the phone.

I used this opportunity to wake up, sensing the call was important, since Paul failed to quiet his voice.

"Okay, thanks for calling me then. Bye."

"Who was that?" I sat on the couch blinking my eyes, forcing them to adjust to the light.

"Eleana." Paul stared at his phone.

"Did she explain what happened to her yesterday?"

"Yep. She was at the doctor's. She had a miscarriage."

Chapter 4
The Greatest Risk

Silence filled the room as Luke looked at me, and then we both looked at Paul.

Luke said, "I don't believe it. It's too convenient." His smile turned up on one side, and his eyes gleamed at me. I wanted to stare back, to dive into the depths I could only imagine were there, but instead I ruffled my hair to distract myself.

"I have a lot of work to do then. I better get a shower," I said.

"What are you going to do?" Paul asked.

I looked back over my shoulder. "I don't know, but when I do, I'll fill you in." With force, I delivered a smile to keep Paul upbeat. I knew his head spun from one minute a father and the next, not. It made it worse the more we analyzed it. He needed more information. That would be the only way I could help.

After my shower, I borrowed Paul's phone, stealing Christina's number out of my contact list. My longest and best friend in the world would need to know I wasn't coming home. I could hear the squeal when I told her where I'd gone.

Nothing had turned out the way I thought it would since I had arrived. When life was unpredictable, disappointing, or flat out altering, I told Christina. Bouncing my thoughts off my best friend always gave me insight. Today, I hoped for the same. When I told her about Luke and Kayla, she responded with suspicion. When I told her there was no longer a reason for me being here, that Eleana had miscarried, she went silent.

Then she asked, "Is it true?"

"That is your first instinct, too? That has to mean something."

"Well, I'm not saying it can't happen. It happens. All the time. I'm just saying I would want proof. We are talking about a life here, and getting Paul out of the equation would be convenient for her, wouldn't it?"

Christina was practical, not headstrong and impulsive like me. She thought things through and was slow to speak. Hearing her say what I felt in my gut was like the best of two worlds coming together, pointing me straight to my next goal: to get proof, even if it meant I strapped Eleana down and scanned her stomach myself. I told Christina about my phone but promised I would keep in touch.

"Get me something cheap, just something from Italy." She said it like this was the dreamiest place in the world.

It was impossible to leave for the market without my usual sidekick, Luke. Kayla opted to stay behind to get some clothes washed, her response to the confusing situation, no doubt. Paul took off. He said he had to take care of something at the embassy, but I think he just needed time alone. All the Marines stationed in Rome were there to protect the ambassador and the U.S. citizens. Luke, being a sergeant, had chosen Paul to assist him.

Today, Paul left to chart the new embassy work schedule for Luke. Everyone was occupied but Luke, who mumbled about some report he had to write later but not now. He told us the name of Eleana's boyfriend, Primo Greco, which he had learned from the bartender. When we searched the internet about him, we found nothing.

Once on the street, Luke hung back and began to act like a spy. When we arrived at the market, I looked through postcard stands behind a swarm of Indian teenagers, and a propped-open door. I tried to watch Luke and mimic him.

If she miscarried yesterday, would she even be here? I thought this would probably be a waste of time. Did her family even know about her pregnancy? Luke used his pointer finger to motion me to come to him when he caught my eyes. I walked over.

In a whisper, I asked, "Yeah, what?"

He returned the same whisper. "I'm hungry."

I pushed him away. "You jerk."

"Come on, let's go get a bite." He rested his hand on my back and sent heat frissons in every direction.

"Okay." The word came out of my mouth, airy and weak. We both turned and walked down the street toward the restaurants. We found another café with chairs outside (my favorite) to enjoy the warmth of the sun.

Spending time with Luke filled a void from missing Shawn, I told myself. My mind wandered to how accommodating he had been.

"I want to thank you for letting me use your computer to keep in touch with some people back home."

"Probably have to check in with your boyfriend, don't you?"

"Not anymore."

"What happened?"

"Um." I stalled. "Not sure."

"He's a fool then."

I looked up, confused.

"If he hasn't told you how he feels. Leaving you wondering is dangerous."

"Dangerous for whom?"

"For him. Look around. You're in Italy. Does he think no one would try to snatch you up here?"

I looked around, and a guy walking by winked at me when I made eye contact.

"See," Luke said.

"I didn't come here to get involved with a guy. I came here—"

"I know, but other things just happen sometimes. Things you don't plan."

"Don't you worry, I'm at no risk there," I said.

"The greatest risk is when you think you're safe." Luke's eyes were like melting ice. Immutable.

After lunch, we returned to the market and noticed a young man speaking to an auburn-haired girl, obviously upset. He had medusa curls falling to his shoulders and tiny eyes. Rubbing her back and talking to her ear, he attempted to soothe her worried face. Pouty lips and flying hands conveyed a story he half listened through while making eye contact with another girl.

"I'm not sure if that's her. Is that Primo?"

"I think so," Luke said.

A woman walked up and consoled Eleana as they disappeared in the crowd. Primo came near us and turned down the main street.

"Hey, let's follow him instead," Luke said.

We jumped and weaved through the crowd but didn't lose sight of him.

Primo dove in and out of the shops. He exited by the north side of the market and turned right, down a less crowded street. He headed away from the apartment, toward the city, a place I had not yet explored. I stood frozen after I rounded the corner and saw Primo staring right at me.

Luke grabbed me, pressed me against the building, and whispered into my ear, "Act natural. Pretend we're lovers."

The nervousness from Luke's proximity burst into action as I took my arms and wrapped them around his neck. He twirled me around, and I forgot where we were and why we were here. I lost my bearings in the spin until Luke propped me against the building. His eyes stared at me as his hands held my face. His eyes were like the Caribbean Sea. Again, I fought back the urges inside of me wanting to dive into them, into him.

His eyes dropped to my lips and said, "I saw him go through a red door over there, at that stone building."

I blinked a few times and gained my bearings, trying to follow Luke as he took off down the street. Remembering who he was, or *whose*, I pulled my thoughts together and knew the intimacy was a ruse. We walked over and saw a building with an iron staircase leading to a terrace. It sat ominous, clouded in mystery. Large bonsai-looking trees shadowed the balcony. The building had no markings, no numbers, nothing. Across the street, a more modern office building stood. After doing a little checking—okay, Luke peeked in their mailbox—we found the address. 721 *Via dei Ramni*.

He pulled out his phone and looked for the address on the Internet. It belonged to *Pizzamiglio*, a dentist.

"What dentist doesn't have a sign out front?"

"A very good one," Luke said.

I stood there searching the shadows of the building's recesses for an idea.

"You wait here. I'm going to see if we can get an appointment," Luke said.

I looked at him puzzled, and then I knew his plan.

I watched Luke disappear behind the red door, and all of a sudden Fear stood on the balcony. He laughed at me in a mock serenade, describing the empty and dangerous street. He swirled down the bonsai tree and cautioned me to hide in the shadows. I did. I always did what Fear told me. I stood against the cold stone building and waited.

The door opened ten minutes later. I held my breath to see whose feet scratched down the steps. When I saw Luke, I appeared from behind the tree.

"Worried me a bit when I didn't see you, but good thinking. Let's get a drink, celebrate. Now we know the little punk is rich with a daddy like that, and she's trying to snatch herself a rich guy. Right?"

"The dentist is his father?"

"Yeah."

"Is that too obvious? I mean, passing the baby off as Primo's?"

"No, this makes sense. Life is obvious sometimes," Luke said.

"Maybe that's what she's going to do, but how can we find out if there's still a baby? I mean what if she ... you know, got rid of it?"

"I doubt it; she's Catholic. You never know, though."

"But, she could have miscarried. We have to know."

"Questions for another day. Now, we drink—you, a little less than me." Luke caused me to laugh at myself, remembering last night.

"I'm still recovering. I don't need another."

"One drink is the best way to recover."

"You sound like an alcoholic."

"Nah, it's just the culture over here. It's what we do. So, we drink two nights in a row. You gonna put me in jail for it?"

I rolled my eyes at his drama. I watched him bounce along, commenting about a restaurant in an old building, wondering how much caffeine he'd had today. Amused and happy to go after the rolling entertainment, we ducked into a bar and ordered two shots of whiskey. I told him no, but he politely ignored me.

"I just ordered twelve-year-old Jamison. It's so smooth, even you'll like it." When he smiled, the dimple on his left cheek highlighted a mole.

"What do you mean by smooth?"

"Goes down easy." He nodded as if saying, "Yeah, baby," but he would never be so cheesy.

Luke handed me the reddish, golden liquid, and I stared at it. I didn't want to drink it, but something in me wanted to make him happy. It slid down my throat, warming my body. He was right. It went down easy—too easy.

We both set the glasses down within seconds. I sat there with a simmering heat in my stomach, spreading into numbness.

"We make a good team, you know," he said.

"You think so?" I asked. I didn't think so. We hadn't accomplished anything.

Luke motioned to the bartender, and our glasses were refilled within seconds. "*Salute e per noi.*" Luke lifted his drink for a toast. When I looked at him, confused, he added, "To good health and to us."

"To us?" My hand stuck to the glass, motionless. It couldn't move from the scratched, letter-carved bar.

"To the team?" Luke said with weaker enthusiasm.

"To the team," I agreed and hesitantly lifted my glass to clang with his.

Since the day was a bust, I couldn't figure out why Luke was so excited. He smoothed over the fact that we still didn't know if there was a baby.

I sipped the amber drink. Luke swallowed his in one gulp.

"You're funny, sipping Jamison." Luke shook his head.

"My stomach is on fire, and my head is getting light. I just want to laugh. At nothing."

"At everything." Luke looked at me with fervor.

His piercing eyes were so hypnotizing. I couldn't trust them. His eyebrows flattened to a line, and he looked at me, straight at me without a flinch or movement. I had to break the tension that was beading up and about to fall.

"Why do you look at me that way?" Boldness washed over me, and I wanted to know certain things. I didn't want to wait or sleuth it out of him. Blunt, that's what alcohol did to me.

Luke darted his eyes around the room before returning them to me. "It's complicated."

"Listen, I've just had two drinks. We all know four is too many. Two might be just right, but now I'm not so sure. 'Cause I don't understand a thing you're saying." I put the empty glass down on the bar and twirled it around.

Luke jutted out his chin. "We—you and me—make a good team. I like hanging out with you."

I squirmed in my chair and dropped my eyes before I faced him. Rather than easing the tension between us, I had only built it stronger. "We will get to the bottom of this, I'm sure of it. Do we have an appointment?" I asked, changing the subject.

"No, don't need one. I found out what I needed to know."

"In fifteen minutes?"

"Sure."

"How?"

"My charm, of course." Luke laughed at himself.

I shook my head, puzzled. "You *are* something. What exactly, I'm not sure. But something."

His face dropped all expression and then squinted at me. "You read people. You're trying to read me?"

"What? I think you're—"

"—In serious trouble."

"What? I think we need to go back." I turned away from his eyes. My mind tried to figure out his words and the subtleties inside them. I was convinced it was the alcohol, but I was scared. I wasn't sure if I was reading him correctly or just lusting after him all on my own.

"No, you need some food. Let's go."

I followed him out. This time, I tugged onto his shirt, not that I could justify the thought of losing track of him. There weren't that many people but enough to get away with it. I just liked holding onto him. I watched his feet, and we ended up at a pizzeria. I downed two pieces before I realized how many calories I had eaten—another problem I found with alcohol.

Hours later, still in the booth, the calories and the water all summed up to me: sober.

"Feeling better?"

"Much."

I could close my eyes and still feel Luke twirl me around or feel his breath on my ear. How could I feel this way toward a married man? I thought I was better than that, but I didn't do this, flirt with him. He did. He had been coming on to me ever since I got here. This was all his fault. And poor Kayla, she was so sweet. How could he do this to her?

"You don't seem to spend much time with Kayla. I mean your schedules ..."

"Concerned?"

"Just observant."

"Yeah, me too."

"What have you noticed?" I asked.

"We are *not* ready for that conversation."

"What does that mean?" I looked away from his dilated eyes. I felt as though an anchor wrapped around me, as I fell deeper and deeper into them. I hoped he hadn't noticed.

"Well, by all means, little Miss Daisy, tell me what you notice then."

"What I notice?" I sensed his joy in toying with me.

He nodded.

"I just told you. You and Kayla have schedules that keep you from seeing each other." I kept drinking water to clear my head. I reached for my rational thoughts that guided me through moments such as this, but they eluded me.

"She's not clingy."

"I see. She gives you freedom but keeps you from being lonely. That makes sense."

"Don't be so sure you see everything." Luke downed a fourth of his beer.

"Oh, am I wrong? Feel free to enlighten me."

"I'm having too much fun watching you try to figure it all out." He grinned at me in a confident, cocky way that pissed me off.

"Well, whatever it is, I don't see or know yet. Be sure I will." His ability to hold his tongue frustrated me.

"Oh, I'm counting on it." Luke kept his smug grin.

"You ready to go? The fun here's all sucked up." I finished off the water.

"Don't be such a poor loser, Maggie. It's not becoming."

"Don't worry how I look, Mr. I'm-so-mysterious."

"You look just fine." Luke grinned larger and finished off his beer.

"Smart ass." I stood to leave.

So what if I was a poor loser? Men who couldn't be straight with me managed to steal all my patience. Why did men have to hide everything? Maybe he was a sleaze bag and nothing more. Deep down I didn't want that to be true, though, so I kept looking.

We arrived at the flat in time for Luke to see Kayla for thirty minutes before she left for work. They were upstairs for most of that time. I settled on the couch and read my book. My stomach bloated and my eyelids hung, but the day raced away, making it too late for a nap and too early to go to sleep. I could hear them talking upstairs, and the possibilities of what they were doing prevented any reading. Could he flirt with me all afternoon and then go up there and have sex with his wife? This situation made me more furious by the hour.

I heard a giggle.

I had to do something else as a distraction and decided to use the computer. I sat to find thirty emails and none I wanted to read. I clicked links with the mouse, going straight to Facebook. I just wanted to see Shawn's face, see if it sparked any emotion in me. How badly did I miss him?

I hated his new profile picture. He had sunglasses on. I wanted to see his brown eyes, the way they glowed amber, like a fire inside of a jewel when he looked at me. I clicked to a close-up picture to stare into his eyes. I tried to find something annoying about him.

No matter what I liked or didn't like, Shawn didn't know how to talk to me. After five months, he couldn't tell me how he felt about me. Luke's words echoed back in my mind, "The greatest risk is when you think you're safe." I closed the window and knew I wouldn't be getting on Facebook again for a long time.

"Hey," Luke said from behind me.

Startled, I clicked out of the rest of the computer windows and twirled around. "Hey, guys."

"I'm off to work. See y'all in the morning," Kayla said.

"Hope the shift goes well. Are you awake enough?" I asked.

She nodded. "My body is used to this."

"Good," I said.

"See you in the morning," Luke said from the kitchen.

Kayla left, and I didn't move from the computer chair. I noticed the clock on the wall said six-thirty. Luke would leave for work at eleven-thirty. Five long hours alone with him in here. I hoped he behaved. I pictured struggling to push him off me. Could I even? What was I thinking? Luke wasn't my old boyfriend, Andy. Why did Fear have me run through the what-if analysis, risk assessment, and character motivations of every person and situation? Luke possessed a self-control Andy never had. I didn't trust my first impressions, though. In the beginning with Andy, he was a gentleman, sweet and courteous, but he revealed his true nature in the end.

Luke walked over, looking at the screen. "Did you get to send off some emails?"

"Sort of."

"Well, what do you want to do now?"

"Don't you need to sleep?"

"No."

"Wow, I'm ready for a nap. Can't even imagine how you will be able to stay up all night."

"You have that post-buzz drowsiness, and that food didn't help. What you need is some caffeine."

"No, no thank you. That will be sure to keep me up all night."

"I need some. Won't you at least help me stay up and watch a movie or something?"

"A movie? I'm always in the mood for a movie. Which one?"

"Let's go see."

"Go ahead. I want to get something first," I said.

I went into the kitchen and made popcorn I found in the cabinet. I had learned where the plates, glasses, and cabinet food were organized. After slathering the puffy white kernels with melted butter, I took the large bowl upstairs.

Luke looked pleasantly surprised. "I love movies and popcorn."

As soon as I entered the bedroom, I became stiff again, like waiting in a doctor's office. I sat in the chair, the only place to sit except for the bed, where Luke lounged against pillows.

"I won't bite you. But, I would like some of that popcorn."

"Here you go." I handed him the bowl and sat back in the chair.

"You can sit here. It's much more comfortable. I know you would with Paul. What's the difference?"

Maybe I'd been making too much of all this. Maybe that was just his personality: a big, harmless flirt.

He had a point. He called me his little sister. If he were Paul, there would be no discussion. Kayla's tasseled blue and green island shams stood straight against the headboard with a chenille throw folded at the bed's foot.

"Sure." I stood, grabbed a pillow, and lay on my stomach with the pillow under my chest. Luke rested against the headboard. "Which movie is this?" I asked as the previews played.

I couldn't help but be self-conscious of my butt, now regretting the position I'd selected. I couldn't change it without being obvious. I didn't try to flirt or look attractive to Luke, but I wondered what my body language said to him.

"*True Lies.*"

"That's a good one— poignant for Special Agent Luke, too."

A pillow hit the back of my head.

"I wish Paul had warned me what a smart ass you were," Luke said.

"I thought he had. *Quipped tongue*, you called it?"

"That doesn't begin to describe your tongue."

I turned around fast and looked back at the TV. Was I imagining that? I dropped my face into the pillow below me.

"If your neck hurts you can lean against here." He pointed to the headboard.

"I'm good. Thanks."

I stayed awake, even though I'd seen this movie many times. Luke laughed with his whole body at the scene of Jamie Lee Curtis's awkward attempt to help the phony spy. When I asked why he laughed, he said she reminded him of me.

"Thanks. I think I'm better than *that*."

"Don't flatter yourself."

I looked back and saw a hint of a smile. "You probably think you're

Schwarzenegger?"

"I could be."

I laughed so hard, I rolled over. Luke hit my head with another pillow. "Ow."

"Serves you right."

"A mean streak? Knew you had one," I said with confidence and threw the pillow back at him. He caught it before it hit him. I became aware of our playfulness, turned my head back around, and became quiet. I didn't understand how it could be so easy with him. I repositioned to sit beside him and removed my butt from his view.

Luke rested back and returned his attention to the movie. Jamie Lee Curtis's pole dancing attempt embarrassed me to watch it. I looked around for a magazine, for any distraction. In my peripheral vision, I noticed Luke enjoying the scene. Her seductive dance went on way too long.

"This bother you?" he asked.

A nervous laugh came out. "It's a bit weird."

"Why?"

"Watching it with you, I guess."

"Oh, I thought maybe watching anything like that would make you uncomfortable."

"Why do you say that?"

"You're still young. There's so much I can tell you haven't ... experienced."

I didn't want to confirm or deny his thought. But wanted to know why he even thought it. "I don't care for porn, if that's what you're referring to."

I knew it wasn't what he meant, but I refused to tell anyone my only knowledge of sex had been through a rape. I remembered Texas when Shawn and I were in a heated kiss on the couch. He always wanted it to go further. I couldn't, nor could I tell him why.

"Not exactly," he said.

We dropped the conversation until the end of the movie, when Luke said, "I have to eat something before I go."

He went into the kitchen, and soon the wonderful scent of sautéed onions filled the small flat. I snuggled on the couch with my book and a green micro-fleece blanket. Luke came to me with a plate, demanding I taste his omelet. His fork hovered with dripping cheese toward my mouth, forcing me to taste it. I opened my mouth, finally agreeing, and he fed me.

"Mmm." My eyes closed. "That is so good." When I opened them, Luke sat motionless, holding the empty fork at my lips. He stared with a gaped mouth. I moved my eyes left and right, dodging Luke's frozen look. He turned around and went back to the kitchen.

"Good," Luke said as he faced the other way.

"Did you make enough? I guess I could eat." Bad habits were forming.

"Sure, I'll get you a plate."

Luke ate in silence and then put his dishes in the dishwasher. "I'm gonna take a shower and get ready."

"Okay." I sat and read my book in my pajamas.

Luke came down with his hair still wet. I tried not to look long but kept watching him as he walked around the kitchen. I began to memorize the lines of his body, the folds of his khaki shorts, and even the occasional freckle. A faint cluster sat on the bridge of his nose and spread to each side. A mole hid behind his right ear, and two graced his neck.

He walked into the living room carrying his dry cleaning. "You look cozy. Hope you sleep well."

An overwhelming need to stand filled me as I saw his pressed uniform, feeling proud. "Thanks for all you do."

He looked at me, confused.

"I mean for all you have ever done to make Americans safe." I tucked my hair behind my ear and looked up at him. "I just want you to know I appreciate you and all soldiers."

"I would suspect so, having a brother who serves."

"I was never happy about it. I thought he deserted me." I sunk back onto the couch. "I'm older now and understand."

"Growing up right before my eyes," Luke said with a smile.

It made my chest swell. He did not make me feel like a little girl anymore. He looked at me differently, and I liked it.

Chapter 5
Fish, Heads, and Eyes

The next day, with no one else around, I had time to think. And, since Luke and Kayla were sleeping and Paul was working, it was my chance to go down to the market alone. I started with a huge cappuccino and a pastry from a café on the way. I imagined all the pampering this city could give me. Indulging myself to some, I bought a pair of jeans without even trying them on. It was something I would usually never do, but they were so cheap I could take the gamble.

The display of food down the streets sent me into a sampling frenzy. The fruit looked as if it had been picked off a tree that hour, and the tomatoes were plump and ready to be sliced. A mood for a fruit salad hit me, and I bought fresh nuts, apples, and oranges. Then, I found raisins, pineapple, and shredded coconut. When I had purchased everything, I walked through the fish area where Eleana worked. I stopped and pretended to look at the halibut while I searched for the auburn-haired woman I had seen yesterday. I didn't see her.

"*Posso aiutarla?*" an older gentleman asked me.

I shook my head and squinted. "*Non parlo italiano,*" my go-to quick answer when hoping the person knew English. I knew some words by now but not what he'd said.

"Can I help you?" the gray-haired man asked.

Relieved, I looked down and pondered over the fish. "I ... I love fish, but why keep the heads on?" The fish eyes grossed me out.

"You Ah-merican? *Si*. Come, I teach you to find good fish." He walked me down the long table. "Don't be shy."

I gaped too long at one of their eyes. I thought I could throw up.

"What kind of fish you like?"

"I don't know. Halibut."

"*Si*, good fish. Here is. Tiny little eye, but clear. Look scales are shiney."

I turned away and focused on him. His big smile revealed a missing right bicuspid. Thick brown patches on his right temple and freckles scattered across his forehead revealed his age. White hair partially encircled his head, leaving a shiny gleam to his smooth top.

"But why the head?" I asked.

"You must have the head. Cloudy, no good. Clear ..." He kissed the tips of his fingers. "Magnificent." His accent lay thick.

I grinned at his animation. "Oh, I see."

"You can tell by the scales and gills, too, but most people don't want to look that close."

"It does look fresh."

"How many do you need?"

"Oh, well no. I ..."

"You have a no one to cook for?"

"I'm visiting, staying with another couple."

"Has romance not found you yet here in our good city?"

"Oh, no. I'm all good. Thanks." I thanked him, as if he could order me up a nice Italian on a plate. I didn't see an Italian though. I saw a tall blonde from Orlando. I forced the image from my mind. Then, I saw caramel eyes. This was crazy.

"You need to find a good man to marry like my granddaughter. Come here, Eleana." The name startled me. I jerked my neck to look for someone. No one came.

"She is to marry a *dentisto's* boy. We so proud. I knew she would do good. She is so beautiful."

"That's great." *Great for ya'll but not so great for my brother.*

"You. You pretty too. I introduce you to good man, *si*?"

"No." Why can no one understand I am not in Italy to fall in love?

"You are shy, I see. I know good customer. Be here tomorrow at two o'clock. I show you. You come? Right?"

"Here? Tomorrow?"

"*Si*, two o'clock."

"Okay. I mean, *si*. I'll be here."

Curiosity expanded like helium in my belly. I wanted to meet Eleana in a natural way, and through another encounter with her grandfather, it might just happen. I bought the halibut, hoping the others were in the mood for it.

When I returned to the apartment after lunch, they were still sleeping. I wanted to burst in and tell someone about my day. I waited until four o'clock, when Kayla came down and revealed Luke did not go to bed until after noon from a twelve-hour shift. Kayla showered and ate, and by six-thirty she was gone again. Twelve-hour shifts at the hospital must be awful.

I decided to go out. I freshened up and went hunting for my shoes.

"What ya doing?"

Startled, I flipped my head up from peeking under the couch. "I ... was going for a bite. I didn't want to cook for one."

"Let me change real quick, and I'll join you."

I loved how no one ever waited for invitations. Luke came back downstairs, wearing jeans and a polo shirt. He slipped on some flip-flops and flashed me a smile. "What are you hungry for?"

The door shut behind us, and we walked into the elevator. He turned to me and stared, waiting for my answer.

"I think I want a great spaghetti."

"Of course, let's do Sargentini then."

"You lead the way, Sarge." I couldn't help but play on the word from the restaurant, but then I thought of Luke's Marine title, his authority. He must command a lot of respect.

We walked the narrow sidewalks, dodging protruding steps and lampposts.

"You enjoyed today by yourself, I bet."

I told him how I met the grandfather, what I learned about Primo—the fiancé—and my near meeting with Eleana. "He also said I needed to meet a good Italian boy like Eleana did."

"Oh, he did? What'd you think about that?"

"Nothing. He was just trying to get me to meet someone he knew, so I'm supposed to go back tomorrow and—"

"Got yourself a blind date?"

"No, I'm meeting him, so I can meet Eleana. Maybe I could befriend her and find out if she's pregnant." My arms whisked the air as I tried to get the story out.

Luke had a permanent grin.

"Stop it. You're enjoying this way too much." I hit him in the arm. "Why are you smiling? Stop it!"

"You're so funny."

"Why?" We arrived at the restaurant, and Luke opened the door and waited for me to pass under his arm. I stopped and waited for him to answer.

"So uncomfortable it's adorable," Luke said with his grin larger than natural.

I turned away and walked ahead until I had to stop at the hostess stand. The door shut behind Luke, forcing him to stand too close. I could feel his body behind me, treeing over me, absorbing the light, and putting off heat.

Was it just me? I had to get a grip. I kept telling myself to see Luke as my brother, but it just kept getting harder to do. My mind wanted his hand to reach for mine, his arm to wrap me in safety. I wanted him to lean over and kiss me after he'd stared too long. When I noticed my train of thought going to unhealthy imaginations , I shut it down. I knew better. He was Kayla's! I had to stop doing this to myself. I missed Shawn and nothing more.

Candles stood on white tablecloths, and I wondered if the restaurant would be expensive. When we sat, I began to read the menu to divert from the awkwardness.

"Ever had wine? It's the best accompaniment to Italian food." He held the wine list in hand.

"Long time ago, when I was fifteen." I pushed away images of a teenager fitting in at parties at unknown residences.

Luke grinned but kept his eyes on the menu. "Did you like it?" he asked.

"Better than beer probably."

"Can I order us some?"

I couldn't refuse his politeness. "Sure. Whatever you think would be best."

He ordered for me, and it reminded me of chivalry and being treated like a lady and not a girl.

"You know I bought halibut for us all tonight? Thought I'd cook for y'all."

"Really? That's nice."

"Maybe tomorrow night?"

"I go in at seven tomorrow night. Sorry. I think Kayla's off, though."

"Do you guys seriously have opposite schedules?"

"She works Monday, Wednesday, Thursday, and Saturday, then the opposite days the next week. I'm the one that swings through different shifts."

"A swinger? Really?"

Luke laughed with his whole body at my joke. I liked surprising him.

I used my best manners, putting the napkin on my lap, starting with the smallest fork, etc. I sipped wine and took care not to bang the stem against my plate as I set it down. Luke looked much more relaxed at this than I did. He knew Italy. He relaxed with me too much. In some ways, this should be bothering him.

The dinner disarmed me. I imagined us in a bubble of *if only* and *what if*. Then I looked down and saw the band on his finger. I turned quiet at the end of the meal while Luke busied himself with the check. What was his motive? Could he not help himself? Wouldn't I like to think so, or was this all a game to him?

When we walked back in the dark, bar lights led the way. In the still moments without conversation, again I reminded myself to think of Luke as my brother, to lend my mind to rational thought, so the irrational never came out. But, moments like this, when Italy came alive and sweetened the air, made it hard to think rationally. In the silence as we walked, he didn't force conversation. I wondered if his guilt had set in.

Back at the flat, I changed into my pajamas, consisting of plaid shorts and a spaghetti strap halter. I crawled under my covers and continued reading my novel. Luke came down in his plaid bottoms from the first morning. He drank a glass of water at the sink.

"So, is this how you're going to finish your night?"

"I usually do."

He sat on the coffee table, staring at the book resting on my thigh.

"What's it about?"

I looked at the front cover as if I forgot the title. "Ah, you know, chick-lit." I tried not to focus on his smooth chest, his tiny brown—

He interrupted my thoughts, wanting to know about the plot and characters.

I explained the main character was in her thirties and still not married. She ran into her ex-boyfriend and his old best friend. They were both interested in her, but the ex was engaged.

Luke didn't drop it as I assumed he would. He wanted to know how I wanted it to end. Sometimes, he could act so crazy, maybe from too many shells going off around him.

"I don't know. I'm just reading it."

"No, you're not. You're already formulating how you want things to go."

"Since when does a badass G.I. even care about a romance?"

"I care what you think." His eyelids dropped, relaxed. It looked sexy.

Nothing could shake his serious tone. I sat there weighing the statement loaded with more than a chick-lit analytical comment. "Yeah. I wonder if she means enough to him to leave the fiancé. I doubt it and think the best friend will win her heart in the end."

"See. That wasn't hard."

"What wasn't?"

In a jazz radio voice, he said, "To tell me what you're thinking."

"Didn't know it was a big deal to you." I tried to mock him—to do anything to shake his seriousness.

"No need to belittle," he said and turned his legs around while he sat on the table and faced me.

"What? You're not talking normal." My heart raced as his body sat closer.

"You haven't met many people. It's just psychology." His eyes stayed on mine.

"You don't have to teach me. I aced psychology, thank you."

"Yes, I see you are well versed in communication." His sarcasm sat like a cherry on top of his sentence, begging to be eaten.

"Oh, please, Carl Sagan, since you think you are an expert, do 'verse' with me."

Luke laughed with his head thrown back. "Touché, but let's ... let's just talk—unless you'd rather find out what the ex does."

"What did you have in mind?"

"I don't know. Tolstoy? Jon Stewart? Oprah?"

I laughed. He sat there with his legs wide, like men liked to sit. Was it because it was too difficult to close his legs from his large ... I tried to think of Tolstoy, but all I could think of was Jon Stewart laughing at me for looking at a guy's crotch.

In my mind, the video on his show was of me looking and Jon said: "Pajama girl checks out the battle of the bulge." The idea of the battle made me laugh. When I glanced back and saw nothing visible, relief showered me. The bagginess of his pajamas kept his status private.

"What are you laughing about?"

"Nothing." I couldn't stop my nervous laugh. This time, I did mock him, unintentionally.

"Doesn't look like you want to talk," Luke muttered as he rearranged himself on the table and stood. As he did, his inseam came even closer, and I tried to look away. My awkwardness became apparent enough for Luke to look down and laugh at me. My face flushed red. I could always blush too much.

In soccer, I looked like I would pass out. I now knew it was the Native American heritage that ran through my veins, clear up to the top layers of my skin. I loved my Indian heritage—a mix of Indian with the Dutch. I was a blonde, tan-skin girl, a dichotomy of blends that went much deeper than the color of my skin.

Luke walked to the kitchen and ate a peanut butter sandwich and banana while staring at a book on the counter. When finished he said, "I'll see you in the morning. Enjoy your book."

"Thanks, night."

"Night."

Guilt from spending so much time with Luke and the thoughts I had of him brought Shawn to my mind. After Luke left, using his computer again, I checked my email and found one from Shawn.

Not too happy how I handled our phone conversation. But, I'm staying busy with intern applications and picked up a lot of shifts. I hope everything is going well with Paul and Eleana. I hope you are well. I would love to hear about Italy. I bet it's amazing. I'm still trying to wrap my mind around Texas. We were doing so well before you went to visit your mom. When I came into town, I could tell something about you was off. When I kissed you, you were tense. Then, when we had the "Interactive Interview," it just blew up and you broke it off. I understand you're going through a tough time right now in your family, but I wish you wouldn't shut me out. We will always be friends and friends talk.
Shawn

Why didn't Shawn understand it was too hard to be his friend? I wanted all of him, and he couldn't give it. He didn't know how to give it. I'd accepted it. I wanted to be pissed at him. How dare he try to be all nice? Friends. Why do people always want you to be their friend? They think you're great, beautiful, and smart, but … It's rejection, so just say it. Why the hell couldn't people just say it anymore?

"What's wrong?"

I peeked over my shoulder and saw Luke, then the slippers on his feet which made me not hear him walk up. "Nothing. Just reading email. Back again?" I logged out and walked to the kitchen.

"For some tea. Things okay with the boyfriend?"

"He's not my boyfriend anymore," I said in a snap that caught Luke off guard.

Luke leaned against the sink as he waited for the water to boil.

"Sorry," I said, knowing there was no need to talk to him that way.

"*Nessun problema.* So, how serious were you two?"

"Dated five months."

"That's not what I asked."

"That's the longest I've ever dated anyone. I think it says a lot."

"So, you guys were doing it. Okay."

"Ew. No. Why?"

"Did you just say *ew*?"

"I mean, why would you jump to that conclusion?"

"I wouldn't normally, but you said it was 'the longest.' Why did you say *ew*?"

"Would you stop asking me that? It meant nothing."

"What flies out of people's mouths is usually the truth, maybe abstract, but the truth. What I want to know now is, did you mean it about your ex or sex in general?"

I walked off, pissed, my jaw clenched. Keeping my mouth closed, I ran my tongue along the bottom inside of my teeth, back and forth, searching for a response. I had done it ever since I stopped sucking my thumb at age eight.

"I'm not going to force you, but I hope you'll tell me."

If he had forced me, yelled at me, or demanded, it would have been easy to run away; but Luke was none of those things. I'd dealt with forceful men. I didn't know how to deal with Luke on any level. Diving into this subject made my heart jump. I looked around for Fear. He stood in the corner, shaking his head. I wanted to know what Luke would think if I answered, but the risk was too great.

"Just some history. You don't need to bother yourself."

"Why do you do that? If I'm asking, I care. So stop acting like it's a bother." He walked up to me. "Anytime someone does anything nice for you, you start apologizing. Either you don't want to see it when someone cares, or you're suspicious of it."

My vision blurred as my throat constricted. I tried to turn away and get a glass of water, but Luke stopped me and placed my arms up to his chest, dropping my head. Being close to him, smelling his scent, I felt hidden and safe enough to fall apart. I tried not to fall too far, but then all the thoughts of rejection, loneliness, and fear imploded inside me. Luke held me tighter as I shook. When exhaustion set in and I could no longer cry, embarrassment washed over me. I pulled away from him as the water hissed on the stove.

"It's okay, Maggie." Luke poured the boiling water over a tea bag and squeezed a lemon into it, grabbing my hand. "Come to the couch." He covered me with the green blanket and handed me warm tea.

I took a deep breath over the cup's steam. Luke and I faced each other, leaning against the couch arms.

"For someone who can talk a lot, you sure can clam up," he said.

A forced laugh left my gut. I sipped the tea, too embarrassed to talk. I just wanted to change the subject. "Mmm. Just what I needed."

When Luke looked at me this time, I wasn't uncomfortable. A calm came over me as our unison breathing filled the room.

"I'm just not the kind of girl that vomits my emotional crap all over someone."

"Yuck."

"Good, so we agree you don't want to hear it."

Luke shook his head and laughed, holding up his hands. "Listen, nobody is holding a gun to your head. You're not ready. Fine. I'm here if that changes."

"See, if a girl told me that, I wouldn't feel so weird, but you are definitely not a girl."

Luke looked down at his lap. "No, definitely not."

It made me laugh, unforced this time. "You're crazy."

"Maybe." His eyebrows were low and his voice smoothed over.

"I don't have you figured out at all." I shook my head.

"Same here."

"Stop trying then." I threw the small couch pillow at him.

"Too much fun," Luke said. He squeezed the pillow like a chokehold.

"See, there you go. You're killing me."

"In what way?" he asked, pleased by my comment, pitching the pillow to the floor.

I shook my head no. "You ask too many questions."

"I thought that was your job; you're the detective."

"I know nothing about you." I squeezed my eyes with the palm of my hands and ran my fingers through my hair.

"You have to have all the answers, don't you?" Luke asked.

"I'd like to."

"Why do you have to control everything? Why can't you just let things happen?"

I sensed myself losing control of the conversation, of my emotions, and of him.

"Why are you clenching your fist?" he asked.

"Stop. Just stop." I sat higher by pushing on the couch with both hands.

Luke moved to the center of the couch, toward me. "Why do I make you so uncomfortable?"

I twisted my neck to the side, unable to face him, but couldn't take my eyes away. "You see too much."

"And why can no one see?" He inched closer.

"You aren't *no one*."

He leaned against my knees pushing them into the back of the couch while he inched closer. I swallowed. The air turned thick. I blinked, trying to interrupt eye contact.

"I hope so." Luke moved closer in confidence without hesitation.

"No." The word sounded amplified in the room. "This is too much."

He leaned back with a sigh. "Yeah, I forget. You're just nineteen."

"Don't do that. I mean, you're ..." I couldn't say it, but thought it. Luke was married.

I pulled my knees to my chest tighter, rubbing my face with my hands. Luke stood. I could tell he knew the words on the end of my tongue. I thought he would leave, but he sat back down, just as I had let out a sigh.

"Wait, is that the only reason? Cause I thought maybe there was something ... between—"

"That's a big reason."

"Sorry. I know." His face appeared humble staring downward. "I just can't get you out of my head."

"Really?" I said, more high-pitched and girlish than I wanted.

"How did you not know?" he asked.

"I just don't go around thinking people are into me."

He laughed at me and took a deep breath. "Are you seriously this naïve?" His eyes widened.

"Stop it." I pushed on his chest.

"Did you just cop a feel?"

"No." He could be so impossible, making me laugh at the oddest moments.

"You're so adorable, Maggie."

I bit my lip for strength. His eyes dropped.

"No, we are not going to do this." My pointer finger waved.

"You're right." Luke stood up and walked to the kitchen, drank his usual glass of water.

I kept my stare on him.

"Hope you sleep well, Sis." He hit the kitchen light, and I heard the weight of him walk up the stairs.

I turned off the lamp and lay on the couch with my covers up to my chin. "Hope you sleep well" twirled over and over in my mind. How was I supposed to do that?

Chapter 6
Where Secrets Hide

The couch's springs felt like bowling balls, leaving me with tense muscles. I flipped side to side, never sleeping longer than an hour at a time. After waking for at least the seventh time, I heard Kayla at the door. I knew it was about time to get up, since I had been hiding my eyes from the sun under a pillow for at least two hours. She walked into the apartment and upstairs. I was so relieved nothing had happened between Luke and me. I liked Kayla. In a brief moment the night before, looking into Luke's eyes, I knew I wouldn't have resisted him if he tried to kiss me. Coming that close and imagining it caused me to dream it had happened. After that image, I woke to Luke's voice.

"Coffee's ready. Sleepyhead."

Eggs were frying. Shit, why did he have to be so perfect? "I need my beauty sleep. I have a date today," I yelled into the kitchen and put the pillow back over my head.

"Yes. Your date. Stay asleep."

I took the pillow off my head and peeked into the kitchen. "What is that supposed to mean?"

"Nothing, Miss Paranoid."

I buried my head back into the couch. How did he know where all my buttons were?

Any more sleep became impossible, so I scurried to the bathroom to avoid talking to Luke. He noticed but said nothing.

I did everything I could to stay in the bathroom longer, coming out only to retrieve my clothes and hurrying back in without being noticed. My stomach growled as the apartment filled with the smell of caramelized onions. After applying make-up, I peeked out and didn't see him again. I snuck into the kitchen and looked for leftovers, hoping it was his amazing omelet he cooked often. While standing over the pan, shoving some cheese in my mouth, Luke popped down from the stairs.

"Can I get you some more?"

I shook my head and poured a cup of coffee. I sat on the couch to eat, bothered. By eating it, was I sending a message to him that I wanted him to flirt more?

Dressed in shorts, a Lucky t-shirt, and flip-flops, Luke looked over at me and asked, "Are you ready to go?"

I gulped the hot coffee. "Go where?"

"It's eleven. We should head that way."

"Why would *we* head anywhere?"

"Trust me, you're going to need someone to make sure you don't get in over your head. I'm not even going to listen to you tell me you have this all under control. I'm going whether I follow you or we go together."

I threw up my hands. "Why so early?"

"Some places I want to go first."

I rolled my eyes. "Whatever, G.I. Joe."

"I love irritating you."

"Well, you're good at it." I put the empty cup in the sink. "Tell me, do you always get your way?"

"Usually."

I found his smile upsetting. I didn't like the control he seemed to have over me. "Lead the way, Bourne."

Luke headed for the door with a smile on his face.

We walked in silent observation of the bustling college section of Old Town. A tall young man called to his dog as we strolled through the park. I could almost translate the "good boy" as he praised his dog for returning a tennis ball. After a week, my learning by osmosis had taught me about twenty Italian words. Luke, however, could return a three- to five-word response and get most of what he wanted without too much trouble. I couldn't imagine him having a long conversation with an Italian about his life unless they knew English, though.

Luke walked ahead of me, as if we were maneuvering through a jungle. His body bushwhacked a pathway. I sensed his protection mode on alert. One time, I rounded a corner and he caught me in his arms, stopping my momentum, so I didn't run into two men carrying a menu sign into the nearby store. We stood and waited until the sidewalk cleared again, and Luke held on until he dropped his hand to signal it was safe to continue walking. He had nonverbal cues that were as clear as a traffic light, and I followed them with precision.

"Let's get some coffee here so we can watch Eleana until it's time to meet the old man," Luke said.

He led me to a crowded café with iron chairs lining the front. The uneven cobblestones made the chairs unsteady, but no one cared. Luke pulled mine out and waited for me to sit before taking his own. The waitress brought two menus.

"I feel totally out of the loop by not having my phone. Have you heard from my brother?"

"We talk every day, Maggie. What do you want to know?"

Guilt spread from my gut to my face. I never needed to talk to my family on a daily basis. I detested any phone conversation over five minutes, frequently leaving my phone uncharged or temporarily lost. In Italy, it didn't work at all.

"When will he be back over? I would like to fill him in and cook that halibut."

"We both work tonight, but I think we're off tomorrow."

"The fish's eyes might get cloudy, but that will have to do."

Luke laughed. "Do you know what you want?"

The waitress arrived, pen ready in her hand. *Aveta*.

She asked what we wanted to eat. Luke responded in Italian. He rattled off a beautiful sentence. I could decipher *Americano, espresso,* Splenda, and *per favore*.

"*Cappuccino, per favore*," I said in my best Italian accent.

After the waitress took our order and left, I asked, "*Americano?*"

"Yeah, it's good. Do you like iced coffee?"

"No, that just sounds wrong."

"You drink coffee long enough, you'll take it hot, cold, and through an IV."

I laughed. "Well, do you like Italian food?"

"Absolutely. It reminds me of what a mother would have cooked."

"Would have?" I stepped into unchartered territory, maybe even a minefield. I searched around the room for Fear but didn't see him and proceeded.

"My mom ... is dead. My father, too."

I pretended Kayla hadn't already told me. "Oh, my gosh. I'm so sorry. How?"

Luke spoke with an even calm to his voice. "Murdered," he spoke with no expression changes. It seemed as if his black pupils spread out like ink removing the blue. I had not seen this expression before.

I sat there, hearing about Luke's life, his face paler than normal, feeling my heartbeat rock my still body back and forth. I didn't know what to say.

Luke continued. "Not what you were expecting? I was fifteen when I heard the shots. We ... I ran to my father's closet to hide. Ten minutes later, the door opened. Someone dressed in black held a handgun with what must have been a silencer. I blended into the dark behind a long wool coat. I guess it's the only reason I'm alive." Luke recalled the details with a cold detachment.

"A silencer? What were the shots you heard then?"

"My dad's gun. He took one of the guys out before he died."

"There was more than one?"

"Apparently. The one who opened my door had a ponytail; the dead one didn't."

"Who in the world would do that? Who would want to kill you and your parents?"

"That's the question, isn't it?"

"Are you still in danger?"

"For a few years after, I thought so. I prepared physically, studied, and stock-piled weapons, but no one ever came for me. For whatever reason, my parents were killed, and the assassins must have been satisfied that I had no idea or posed no risk to them."

"Assassins?" I fidgeted with my napkin.

Luke took a deep breath and looked around. He leaned into the middle of the table as I joined him there. "My parents worked for the NSA," Luke said and leaned back to finish his water. "Do you know what that is?"

I sat back and dropped my arms, nodding, dumbfounded. "That's just crazy."

"Yeah, sounds like a Lee Childs novel or something."

"You handle it so well."

"Good, glad I've got you fooled."

Luke's vulnerability surprised me. I didn't have conversations like this rehearsed. Everything about Luke made me feel unprepared. I refolded my napkin in my lap over and over. I looked up, and he watched me, waiting.

"I think you're amazing," I admitted.

His chin almost to his chest, he stared at me through his eyelashes, and then one corner of his mouth rose. "Then I have you totally fooled."

"Stop. I'm serious. You are ... very brave—in everything you do."

"No, in some things I'm a coward. You just don't see it."

"Why so disparaging?"

"Damn, college girl, just speak English."

"Why so demeaning?" I refocused the question to what I truly wanted to know. "Why are you opening up to me?"

"Why not?"

He made it look so easy. He made disclosure look healthy. I had done it before with Andy, but I never liked how I felt afterward. It felt as if I'd lost control over the relationship, and he used everything he knew about me to control me, berate me, or seduce me.

"I'm not sure how to take you."

"Then just take me." He paused, about to speak. "At face value."

I laughed and started to fidget again. "At face value? That may be dangerous."

"I'm used to danger, remember?"

His stare dropped my heart into my lap, and a new beat began. I wasn't used to feeling this way just from a look. He woke parts of me I had squelched for a long time. Luke made me feel alert. My heart raced, the adrenaline pumped.

"In my experience, danger means pain, and I'm not signing up for any more of that." I was on the verge of crying and being turned on at the same time. I was afraid of the desire creeping up within me.

"Phew. Pain? More like money. I'm sure everyone doted on little Miss Maggie."

"What?" Blood rushed to my face. I raised my voice. "You have no idea who I am." I pushed my seat back, wanting to be anywhere else but there.

"Whoa. I was joking." Luke laughed, more nervous than mocking.

I leaned back in my seat and folded my arms.

"I guess I just assumed a few things. I'm sure it wasn't like that. No one's life is a bed of roses."

"Far from it, Luke." Anger at his assumptions pushed aside any desire.

"Sorry, I didn't mean to hurt you."

The chair scraped against the stones as I pulled it in closer to the table, picking up my coffee and taking a sip.

"I would very much like to know your story."

His request made me cringe. My story? No one wanted to hear my story. Again, he ignored the proverbial doors I shut and tried to go through a window. "I bet you would."

"Yeah, I would. I don't want to assume or guess. Something tells me you are more than you appear to be."

"That's not how people see me at first?"

"No. For instance, this Italian you'll meet will hear how you are an American college girl. Beautiful and smart, he will think you're the answer to all his problems, assume you have money and are willing to share it with him. He will think your body's flawless, just like all those models he sees in the magazines. He will dote over your perfectness, knowing he is unworthy to even be with you in all his weaknesses."

"Now, you're making fun. People do not see perfect anything when they look at me."

"And again, you are naïve," Luke said it just as seriously as when he talked about his parents. "Your story, please."

I took a deep breath and jumped. "Mom and Dad divorced when I was six. My mom didn''t handle it well. She wasn't able to be there for me—became an alcoholic, went to rehab last year, and is sober now and happy in a new life and marriage. And, well, my dad is dead."

"I don't want to be rude, Maggie, but I know all those things. I want to know about *you*."

My chest seized for a moment. Again, I wasn't prepared. I had a pat story I usually gave, and it freaked guys out so much they never asked again. I didn't know how to respond. My breathing quickened, and I swallowed several times before answering. "I guess I'm surviving." I tried to say something honest. Uncharted territory always made me default to balls honest statements I would regret later.

Luke smiled, pleased, I supposed. He waited and watched me think as I took my pink pearl and held it to my lips, sucking it like a pistachio. A solitary natural five-carat conch pearl, near round and baby pink hung by a gold chain given to me by my dad. He told me the story many times before he died. He bought it at my birth, pink for his baby girl, different, because he knew I was special, and one pearl because it represented me and the beauty I would become.

Nervousness set in, but I ignored it. "I loved my daddy. His death was the worst thing in my life, and that's saying a lot for someone who was *almost* raped and almost died three times." I kept the truth to myself about my ex-boyfriend, Andy. No one wanted to hear it. And, I hated the pity that would follow.

"Oh, Maggie." His voice streamed soft and strong like waves in the ocean.

"It's okay, I'm fine now. I'm stronger for it."

"I can see that, but I thought you would rely on someone. But, you don't even rely on your big brother. It's almost the other way around. I wonder, who holds you when you need to break down?"

Who was this guy? Asking me the questions no one wanted to know? The questions no one should ask?

"I don't. I can't." Who was I, answering them?

Luke raised his eyebrow and sat back in his seat.

I remembered last night in the kitchen. "Well, not usually." I smiled, looking for mercy. The conversation had gone far enough.

"Uh huh." He left it at that. His firing range had stopped.

"We haven't finished our coffees or discussed a strategy." I looked over at the market where we both had surveyed throughout the meal without seeing Eleana. I noticed the old man tinkering around, refilling ice around the fish and serving customers.

"Nice switch, I'll give it to you. First of all, just be yourself, and he will fall easily enough, but find out if he knows Eleana or Primo."

"Right."

We discussed the details, and I took directions like a soldier. He helped me think like a spy. It put me in the right frame of mind. We still had an hour before time to meet the old man.

Without waiting for the waitress to bring the bill, Luke tossed some money on the table. "Let's go." He grabbed the hand that rested next to my glass. I threw my napkin and tried to follow, almost tripping over the chair leg.

"Where are we going?"

"I want to show you a place." Still holding my hand, Luke stopped to face me, people streamed around us as if we were rocks in a creek. "If for any reason you and I are separated, I want you to meet me here."

"Right here?" I looked around puzzled.

"No, where I'm about to take you."

"Oh, got it."

Luke continued to walk, pulling me by the hand. He zipped through the crowd, the light poles, and the newspaper stands. I started to sweat. We moved fast through the populated streets as the sun beat down on my head.

"Lemonade?" I yelled to him as we approached a sign, advertising it freshly squeezed.

He half turned his head and said, "In a minute."

I took it as a no. We had gone five blocks, and with all the turns, I doubted I would ever find the market again, much less this new place. I tried to remember landmarks: a tan building on the corner, the Dior sign, pink flowers hanging on the side of a pink building, and a graffiti painting of a man sitting down. I didn't try to guess where Luke led me, only to remember how to find it again. The problem was I only noticed the loudest but changeable landmarks, like a yellow Ferrari, a pink bike helmet on a guy parking his moped, or a couple sitting at an outdoor café, kissing. Just as we passed the kissing couple and turned right at the corner, we turned to the next door, a wrought iron gate leading into a courtyard. I ducked under the heavy pink blooms drooping overhead. I followed Luke on a flat stone path embedded in short green grass. We came to a stone and sand patio outlined with terracotta planters, red and pink blooms flowing over the sides. Another iron door barring a wooden door behind it opened from a key in Luke's hand.

Inside, a small, sleek kitchen greeted us with a dark wood table and four chairs. I stepped my foot onto old red hexagon tile. I looked up to see the ceiling extended with restored dark wooden rafters. Luke let go of my hand while I twirled around, bringing the whole room into view.

"What is this amazing place?"

"Here, take this key. Keep it on you always. If we get separated, I want you to come here and stay until I arrive."

"Okay."

"Don't leave here, Maggie."

"I don't know how we would get separated. Your paranoia is a bit of overkill, but I love this place. It's great." I walked farther in and looked around the small flat with plaster walls and old-world hardwood floors. I peeked, afraid to be alone in a bedroom with Luke, and noticed a four-poster bed dominating the small space.

I turned to him. "Seriously, how do you have a key to this place?"

"Don't worry about it. It's safe. Just don't let anyone see you enter."

"Oh, sure," I said. "Bathroom?"

"The door on the other side of the bed is the only one."

I walked into the bedroom, darkened by the thick curtains. The room resembled a hotel room without one personal item. I went into the bathroom, used the toilet, but didn't flush yet. I knew there had to be some sign of Luke in this place. I opened the mirror cabinet and found toothbrushes and paste, a razor, and a tube of lipstick. I had never seen Kayla wear any, only lip-gloss. I took the cap off to see the color. Bright burgundy red, a color no blonde would ever be able to wear with its purple tint, a brunette color only. I began to think Luke had never been faithful to Kayla, and I wasn't anything special, only another conquest. I put the lipstick back where I'd found it and returned to the kitchen. I hoped he didn't have any aspirations to bring me here for some kind of tryst behind Kayla's back. It was never going to happen.

"Well, let's go. We have just enough time to get back for your date."

"And some lemonade?"

Luke smiled. "And some lemonade."

Chapter 7
Lucky Fiddler

It took less time to get back to the market compared to heading to the villa, but it was time to see Giuseppe after our lemonade stop. Luke disappeared through an outdoor rug shop located next to the market.

When the old man finished with a customer, I walked up to him.

"Hi. Do you remember me from yesterday?"

"Of course, I do. A sweet flower like you."

"Thank you." Old and young were so poetic here.

"You meet my grandson, Merrico, si." He called the same name aloud with long syllables—*Murr-eee-cooo*—and a tall skinny Italian man came toward us. I guessed him to be Paul's age. "Merrico, this is the girl I told you." His added vowels to the end of words, sounded like singing. The old man held his hand out waiting for something.

It dawned on me. "Margaret."

"Oh, Mar-gar-rette." It rolled off the handsome man's tongue. "So nice to meet you." His English floated out smoother than his grandfather's. He looked young but educated. His manners surprised me, taking my hand in a shake and turning it into a chance to feel the softness of my skin. His presence made me aware of my own.

"Very nice to meet you, too."

"Come, a walk will be nice, no?" He leaned forward and waved his right hand for me to walk by.

I found myself wanting to mirror his manners. "It would be lovely."

"Have a good time on this beautiful day in this beautiful world ..." The old man continued as his voice trailed off.

Merrico still held my hand, as if my skin were the shell of an uncooked egg. "Are you are American?"

"What gave me away?" My smile widened.

Merrico laughed to the sky. "I love humor. How long are you in Rome?"

"I'm not sure, visiting friends. It's open-ended."

"O-pen end?"

"I'm flexible on my departure."

"*Si*, that is good for me."

I laughed at his cockiness.

"Such a beautiful laugh and a breathtaking smile, but it is your eyes that hold me. We do not see many cerulean eyes in Italy."

His eyes, not as dark as most Italian's, had flecks of green that caught light from the mid-day sun. I pulled away from his stare and peered into the distance to find Luke's short haircut and squinty slits looking at me with a pensive expression. I turned away to cross the street with Merrico. We walked away from the market. I followed his lead while he talked of his great city. I agreed with him on its beauty, a word they used repeatedly for an adjective that could describe anything from wine and women to places and clothing.

"What do you do?" I asked.

"I manage the Alla Rampa Restaurant."

"Nice. How did you land that gig?"

Merrico squinted, as if trying hard to understand. "Land gig?"

I would have to leave out all slang that seems so pervasive in my speech. "How were you able to get a job like that?"

"Oh, *si*. Understand. My uncle owns the restaurant, and I am his only nephew responsible enough." Only his eyes smiled.

"Your English is so good. Where were you educated?"

"I have a marketing degree from La Sapienza."

"Impressive." I'd noticed it in a table book at Luke and Kayla's, a beautiful campus of architecture and the reason for my response. I had no idea how it ranked among colleges in academia.

"I hope so. You are in college?"

"Yes, I go to SCU. I mean South Carolina University. Do you know where that state is?"

"Carolinas, yes, on the Atlantic coast."

"Yes."

"Columbia?"

I'm always amazed when people from other countries know American geography better than some Americans. "Wow, do you know how many Americans don't know that?"

Merrico smiled, and like a preschooler interrupting a book reading, he asked more questions than I cared to answer. After walking four blocks, I attempted to find the answers I had come for.

"How do you know the old man at the fish market?"

"Giuseppe? He's my grandfather."

I remembered the old man introducing Merrico as his grandson now.

"Does your grandfather typically find you girls to talk to?"

Merrico blushed. "No, well ... he knows I'm partial to American women." He paused, deciding something in his mind. "*Mi madre* was American."

This caught me by surprise. "I see your partiality. Does she live here?"

"No, she died when I was ten. Beautiful, she was."

"Oh, I'm sorry."

"It was the day tenderness left. Don't get me wrong, my papa's a good man, but he is demanding."

"I know the type, but maybe it's made you 'responsible'?"

"You listen well, Maggie. Feel free to forget all that, though. Such a heavy conversation for a first meeting. Don't you think?"

"It's best when the conversation is meaningful, and this is."

"I'm glad you are enjoying it."

"Then, your cousin is getting married?"

"My cousin?"

"Giuseppe told me his granddaughter is getting married. He wanted me to meet her."

"My sister is getting married."

"Well, yes, that works, too." I tried to contain my joy, as it would appear unusual for the news.

"You should meet her. She is completely happy. She has wanted that boy since she was fifteen."

"Sounds like a fairytale. Do you believe in those?"

"I believe who you marry should be your friend. It doesn't matter where they are from, but you have to be able to talk. My papa had that with my mamma. My grandfather was not happy about it."

"Giuseppe?"

"Oh, no, not at first. But my mamma won him over, and now he wants me to marry an American."

I shuffled my eyes from him to the pavement. Now we were going deep for a first conversation. "How about some ice cream?"

"You are funny little poppy."

"Poppy?"

"You remind me of a blue poppy in the wind. You jump up and down so fast and speed up and slow down when you walk. I have been trying to keep your pace. Are all Americans fast like you?"

I laughed at his description of my nervousness. "No, but maybe younger ones are."

"Always in a hurry. I will teach you, Poppy, to slow down and enjoy ..." He gazed upward and opened his arms, stretched forth toward the buildings, and took in the view. "Life." He looked back over at me. "You don't want to rush it, do you?"

"For such a young man, you speak with wisdom." I knew it flattered him, I just hoped I wasn't obvious.

"It is our life ... to go slow, to enjoy. I think I will like teaching you that."

"Americans have a hard time with guilt unless they are productive. That may be why they have so many hidden pleasures." I imagined the porn on the internet, the couple engaged in infidelity, and gambling.

"Hidden pleasures? Oh, Poppy, what are yours?"

I blushed, and Merrico smiled his pleased grin. I found myself increasingly uncomfortable with him, wondering if he was safe after all.

As I approached the market, I saw Giuseppe and waved. Luke still followed me, but I knew not to stop and engage him. Merrico and I said our goodbyes, and I promised to see him again. His eagerness telling me, "I can't wait," made me feel giddy and creeped out at the same time. Two blocks from the apartment, Luke walked over to me.

"You two looked like you were having fun," he said.

"It wasn't as bad as I thought."

"Well, what did you find out?"

"Eleana's his sister."

"And is she pregnant?"

"I don't know. There was a point where it wasn't appropriate to ask. If I had stayed with him any longer, he might have proposed."

Luke smiled. "Proposed, huh?"

"He was just coming on a little strong."

"I'm not surprised."

I told Luke how Merrico's uncle owned the Alla Rampa restaurant, where he was the manager, and the grandfather ran the fish market. It appeared Eleana wasn't poor.

"She did make Paul think of her as the poor girl who worked at the fish market. Interesting."

"And, from what I can tell, she doesn't have to work there much."

Luke walked without saying a word. We arrived at the apartment building. In the elevator, he turned to me.

"She never wanted Paul as her boyfriend but as a sperm donor."

It made me sick to think about it, but I knew that Luke might be right. That made the most sense. I hoped we were not getting carried away with our suspicions, blind to the idea that Eleana wasn't pregnant.

I spent the evening alone with Kayla while the boys worked. Woven through our conversation, I wanted to know if she knew about the villa, other women, or if she had any clue at all. I enjoyed being with her. Every moment I smiled with her, I felt more compassion for her and anger towards Luke.

I filled her in on the current events. We both hypothesized every scenario. It boiled down to speculation and assumptions. If Eleana was still pregnant, was she trying to pass it off as Primo's baby? Had Eleana miscarried? Was she being coerced or controlled in some way?

The only way to know the truth would be through Eleana. The desire to know chipped away at our brains until I stood and said, "Come on, I can't sit here all night. Let's at least go to her neighborhood and look for her. We should be able to spot that Winnie the Pooh in the dark."

"I don't know, Maggie. Without Luke or Paul?"

"What's the big deal?"

"I think we would stand out."

"We won't at Fiddler's."

"Well, Luke doesn't like me to go out in that part of town at night."

"Are you kidding? It's a college area; it's not the hood, Kayla. We can ask around. Who knows? They might even be there. I just can't sit here."

"Well, maybe just for an hour."

I agreed to anything that got her out of that apartment.

"Maybe we'll get lucky." I raised one eyebrow at her.

"I don't want to get that kind of lucky. I mean, you can. I'm not. But then again, you shouldn't."

Still laughing, I told her, "Umm, I meant with information. Just a joke."

Kayla headed upstairs and returned in jeans, a white shirt, and flip-flops. When she wore tight clothes, she could be cute, showing curves. Otherwise, she was stick-straight.

We headed outside, and the sky winked at us, full of stars with a large moon. The sky could be the ocean and the stars, tips of waves. We heard the beat of music far in the distance and walked toward it. The pub scene in this district pulsed electricity as our skin vibrated to the music. The numbers of people walking around made those driving come to a halt in a three-block radius. We walked past the dark alleys toward the brighter lights. When we approached the crowd, we started to get looks, but the gawkers kept walking. Kayla started to let it bother her and moved slower.

"Keep the pace."

"Their googly eyes. It's freaking me out," Kayla said.

"I know, but if we stop, we're not safe."

She walked faster. Five minutes later, we opened the door to Fiddler's Elbow. I looked over my shoulder to see if anyone had followed. I looked around and tried to understand this corner of Rome. It turned out to be a small community of old people and young college students. Merrico's college sat a mile away. This district contained the nightlife in Rome for anyone under twenty-five. It reminded me of Columbia, and I didn't feel as afraid as Kayla. She never went to a large university and had dropped out of community college to travel with Luke.

Inside, the atmosphere bounced with people standing shoulder to shoulder. We parted the crowd and made our way to a corner of the bar where the bartender could talk to us. The same one Luke spoke to a few nights ago.

"Hey, two Smittywicks, please."

He turned without a word and filled two beers from the draft tap. "Four euro. Kayla?" He looked past me.

"Hey, Rufallo."

"Where's Luke?"

"Working."

Rufallo looked over at me with a squint. "You two alone?"

"Yeah, we're looking for Primo or Eleana."

"Oh, they might be in tonight, usually are on Fridays."

I smiled so big it alarmed him.

"What are you up to?"

"Oh, no, nothing. Just want to meet her."

He continued to address Kayla. "Why she want to meet her?"

"She met her brother today—a real looker. I think he likes her."

"His new beautiful waste of time." He smiled with contentment and returned to his other customers.

"Whew. Great thinking, Kayla. He wasn't too nice calling me a waste of time."

"It's a compliment over here."

"Oh." We tipped our beers toward each other and giggled.

We stood in our little corner, unable to move, but at least we had a direct view of the door. I stood taller over Kayla in my wedge heels and kept my eye out. She entertained me with stories of Luke. When she told stories about him, she never described him being romantic or loving, but as Luke, the protector.

An hour later, I had managed to drink my beer, but now the decision to leave or order another one pressed on us. Kayla opted to stay, surprised she didn't feel so afraid without Luke. It turned out to be a good call, because ten minutes into our second beer, Eleana walked in with a girlfriend. I watched as she made her way through the sweaty bodies to the bathroom.

"Now the night just got interesting." I said to Kayla and motioned for her to follow.

We walked into the packed ladies room. We stood two people behind Eleana, while she spoke something loud in Italian as she wiggled the pee dance. Her friend tapped the girl in front of her and said something I couldn't hear. One by one, her friend talked to the girls, and they both moved forward, passing everyone in line.

In a few minutes, Eleana came out and thanked everyone. That word in Italian I understood. She washed her hands at the sink. Her friend joined her and applied lip-gloss.

"*Guarda me. Questo è ridicolo. Non riesco nemmeno a venire fuori molto più a lungo.*" She fidgeted with her shirt while she looked around.

"*Non voglio di sentirla. Che sei ancora più piccolo di me e sei tu quello per avere un bambino.*"

I looked at Kayla. Her widened eyes confirmed she heard the word bambino, too. But, I knew she understood more than that. We had to get out of there. I pushed Kayla to go through the door and looked back at Eleana to see if I could see anything at her stomach, but nothing protruded. I looked over at her face and a large smile with eye contact greeted my stare. I smiled back as if a bystander and turned to navigate through the tight crowd of pawing hands, out of the bathroom, and through the pub.

Kayla forced me to speed-walk in heels. She never even brought up a strange looking man or a burnt-out streetlight. We breezed by everything too fast to analyze it or be afraid. I got inside and plopped on the couch with my full body lying flat.

"Oh, my gosh. That was so close. Okay, what did she say?"

"Eleana was complaining that before long, she wouldn't even be able to come out in public. Her friend told her she looked great, that she was smaller than her, and Eleana was the one pregnant."

I laughed, holding my sides in with my arms. "We did it." I sat up. "My brother's going to be so happy. He's really having a baby." Then, my smile faded as I thought of Paul. This had pain written all over it.

I slept well knowing I had at least found out the truth for my brother. Kayla invited me to sleep in the bed with her, to have a mattress and a night free of the lumpy couch. She assured me Luke would take the couch, because he slept there a lot anyway. As uncomfortable as it would be to lie where Luke slept each night, I was more thrilled at the idea of a bed. I accepted without hesitation. I realized I had failed to think through the logic of my position when Luke came tiptoeing in, undressed down to his snug boxer briefs.

"So sorry. I'll just go to the couch," I whispered, pulling the covers up and to the side, trying not to disturb Kayla.

"I didn't see you. It's okay, I'll take the couch." He stood there shirtless and yawned, stretching his chest and arms, but didn't leave.

I shook my head. "Don't be ridiculous; it's a blaring nuclear holocaust down there it's so bright. You won't be able to sleep."

"I could pass out on the sun." He stared at my feet and back up to my face, stopping over the middle too long. "You're the one who won't be able to sleep anymore," he said with a grin.

I noticed one of his pec muscles twinge tight. I sensed he wasn't talking about the light coming through the window anymore, but him. He stood straight, his jaw raised. Even in the shadowed room, I could see his eyes peering right through me, always saying more than his words. He licked his lips. I then realized I stood there arguing with Luke in my four-leaf clover underwear and green cami. I looked down at my braless cleavage while heat flushed my face, and I took off walking as fast as I could. My arm grazed his while it swung past him. His arm touched mine a second time from behind me, not from my swing, but he must have reached out.

I made it to the top step before Luke laughed and whispered louder, "So, did you get lucky last night?"

I gave him a dirty look and ran down the stairs. I stopped at the sink, looking out at the silhouetted trees in the park and drank a full glass of water. Why I waited there, I didn't know. As I asked myself this, I knew. I hoped

Luke would come down. When I realized my motivation, I jumped on the couch and threw a blanket on me, not taking the time to turn it into a bed with sheets.

"Stupid. Stupid. Stupid." I repeated to myself. I can't believe he saw me in my underwear, the four-leaf-clover lucky ones of all panties. I did put them on last night hoping to get lucky with information, and I did. But, Luke turned everything into sex. He stood there so smug and confident about his body, wearing those snug boxer briefs. I cringed, thinking of it. I wanted the image out of my mind but couldn't purge it.

Chapter 8
Playgrounds

The next morning, I avoided Luke as best I could in a one-bedroom flat, making it nearly impossible. We all slept in late, and when he ate breakfast, I used the half bathroom downstairs to change clothes, brush my hair, and do my make-up. When he took a shower upstairs, I ate breakfast. When we were both in the room, Kayla's presence deflected any one-on-one conversations. Later in the afternoon, Paul arrived with some tiramisu, raving it was Rome's best.

"Where did you get it?" Luke asked.

"Pompi, you know the place off Ceneda?"

"That restaurant is expensive," Luke said.

"I know. That's why I only brought dessert."

"No worries, I have dinner planned," I said.

I wanted to do something nice for Paul. Maybe I thought it would somehow lessen the blow of what I had to tell him. I wanted him to know he was loved, and that he wasn't in this alone.

"Since when do you cook?" Paul asked.

"Since I took Adult Living senior year of high school. I can cook anything now."

Paul addressed Luke. "I don't know if I would believe all that."

"Yeah, you might have to prove it," Luke said.

"You brought the best dessert in Italy. Now, we need the best meal. You two beef-heads probably won't think it's the best meal in the world, though, since it's fish. But, I will try to prepare it perfectly."

"Fair enough," Luke said.

Kayla walked down the stairs after hearing part of the conversation. "I just hate that I'll miss it," she said, eyeing the box Paul brought. "But, the tiramisu looks ready. I believe I will have to make sure it's okay before I leave for work." She opened the box and rolled her eyes with a moan of pleasure.

"Okay, I can't watch this or I'll eat some too," I said and left the kitchen.

I could hear them all *oohing* and *ahhing*, even in the living room, but at least, I didn't have to watch them. I wasn't the kind of girl who could eat dessert before my dinner. It was something my dad drilled into me, no doubt.

I sat on the couch and pulled out my journal I had brought from Mom's house, trying to distract myself.

I wrote most of this journal at age twelve. I had wanted to write down everything I could remember, even when some things were already fading. I wanted to capture every memory. If I could keep them, I wouldn't lose a part of me. Of course, only a little girl thought that. As an adult, I had found forgetfulness could sometimes be a blessing.

I opened the cover and found my name written in my less-than-perfect twelve-year-old handwriting.

This journal belongs to: Margaret Dulaney. If found please return to: 121 Axton St. Dallas, TX. I flipped a few pages and stopped on the entry date: September 1.

I remember my first day of school. I was so ready. Wanting to learn all I could. Why did they call it kindergarten, why not first year or first grade? We were kinders in a garden? What is a kinder? There was a big playground where I used to run as hard as I could. My messy hair flew free with my voice. I could run and scream, and no one would tell me to be quiet. In that place, I felt safe. My favorite game was "house."

I was the mommy. The big oak tree was the house. The roots divided the house into rooms. It was much better to play when a boy could be the daddy, but they ran off, I guess hunting for food. Another two acted as the kids. I cooked for them, usually acorns. I loved taking care of them. When we had to go inside, I liked to be mommy there, too. The parents were always smarter than the children. I had to do good in school. Numbers came easy for me. They were always the same, the answer never changed. Four always came after three and before five. I liked the order. I liked being good at numbers, seeing my teacher amazed. I wanted to be different, to be special. I hope in this big world there is something special about me.

In a way, the same little girl who wrote those words was somewhere inside of me. I could be transported to a scene and remember every detail. Rummaging through this book was like walking through the closets of my mind. I closed the journal when Luke walked up.

"Whatcha reading?"

"Nothing."

"Please, I like hearing the synopsis."

I looked at the book. "No. This ... this is different."

"Maggie. Come on. It looks cool. It's so old looking." Luke reached to touch it.

I pulled it away. "No. I'm serious, Luke."

Luke took this as a challenge. With a smile on his face, he tried to force it from my hand, but I pulled it down to the couch and laid on it. Luke reached around both of my arms and dug for the book. I had shoved it between the cushions with both my hands still on it.

"Luke. No! Stop it! Please, Luke."

My pleas only made him try harder. Like a dog for a bone, he dug until ... "Aha! I got it."

I turned and saw him standing over me with my green leather journal held high, as if he had just killed an animal from a hunt. Tears filled in my eyes. I said nothing at first, but Luke looked down at me, and I knew he could see the tears that threatened to fall down my face.

Luke's arm dropped. "Maggie. I'm ... I'm so sorry. I thought we were playing." He handed me the book without opening it. He stared at my face and watched me hold it to my chest.

Paul entered from the kitchen. "What you got?" he asked, only catching the loudest parts.

"Nothing. I didn't know the book was so special. I ..."

"Oh, that thing. That's her journal about when she was a kid."

I shot Paul a dagger look as he walked away.

"Maggie, I'm sorry." Luke's forehead wrinkled.

"It's okay."

Kayla had finished her dessert and left for work. I had been reading my book when I told Paul I would start dinner. He mumbled and went upstairs to watch a Jackie Chan movie. While I chopped the onion, Luke walked into the kitchen.

"Crying again?" he said with a timid smile.

I couldn't help but give a slight lift to a corner of my mouth after his attempt to make me laugh. This time, the tears were from onions. I didn't know why I had cried. I'd been pretending to read for an hour, trying to wrack my brain for an answer. The odds of Luke opening the book to one of the telling pages were slim but possible. One of many embarrassing moments he could have read flashed through my mind. I closed my eyes and let the onion tears fall, hoping it would burn away the images that rested behind them.

"I'm sorry I upset you, Maggie. Can I help with dinner?"

I knew it wasn't his fault he had triggered the helplessness I had felt with Andy. He didn't know what Andy had done to me. It settled better with people to tell them I was almost raped. However, when I felt powerless, the same emotions came up inside me. Would I push away everyone who made me feel so vulnerable and weak? Would I blame every man in my life for Andy's behavior? I gave Luke my best "you must be crazy" look for thinking he could cook. Men who looked like that couldn't possibly be domesticated. Then, I remembered the omelets. How could I forget his omelets? I saw his frozen face in my mind.

"Who do you think does all the cooking around here when we aren't burdened down with visitors making us go out all the time?"

I flashed him a grin. "Oranges. Will you peel me four?"

"Hmm, oranges. Nice."

"How was work last night?" I watched his cutting technique.

"Fine. You know I can't talk about it, but if you guys were ever in danger, you know I would tell you. Terrorism isn't the most dangerous thing in this city."

"I know. The terrorist stuff going on in Europe is freaky, though."

He looked over at me. I smiled at him as I cleaned the red plastic cutting board.

"When are you going to tell me about last night?" Luke asked.

"What?"

"Maggie, I know you went out. Without me." His tone sounded disappointed.

"How do you know anything I did?" I jumped to a defense.

"I'm not going to act like your parent right now."

"Then don't."

Luke stopped peeling the fourth orange. "Really? What is that damn chip on your shoulder anyway?"

"Why do you feel the need to know everything I do? You checking on me? Spying?"

"Maggie, I was hoping you would just tell me."

"No, you weren't. Otherwise, you wouldn't check up on me."

"Why are we having this discussion? I'm not your brother or your father."

I put the knife down, grabbed a rag, and wiped my hands. "No, Luke. You're not." I threw the towel on the cutting board and walked away. I realized I had no room to run. I opened the front door and walked out, leaving a slam in my wake.

What was he doing? Following me? Calling every bar in town? Why? He could be so ridiculous. I walked so fast, I decided I couldn't stand still in an elevator and took the stairs two at a time for all five flights. I burst out into the dusk as the sun burned like a sunflower above the horizon. Honeysuckle floated in the air. The scene and scent calmed me. I could never stay mad for long. I experienced only bursts of anger. Once it was out, it was gone, but I needed to understand what caused it. I didn't get mad often, but when I did, I would always look for a way to prevent it in the future.

This way or that way? Life was all about turns and decisions. I had faced two choices in Dallas and ended up choosing Italy. And now, so many more choices spun from that one. After a week, I realized I knew exactly the same about Paul's baby as I did when I arrived. The thought of failing pressed heavy on my chest. Luke's overprotective ways prevented me from discovering the truth about Eleana.

I walked faster. Tears fell down my cheeks for the third time today. I wanted to scream. I wanted to fight the air, to punch something and not get hurt—to matter. I couldn't fail my brother. I walked around the building until I plopped down in a swing at the park across the street. My head fell into my hands.

I wiped my face free of any leftover tears the breeze hadn't erased. Lifting my head, I saw Paul walking toward me against the sky's rich blue, reminding me of the Mediterranean Sea I flew over when I had arrived in Rome.

"Hey."

"Hi," I said, almost inaudible from exhaustion.

"You okay?"

"I don't know."

"What's that all about? Luke and Kayla have been so good to you, and you just open fire on him?"

"I know, I know." I stared at my feet in the pebbles.

"And you don't know why?"

"He is ... he's just ..." I fidgeted, clenching my hands tighter around the chains of the swing. "I just don't understand him." I knew it was more than him checking on me. I didn't want to think about him so much, look for him, want to know his thoughts, or—worse—want to please him.

"Maggie, he's only trying to keep you safe. That's what we do."

"I'm fine. I can handle myself. You know I can, Paul."

"You are strong, Maggie, and fearless at that, but you are a woman, and on this side of town are some dangerous men. I've done some checking. Primo's father is not a good man. It's not like the kind of dentists back home with a billboard of a dancing, happy tooth. Primo's family is involved with tough immigrant criminals, trafficking drugs. He might even be a part of the fifth mafia and have dealings all over Italy."

"Fifth mafia?"

"Apparently, in the spirit of making money, the four Italian mafias have put their differences aside and joined together."

"That's scary."

"Yeah. I'm relieved Eleana miscarried. I don't want to have to fight all that."

I clenched my teeth and tried to force a smile.

"What?" Paul asked.

I stood. "Well."

"What do you know?"

"Eleana *is* pregnant."

"Shit. How do you know?"

"Sit down." I swung the chains toward Paul. "Last night …"

Paul grabbed the swing and threw his weight into it while he listened. In the animation of my story, I watched as a little girl slipped down a slide toward her mother, screaming with pure glee at the top of her small lungs.

I heard pebbles crunch behind me.

"What's going on? Did you punch him and I didn't see it?" Luke asked.

"Ha. Ha. Funny," I said with all the sarcasm I could muster.

Paul glared at Luke.

Luke turned toward Paul with a "What gives?" look.

"Eleana *is* pregnant," Paul continued.

"Again? Wow, you got some good swimmers there, Paul," Luke said.

"Good one," I said.

Paul stood. "How do you know?"

"Kayla and I heard her and her friend talking about it in the girls' bathroom at Fiddler's."

Luke had a contemplative expression, nodding his head.

"That's what I did last night when you were having me followed," I said to Luke.

"I wasn't having you followed. Kayla told me."

I closed my eyes and turned away. I always regretted getting angry.

"Let's just say I did have you followed. Why would you react the way you did?"

I looked around at him. "I'm glad you didn't. And, I'm sorry I jumped to conclusions. But, for the future, I don't want to be followed. I don't want you treating me like a child."

"So, when you're stubborn and run straight over a cliff, I'm supposed to watch?"

"I ... I'm not."

"Everyone needs rescuing sometimes, Maggie," Paul said.

"Well, when I needed it, no one ever came, and I survived. I rescue myself."

"Do you hear how arrogant that sounds?" Paul said.

I walked away and headed back to the building. Luke called out. "I hope you never need to be."

All this from a man who thought there was something between us. He was the arrogant one. He wanted to be in control of everything and everyone. He couldn't get me to fawn all over him, so he tried to control my whereabouts like a child. I didn't even get this kind of treatment at my mom's house.

I went into the house and finished preparing the meal. Chopping off the fish heads proved to be more therapeutic than nauseating. I couldn't take the skin off until after I had cooked them, so they weren't too pretty on the plate, but they tasted great. The boys came in as I set dinner on the table: broiled halibut with a fruit salad and sautéed green beans with mushrooms. We sat at the table and all ate together. Sounds of chewing filled the air until Luke broke the awkward silence. Or fixed it.

"This is really good, Maggie."

"Amazing, Sis."

"Never had green beans like this."

"Thanks."

"I want to know how to make them," Luke said.

"Sure. I'll show you." Relieved the mood started to change and that Luke was pleasant, I tried to be too.

"Okay, you two. Kiss and make up," Paul blurted out. He hated white elephants as much as I did.

Luke and I looked at each other. Little did Paul know how Luke would probably like that, but it would never happen. He sat there swallowing up the table with his arms.

"I mean, you know …" Paul tried to clarify and waved his fork in the air.

Luke took a deep breath. "I'm sorry I treated you like a child."

"I'm sorry I went off on you." I took a bite of the halibut.

"I just can't imagine something happening to you."

I swallowed a large piece fast. "It won't."

Luke stopped mid-conversation, fixed his eyes on his half-eaten food without moving.

"Hello. Earth to Luke." I watched, waiting for an answer.

His eyes refocused, coming out of his deep thought. "Yeah? Sorry."

"Where did you just go?"

He pursed his lips together and shook his head. "Nope. You're not opening that 'green book' of mine."

I took a bite and stared at Luke's fixed gaze on the saltshaker. I wanted to go in there, in his mind, to know what he was thinking. It became what woke me at four every morning.

"We're all good?" I asked.

Luke looked up. "Yeah. I won't *start* following you," he promised and took a big bite of halibut.

"Good. And I won't go *snap, crackle, pop* all over you."

Luke and Paul laughed.

"Good. Glad that's done. While y'all have been jabbering, I've finished. I think it's time for that tiramisu again," Paul said, waiting for a confirmation.

"Sure. Go ahead. Just save me one. I can't eat any yet."

Luke joined Paul, and I started the dishes.

Paul called out. "Put those down. That's my job. Right, Luke?"

"The sponge has his name on it," Luke said.

"Well, you don't have to tell me twice." I untucked the towel from my jean pocket and threw it onto the counter, before plopping on the couch and stretching out.

Paul crashed at the apartment again. I had taken his usual spot on the couch, so he didn't stay over as much. His dump with three other Marines became old to him fast. My arrival may have inconvenienced Paul more than

Luke or Kayla.

    Paul slept on the air mattress in the living room while I prepared my usual place on the couch. Although I knew Luke had already locked the place for the night, I double-checked the door. All three locks were bolted. I grabbed the journal tucked in the couch. I turned to a page and tried to decipher my messy middle school handwriting.

When I was five, Paul and I loved adventures. He was my best friend. We shared a room with bunk beds. I still had the top bunk, but I did not fall out anymore. Paul had to have the bottom. I never understood why someone (can't remember who) read me the book, *Where the Wild Things Are*. I had a nightmare. I'd never had a bad dream. I had two parents who loved me. I knew it every time they held me. But, I had not seen my mom much, and that bothered me. There was a window to the left of my bunk bed, and on the other side, a fenced front yard. I dreamed the large Wild Thing stepped over the fence that came up to his knee and busted his big fist through my second-story window and grabbed me out of my bunk bed and ate me. It was so real. I had a hard time fitting it with all my other memories. The only proof it wasn't real was that I was still alive. Did it mean it was going to happen?

Scribbled at the bottom of the page with better handwriting, from when I was fifteen:

Despite the fear that had already gripped my world, I believed something or someone communicated to me. I knew the difference between Grandma's house and going to my mom's. I knew the difference between peace and fear, and I knew things about people, like whether they were good, just by looking at their eyes. I could look past their eyes, to the dark or light reflecting back.

    I didn't want to live with the wild things in an unreal world. I wanted truth, not fantasy. Were the unknowns about Luke dangerous? It bothered me that I'd never seen him angry. I knew anger. I knew how to handle weak people. If I could see his human side just once, I would know the worst and be prepared. Even yelling at him did not rattle his cage. The only hint to Luke's hidden side was the day we sat on the couch as he stared at my face. I believed I saw light, but I doubted my instincts now. Life had become more complicated than when seen through the eyes of a twelve-year-old child. My world of peace and fear blurred boundaries and became many colors, no longer black and white.

Chapter 9
The Guest Room

The next morning, I woke as always with the five-fifteen sunrise. I forced myself back to sleep, only to reawaken at seven-thirty when Kayla unlocked the front door. I tried to sleep later but was now on a routine that wouldn't allow it. I was the one who usually started the coffee pot, but today, someone beat me to it and drank half the pot.

I lifted my voice. "Hey, where are the boys?"

"Gone when I got here. Check the sheet in the second drawer of the kitchen, under the silverware."

How did the guys leave without me even stirring? I opened the drawer and found a calendar. This would have been handy all week. It was Luke and Paul's work schedule. Kayla came down the stairs in plaid pajama shorts and a cami.

"I know Luke works today. Does Paul, too?" Kayla asked.

"Yeah."

"Sorry. I don't work tonight, so just give me a few hours of sleep, and I'll be up for whatever."

"That's fine. Sounds good."

Kayla turned to go upstairs.

"Oh, hey. Do you have a phone I can call Paul with?"

"Sure." Kayla left to return with her cell phone and then went upstairs with her red eyes drooping.

I dialed Paul's number, already saved in her phone. "Hello?"

"Hey. Did you two forget to tell me you were working?"

"Never came up, did it? Sorry, Sis."

"It's okay. I just wanted to know if you were doing okay?"

"Me? I'm fine."

"Well, could you do me a favor then?"

"Shoot."

"You talked a lot about Primo's family, but can you find out who Eleana's mother was? Merrico said she's an American."

"Hmm." Paul turned silent. "I think she told me her name one time. I just can't remember it. If I can, I'll bring something home about her."

"Okay. Thanks."

"Now that I have you on the phone, do you want to come down here today? It's Sunday, and there's not much going on. I could show you around."

"Really? That would be fun. Better than sitting here all day."

Paul gave me exact details to the American Embassy. I had been here a week and had not visited any monuments. I flitted around the room with a new bounce in my step.

After writing Kayla a note, I dressed for a day on the streets of Rome. I took my shoulder satchel and made a point to remember my passport. Paul told me the address to the embassy and recommended the subway routes. I printed a map from the computer.

After a short walk, I jumped on the subway at Tor Sapienza. Two very long stops later, I changed at Tiburtina. The FM-2 line was packed full of students and old people, the very representation of San Lorenzo itself, but when I switched to the blue line more diverse people and accents flew around announcing downtown Rome. For the first time, Italy became uncomfortable. It was the combination of the dim light, the smell worse than belly-button lint, and the skin flaking off an elderly man onto the back of his seat. It all had me sitting on the edge of my own seat, alert.

I had to go four stops to Termini, and then I could smell fresh air again. I counted in my head and told myself it would only take five minutes. It took seven hundred and eighty-four seconds before the doors at my stop opened. I rushed toward the daylight.

I walked fast and imagined the green rolling hills of the Appalachian Mountains from the weekend trip I took with Shawn two months ago. So far away in my mind now, I had to dig deep to retrieve it. Standing on the stairs waiting for the line to move, I closed my eyes. I saw Shawn's slight smile turn into his signature expression: bottom lip raised, forcing the corners of his mouth down. I still thought about him often, his face popping into my mind at the oddest moments.

In my head, the screams almost became audible as I opened my eyes to the smell of body odor. The tall Italian in front of me had his arm raised, waving to his wife to join him. He must be crazy or just demanding. Did he expect her to fly? The people stood like too many pencils jammed in a cup.

One by one, we finally moved. Everyone pulled out their passports, showing them to two train attendants before they were allowed to pass. It reminded me of the roadblocks back home to catch the drunk drivers on holiday weekends. I made it out to the big, white overcast sky. I took a deep breath and admired it.

I could have switched trains and traveled two more stops, but walking in the fresh air became the only choice for me after experiencing even a tiny bit of Rome's subway system. The sidewalks were wide, and I had plenty of things to see. Carved architecture and centuries-old buildings made me look up more than watching in front of me. When I almost tripped over a rolling suitcase, I focused again in front. I passed a stand selling luggage, stacked neatly like magazines, on the side of the street. To my annoyance, the only ones at the stand purchasing were Americans. Leather was cheap in this country, but an American falling for the faux leather made the over-sized guy look like an idiot. I walked past shaking my head.

The sun beat down as I walked at least the length of a football field. There were no regrets about choosing to walk though when I came to a circle of buildings with a large fountain in the center. I had difficulty crossing so many lanes of traffic. I braved the risk and darted in between cars, causing a flurry of honking and screeching tires. When I made it across, I stood in front of four naked women and a man carved out of stone. My eyes widened with curiosity. Each woman rode an animal, but the naked man sat atop a fish that spouted water out of its mouth. They were old, but the water kept moving like time. If they could put this in the center of their city, it had been at the center of their minds. That meant if Paris was the city of love, as people said, then Rome must be the city of sex.

Circling the fountain, I lost my sense of direction. I pulled out my map and looked for the road I needed, and kept walking when I found Orlando. Del Terme's snack bar enticed me to a drink and pastry to go. I walked and ate as I came to the end of a narrow two-lane street and another large opening. I had to look at my map again. I detested looking like a tourist. Nothing made any sense or followed a logical grid pattern. I kept walking straight and saw a whole line of motorcycles parked in what should be the middle of an intersection.

The streets became a maze. I meant to take *Via Umbria* but spun through and took *Leonida Bissolatti*. At the end of it, I came to ornate iron gates on my right and a police car parked in front, where Paul sat waiting for me. A bead of sweat fell from my temple.

Paul jumped from the drivers seat. "Quite a trek?"

"I hated the subway, so I walked longer than you told me to."

"Oh, my gosh. How far?"

"From Termini."

Paul laughed. "Actually, that's not too bad. Here everyone walks.

Personally, not a fan."

I imagined Paul on the walk I took, seeing an impatient man, tired of sweating. Paul blended in here much better with his dark hair and dark hazel eyes on a skinny frame.

"Get your passport out."

Paul spoke for me at the embassy gate to another guard and showed him my passport.

"How do you put up with him?" The guard asked with a chuckle.

"Gently," I said, smiling.

"Have fun." He dismissed us to proceed to the front doors.

I thought about that as I scanned the pink stucco building that looked more like a hotel in Florida. *Fun?* I thought the walk here was the fun part.

Paul took me through the front doors. The lobby resembled a bank with counters lining one wall with women behind thick glass. It was busy with three lines two people deep, while other windows were unused. The floor tile stretched out seamlessly like a large piece of earth.

Paul swiped his security card at a door to the right of the lobby. On the other side, a guard read my passport again. I walked down a long hallway, following Paul, wondering about Luke. The hallway boasted ornate wallpaper with velvet lines. A hospital linoleum floor would be out of place here. The hardwood floors were old and wide. The tall ceilings were framed with intricate wood on all corners, and sconces illuminated the wallpaper of red and green. Paul took me through another door into a modern industrial kitchen.

"Hey, Sammy."

"Hi, Skin. Who ya got with ya?"

"This is my kid sister, Maggie."

"Ah, a baby sister. Cute."

"Nice to meet you," I said.

"You as well," Sammy said.

"So—*Skin?*" I asked her.

"Oh, short for skinny," Sammy said.

"Of course. He is, isn't he?"

"I try to fatten him up. He comes in here and eats everything I give him, but he never changes."

"You have a great spread here. This kitchen has everything." I looked around at the vastness of stainless steel. Vegetables covered large tables, like the ones in an operating room, and there were stainless sinks twice the size found in a normal kitchen. I counted three refrigerators, two large industrial dishwashers, and four workstations, each with their own double sinks.

"We feed a lot of important people in the dining hall. Have you shown her that yet?"

"No, we just got here. I wanted her to meet you first."

"I'm really glad you did," Sammy said.

Paul didn't notice, but this petite brunette had a crush on him. Sammy wore a double-breasted white chef's jacket, but certainly she had a figure it couldn't hide. Her nonverbal clues gave her away—brushing her hair back on one side, looking up from a hidden smile, and glancing at Paul's butt when he turned to get a drink out of the refrigerator.

When we went into the dining hall, I noticed Paul change. He went silent and turned his head away as a man in a dark suit walked with three other people, all with nearly matching ties.

He whispered, "That is Ambassador Thorne."

"No way."

"Go this way and don't look." I assumed I wasn't supposed to be there by Paul's actions. Paul walked faster, with slight nudges for me to hurry. I dropped my eyes to avoid any eye contact as we walked into another room and out through a French door, into a garden I had noticed in pictures on the wall. Trees blocked traffic noise, and bushes made walls that hid the gray streets beyond. Flowers filled the space like a beautiful woman.

"You're going to love this."

"What?"

Paul led me in a zigzag around some trees to a white marble American flag in a wave.

I gasped. Paul"s patriotism shone as he explained the place he guarded, our little home away from home. The old, ornate building didn't make me feel at home like our apartment did, but out in the garden, it felt safe, and I was proud to be an American. The Italians were letting us live in their guest room, which was how I saw the embassy now. It made me love the Italian people even more.

"Paul, I'm speechless."

Paul's smile spread wider. "I'm glad you like it."

"This was so worth the trip."

"I'm glad you think so. There's not much more I can show you," he said with shrugged shoulders and a grin.

"Look at this garden. It's enough, trust me. Can I wander in it a bit?"

"Sure." Paul talked into a black radio speaker. "I'm assigned here for the next thirty minutes; have at it."

"Thanks," I said and walked around to read the monuments. My mom had a book about flowers in South Carolina I had once leafed through. I looked now for any I might recognize, and I found wisteria hanging, camellias climbing the iron fence, and roses under the windows. However, I didn't know what the tulip-looking flowers with fringed edges were. In the distance, a faint sound of water and a hum of traffic could be heard. As I walked around, I turned and looked back at the embassy and the vast windows. I wondered who stood behind the drawn curtains.

"Should I find you some binoculars?" Luke walked up behind me and caught me unaware.

"No, I still wouldn't be able to see through those darn curtains. I need to speak with Security about that."

"Tsk, tsk, tsk. Quite nosy." He took on a British character complete with accent. "I'm sure we would be happy to make it easy for you. Can I fetch you the videotapes?"

"Ah, movie stars only."

"Fresh out." We smiled at each other.

"You know this isn't a bad place to have to come to work every day."

"It's not 1600, but we have our ways."

He referred to Pennsylvania Avenue, home of the White House.

"Hey, Luke, we gotta go," Paul said.

I didn't hear Luke's radio make a sound. I wondered if he had it turned down.

"Okay."

"Maggie, you'll have to come, too." His voice was tense. We went back to the door where the second guy checked my passport. Luke talked to the guard, and Paul watched and then told the guard, "Keep her back."

Luke and Paul pulled out their guns, hung them down to their thighs, and opened the door. I heard running and yelling, then the door closed.

The guard looked at me as if to say, "Don't even think about it."

We stood there in the long hallway together, alone. I listened for gunfire, and I didn't want to be there. I wanted to see if they were okay. I told myself anyone crazy enough to come in here armed was probably dead, but Fear stood in front of the door and amplified the noises I heard. I had memorized the wallpaper design by the time Paul returned. Relief washed over me as I let out the air I had been holding in my lungs, not realizing I had been breathing shallow, silent breaths.

Paul escorted me through another exit.

"Hey, what happened?"

"Go home." He stuck me in a cab without a clue on his stone face.

It was a strange feeling, being treated like royalty upon entering, but more like the mistress rushed through a side door upon leaving. I hated feeling helpless. I decided I hated it worse than being ignored. Zooming through the streets with sounds of horns, motorcycle engines, and cars passing by, I sensed the weight of Paul and Luke's responsibility.

I had the driver drop me at Santa Susanna, the Italian church for Americans. White stone walls held four statues ruminating in their own individual porticos. Across the middle, it read *Portcard, Paepae Vicar*, followed by Roman numerals. The history of this place was nonessential to me. Maybe it meant more to a Catholic or to an Italian, but for me, I only came to light a candle and say a prayer. The outside resembled the Alamo with its detail, but the interior transported me to another time.

I entered a dimly lit room as tall as it was deep. Arches framed the center square room. Pictures or designs covered every inch of the walls and ceilings. I didn't know what that kind of art was called. Some were flat like paintings, but others were raised. Stone and marble columns stood in the corners. Whole Italian scenes from centuries long ago told a story on the walls. The curvy, pale women of their ancestry in faded colors contrasted with the skinny, sleek youth who walked the streets outside in bold colors. The organ pipes on the back wall stood like golden Roman spears under the bright cascading window. The natural light illuminated the pews.

I moved farther in, to the front. I took a stick and lit a candle from one already burning. I bowed my head and said a prayer for Paul and Luke. Then, I turned down the aisle of the first pew and put one knee down. I wasn't sure if I did any of this correctly, but I watched one lady and proceeded with confidence. She sat a good ten rows back, but I didn't want to see anyone gawking at the scenery. I wanted to remember it was a church. I wanted to feel something.

I tried to imagine my Grandma's house. The only noise came from the deafening footsteps on the wooden floor. With my eyes closed, my mind wandered. I rolled my pearl against my neck and remembered.

I tried every day to live up to my father's expectations. He said beauty was not in the outer shell but radiated from within. Just as the pearl's glow came from layers and layers, so would mine. He placed a different expectation on me than most of my friends had from their parents. They strove to be pretty, obsessed with a boy's confirmation of their beauty. I knew my dad expected more. He expected kindness, gentleness, and self-control.

I opened the Bible tucked in the pew and read the first thing my eyes fell on. It said, "Do not repay evil for evil."

Grandma wrote scriptures on pieces of mail and skinny, torn yellow legal pads. They were tucked into her Bible, *Readers Digest*, or the *TV Guide*. She lived by them, like food. She was like a quiet lake to me, like a day where clouds form at your mouth and ice falls from a branch in the distance, yet everything is white and solid. I lost her when I turned twelve.

I tried to feel her, to feel love, but I couldn't even feel peace in this place. I stood to leave and walked down the aisle of empty pews to the door flooding with daylight.

"Poppy?" An Italian voice called to me, but the light at the door blocked his face.

"Merrico? Hello."

"Ah, my Maggie. I have wrenched my brain, trying to figure out how to see you again, and here you are."

I smiled. "A normal hangout for you?" I looked around and waved my hand toward the ornate ceiling.

"Ah, yes, I see you are on to me. I like Americans."

"This must be their headquarters."

"There is only one I care to talk to." He never looked around. "I won't let you leave me again. Come. This time, I take you to eat?"

"I would enjoy that very much." My manners came over me again.

I lifted my hand so he could carry it in his own. He kissed it first and led me through the doors, holding one open for me. He walked me to his car, a black four-door with a cross emblem on it.

"This will be my first ride in an *Alfa Roméo*," I told him, sitting there looking at the sleek black dash with chrome circles. It didn't look like any American car I had ever been inside.

"Of many, I hope," he said.

I lifted my chin and forced swallow. This charming Italian had a way of threading his desire through every word he spoke.

Chapter 10
Pears and Dates

The drive reminded me of the cab ride from the airport. Drivers in Italy appeared to have a death wish. The narrow streets and pedestrians we zoomed past gave perspective to our speed. Normally, I could tolerate a roller coaster, but knowing we were not on any rails and traveling within the confines of strict parameters made the streets of Rome so much worse than a loop-de-loop in Orlando, Florida. Merrico must have noticed my face turning a shade of green. He drove slower, more like an American speeder. I still didn't remove my clenched hand from the door until we were parked.

"I hope we have not taken your appetite from you," Merrico said, as he led me from the car by hand again.

"I'm feeling much better," I forced out after a wave of nausea.

"Nothing a glass of wine can't fix, *si?*"

I smiled, pressed my lips together, and nodded. As soon as we entered his restaurant, people jumped. He gave two or three orders, and people scurried before we sat. I felt intimidated, as if being worked over. I tried to pull back my enthusiasm without squashing his.

He managed Alla Rampa, a warm, inviting place that glowed with a soft yellow light. The small windows kept the white sunlight to a minimum. We sat in clean linen-covered chairs that appeared to be removed and washed daily. They matched the fine, off-white tablecloths. A hand-painted mural of a window, a picture, and antique pots on shelves decorated the place to look like what I would imagine an Italian grandmother's house would be. A faux terracotta clay roof with a clothesline above it hung behind Merrico. The china and crystal on the table boasted of a five-star restaurant, and my stomach grumbled to make room for the food I smelled.

Merrico's chest puffed out more than the first time I had met him. Here, he commanded the room, made the orders, and knew what tasted good. He took pleasure in ordering for me, an annoyance for any American woman I knew.

When the food had arrived and I had taken a bite, he asked, "Do you like it?"

I looked down at my ravioli covered in spinach. "Very good, unexpected."

"Can you tell what it is?"

I could tell it wasn't filled with cheese. I looked at him, waiting with wonder.

"Sea bass."

I used my napkin to wipe my mouth after every bite as he watched me eat. I deterred his inspection by asking questions. "Does your family come here much?"

"*Si*, one of them, at least, every night." He laughed. "But, I have a big family."

"I thought it was just you and your sister?"

"And my papa, but I meant the extended family."

I nodded. "Do you like it?"

"Like what?"

"Running this place. It's wonderful."

He told me the whole story about finding his chef on a vacation to the Amalfi Coast. He described the employee conflicts. I surmised Merrico's passion didn't involve food, but about making something the best it could be. I felt he would be able to do that with whatever he chose to do. Still, learning about Merrico and not Eleana didn't help Paul.

"I bet your mom would have loved it." I cringed, waiting to see if my boldness backfired.

"I know she would. She loved seafood and pasta."

"Maybe you could name a dish after her."

"I sort of did. A dessert, Pear Bella Helene. Her favorite dessert was apple pie, but when she tried my grandfather's pear crisp, similar to your cobbler, she never ate apples again."

"That's a nice story."

"I'm sure you are getting tired of my stories," he said and pulled the waiter over to order dessert.

"Not at all. I love hearing about your family. How are your sister's wedding plans coming?" I asked as the waiter cleared the table.

"You are the most charming American I have ever met." He paused to smile. "She's planning a wedding at the largest church in the world, so she will be bride crazy for a while."

"Wow, here in Rome?" I said, assuming.

"Saint Peter's."

I nodded, regretting not reading a single tourist map since I had been here.

"You know, the Sistine Chapel?"

My face lit up with understanding, "Oh, my gosh. You have to be kidding. That must cost a fortune."

"I suspect so. It will be in the small chapel, though. Lucky our family is not paying. The rich groom has offered."

"Lucky indeed," I said as I looked at the Pear Bella Helene placed in front of me.

"Will you still be here July fifteenth?"

I almost choked on a pear. Coughing to clear my throat, I managed to ask, "For the wedding?"

"Are you okay?"

I nodded and cleared the rest of my throat.

"Of course, for the wedding. Will you?"

"I'm not sure. I hope so. To see a wedding in the Sistine Chapel may be a once-in-a-lifetime kind of moment, even if it's the small chapel."

Merrico smiled at my enthusiasm. "You never know. It might not be. Wouldn't you love to live here? Surely Italy has wooed you after a week. Maybe, even make you doubt ever returning to America?"

"Are all Italians so transparent?"

"Perhaps, when they see something they want."

I blushed. His attention could be influential, and I wanted to like him. It would be nice not to think about a married Luke or Shawn's indifference. Was it possible to get lost in Merrico's desire for me?

Since I wasn't trying to impress Merrico, I guess I did. When relaxed, the true self is revealed. However, I couldn't see myself with someone who had mastered the art of talking to women.

"Hey, Merrico."

"Hello. *Come va?*" Merrico said.

I glimpsed over and saw Primo walk to the table.

"*Ho avuto modo di avere ancora un po 'di quel cheesecake, Eleana ha una smania,*" Primo said.

Merrico responded, "*Nessun problema. Anthony otterrà che per voi. Sulla casa.*"

"*Grazzie.*"

"Oh, excuse my manners, please. Primo, this is Maggie. Maggie, this is Primo, my soon to be brother-in-law."

I turned to a stretched out hand and shook it. "Pleased to meet you."

Primo's curls were pulled back away from his face, and he appeared tired. "My pleasure." He stared first at my face, then my hand, never smiling.

He looked again at Merrico. "Thanks for the cheesecake. Enjoy your dinner."

"Goodbye," Merrico said with a wave of his hand as Primo walked off. "Now, where were we?"

"Your Italian sounds so beautiful. Please, teach me some." I wanted to know what they said.

He leaned into the table, "*I tuoi occhi sono profondi come l'oceano.*"

"*Occhi?*" I asked.

"Eye."

"*Profondi?* I know. Profound?"

"*Si.*"

"*Sheano?*" I shook my head.

"Ocean."

"Eye is a profound ocean?"

He pulled his head back with a laugh. "No, Poppy." He put his elbows on the table and leaned toward me. "Your eyes are deep like the ocean." He stared into me.

"Okay, now something real that I can use and say to someone else. Like what did Primo say?"

"*Eleana ha una smania?* 'Eleana, my sister, has a craving-for cheesecake.'"

"Oh, that's odd, isn't it?"

"Girls getting a craving for a sweet? Not over here it isn't."

Merrico taught me words I could use like *dov'è il bagno*, where's the bathroom? Then, I tried it out and left the table with a smile. When I returned, all the dirty dishes from our meal were removed, and the crumbs had been raked. The condensation on the sides of two glasses of a chilled white wine danced in the ambient light.

Merrico sat with a smile. I returned one and settled down into the booth. "Nice."

"You like white, or I could call for some red?"

"No, I like white."

"You know what is perfect with wine? A foot rub."

I couldn't help but laugh again at his directness. "I think my foot propped on this table would be most inappropriate," I joked.

"Funny, Poppy." He recognized my facetiousness. "I would like to show you where I live when I am not here."

"Yes. I know, but it's been an exhausting day, from waking early and walking half of Rome. The wine is just the tranquilizer my muscles need before I go home to rest."

"Sore muscles? I have the perfect remedy." He laced his fingers together and popped them.

"Umm, no." I laughed to soften my directness, but I realized I had to be blunt or he would keep asking me back to his place all night long.

As we finished our wine, we walked outside, and the city had changed: fewer cars, fewer people, and less noise. Standing in front of Ristorante Alla Rampa, Merrico tried to kiss me. The bicyclist going by distracted me, and I turned my head to change the mood.

"Wow, he sure got close, didn't he?" I knew I spoke more of Merrico than the cyclist.

"Where would you like to go next, my poppy?"

"I'm stuffed. I just need to go home and rest."

"Very well." He opened the car door for me. I swallowed hard while I ducked down to enter the car, swung my feet around, and watched his eyes lick my long legs before he shut the door.

"What is the address?" Merrico always spoke such proper English, it sounded strange. His hand was already on his GPS.

"319 Pinar."

He typed and then drove away. He drove slower for my benefit, and I enjoyed the ride back, pointing to landmarks. I asked questions and Merrico answered, pleased to teach me. From restaurants to nail salons, he told me all the best places along our route. He drove me to the front of the white building. A week ago, I pulled up alone out of a cab and now from a date.

I thought of Luke. Would he be awake? Would he care where I'd been? Would he be jealous? I tried not to think about him, but throughout the entire afternoon, I couldn't help but remember all the places Luke took me and the alcohol we drank, the conversations we had, even the way he always made me laugh. Why did he have to be married? It didn't matter. He was, and I had to stop hoping that would change.

"Thank you so much for today. It was such a wonderful surprise running into you."

"I hope we can do this again—tomorrow."

"I don't know. I'll check and see."

"You ... have a number? I can ... call you, to ... set something up?"

I suspected his nerves made his English broken, reminding me of his grandfather.

"It doesn't work over here. Sorry."

"Oh, Poppy, don't leave me ... with nothing. Meet me for cof—"

I interrupted. "Gelato? Say ... four o'clock?"

"O-kay. Campini's?"

"Sounds great."

He leaned into me, and I pecked his cheek, hoping it would be enough. He turned his head, and his lips caught the corner of my mouth. I raised my eyes toward him. His skinny lips turned soft and larger in a kiss. It wasn't bad, just different.

"Bye, see you soon."

"Tomorrow."

I walked into the building while Merrico stayed parked, watching me.

I found Kayla in the kitchen making an English muffin with melted cheddar on top.

"Hey, stranger. You went to the embassy all day?"

"Not exactly. I did go but didn't stay long. The boys had an incident with someone, and it was awful, their guns drawn, and everything. They got it under control but rushed me out of there. Then, I ran into Merrico."

"Oh?" She brought her plate and iced tea to the couch. "Do tell." She took a bite and the cheese formed a bridge she had trouble separating.

"I ran into him at a church, and he took me to the restaurant he manages."

"A date, date?"

"Uh, yeah. He was by no means bashful about how he felt about me."

"Oh, my gosh, Maggie. What are the odds you and Paul, brother and sister, would fall for another brother and sister?"

"Wow, no need to go that far. It was just a date, Kayla."

"Can't say it wouldn't help to have access to the family."

"Well, Paul won't ever get a chance after July 15th."

Kayla had her mouth full and motioned for me to go on.

"Eleana and Primo are getting married in the Sistine Chapel. Well, the church where the chapel is ... you know Saint Peter's?"

With her mouth full, she screamed anyway, kicking her legs out of their crossed position. It made me laugh.

"I know. It's crazy, isn't it?"

"You've got to be kidding," Kayla spewed out of her mouth after she swallowed her food.

"The groom is paying, of course."

"Of course."

"Merrico wanted to know if I would be in town. He wants to take me."

"Maggie. This is huge."

"I know." The gravity of it all hit me. "I need to know how this can help me to stop the wedding. This has to be a good thing, to be able to be there."

"It would be nice if there wasn't going to be one in the first place," Kayla said.

"Yeah." I let out a big sigh.

Paul needed a miracle. I remembered the candle I lit today. It felt empty. I stood to pour a glass of water and breathed a prayer for Paul while Kayla placed her empty plate in the sink.

"I bet it would be a beautiful wedding." Kayla looked up, imagining.

"How big was your wedding?"

"It wasn't. Pretty ... small." Kayla stumbled over her words.

"Justice of the peace?" I smirked.

"Yes, but no, Maggie. You don't understand. I wish you knew him the way I do. Luke's the greatest. I know you would feel the way I do if you just understood ... him."

Guilt flooded my face and dropped to churn into my stomach. Acid rolled around with the water I just drank. All the thoughts I'd had of Luke smacked me in the face.

"You're still mad at him?"

"You know about yesterday?"

"Not all of it."

"Kayla, I'm sorry. He's great, I'm sure, for you. I just don't like someone trying to make me feel weak so they can take care of me because they're uncomfortable with any other relationship than the ones they can rescue."

"Maggie, you have such a big heart in there, surely you can see. He likes to hold onto those he loves. He's lost so much. You can't blame a guy for not wanting to lose more."

"I don't see what that has to do with me." The conversation had become too close for comfort, discussing Luke with his wife. I didn't want her to be jealous, even though it was the last thing I ever sensed from her.

"But, I can see how he would never want to lose you. He is so lucky to have you."

The apartment simmered with an orange light from the windows. A warm breeze blew in, creating an atmosphere of friendship between us.

Her eyes lit up talking about Luke. Her love for him was unconditional. I could never hurt her. I could never dash her view of him, even if it was sentimental, romantic, and unrealistic. I wanted the world to be as great as in Kayla's eyes. How could I ever ruin that for her?

She did a bunny-hop with joy, looking like a kid in her capri pants. Then, she grabbed me and hugged me, believing everything was good again.

"I see why Luke married you," I smiled, but hers faded. She turned around and washed her plate, placing it on the rack. "Is there something wrong?"

"No. I'm fine."

"I'm sorry. I reminded you of your wedding day that was less than it should have been." I turned her hand over. "At least he gave you an incredible ring."

"Oh, that's m—his mother's ring."

"Wow, okay, he's, at least, sentimental. That's nice, real nice. It's beautiful."

She withdrew to clean the table and windowsills and straighten the desk.

After another hour, I turned to check email, but the boys walked in.

"Hey, ladies," Paul called out with a large McDonald's bag in his arms. "We brought dinner."

"How did you know we were too tired to make anything?" Kayla said.

"I was, too. Plus, I needed a burger fix," Luke said as he placed the bag on the small table, and we all filled in the chairs while he passed out the food.

Despite eating three hours before, I made room for part of a burger, salty fries, and a real bona fide iced Coke. I loved it.

"I bet they had to ship the fountain machine in from the States, and then no one knew how to hook up the ice maker to the water supply, so it sat there for two weeks before a guy from America came."

"Don't be hatin' on my Italian McDonald's."

"Sorry. All you've done is make me homesick, but right now ..." I raised the burger in the air. "I love Italian McDonald's." I took a huge bite and smiled.

Kayla put a handful of fries in her mouth and chewed with the tips hanging out.

"My gosh, Luke, if we hadn't come sooner, they would have eaten their own hands."

We all laughed.

Chapter 11
Hot and Homemade

The guys were tired from an eventful day. The threat to the embassy wove through the words they didn't say, as they tried hard not to mention what happened today and to act normal. Both Luke and Paul settled into bed early, meaning Paul crashed on the air mattress on the other side of the couch table. I had to be quiet.

I was glad I had a clip-on light to read my novel, the same novel Luke had questioned me about. Somehow after that conversation, I began to care about the book, the characters, hoping he would ask me again. However, tonight while reading the pages, I had to reread the same paragraphs, because I couldn't stop my imagination of Paul checking someone's passport, only to have the man be a suicide bomber with a bomb strapped to his chest. I didn't want to think about it. I forced the novel's words into my brain like feeding a pill to a cat. But, over and over, I spit it out.

Paul snored. Did I know that about my brother? Restless and exhausted, I stood, folded my sheets into a pile, went to the kitchen, and fixed a bowl of Cheerios. I stood in the near dark. The light from a computer's screen saver, a digital clock, and a stove guided my movements. I walked to the window where shadowed, sepia-lit streets stood motionless as if a photograph.

"No, don't." The spoken words startled me.
I turned and saw Paul roll over, talking in his sleep. I knew my brother to be strong, but ever since the playground when I told him he would be a father, I found him staring or not paying much attention when people talked. I walked over to him and stood for a second, wondering.

"Don't. Just let him sleep." This time, the audible words made me jump. I turned and found Luke watching me from the bottom step of the stairs. "It may not seem like good sleep, but it's better than waking up and thinking about it."

"I guess you're right," I said as I stood frowning over Paul's wrinkled face mushed into his pillow. When I turned back to Luke, he stood within three feet, and his brown, leather fur-lined slippers stood out to me. "What is the deal with those shoes? It's summer."

He glanced down at them and wiggled his toes inside. "What, you don't like 'em?"

"I, well, they just don't seem ... like you."

He snickered. "I wear them to keep my elephant feet off the hardwoods so I don't wake Kayla."

"That's nice of you. You are thoughtful in ways I don't expect a big tough Marine to be."

"Are you trying to stereotype me? Let me see ..." Luke changed his voice to mock mine. "I'm not a type, I promise you that," he added a feminine wave to his hand in the air.

I couldn't help but laugh. "You're not the same guy I thought you were." I pushed his left shoulder, knocking him off balance while he let out a natural laugh.

"You're not the girl I thought you were."

"Not a baby?" I followed Luke into the kitchen.

He leaned both hands against the stove behind him and faced me, watching me approach. His eyes dropped to my bare feet and climbed until he stared into my eyes. "You never looked like a child." He paused, without any smile lines in his face. "And no, you don't act like one." He stepped toward me and took my left hand. "Listen, Maggie, I want to tell you ... I'm sorry."

My eyes fixed on my hand in his. "A-bout what?"

"For treating you like a child and giving you such a hard time."

Being this close to him unnerved my whole body. It got hotter, as if someone had been cooking. My pulse quickened, and I pulled my hand from his grasp and stepped back. "It's okay. I wouldn't have wanted it any other way."

"What does that mean?" Luke squinted at me confused.

I looked down, then anywhere. Nowhere felt comfortable. His mere presence was unsettleing. "I don't know how to take you ... nice and all." I held one hand to my chest, rubbing it with the other.

"Did ... I electrocute you?"

I pushed him backward. I needed air. "You're so weird." I gave him the *strange* look.

He only stepped closer, backing me against the sink. "Why are you so uncomfortable when I'm nice to you?"

"I don't trust it." I eyed him suspiciously, throwing alarms to him, hoping he would back off.

"Maggie, you have great instincts. You know you can trust me. Deep down, you know. You're just letting your brain tell you, you can't."

"I don't even think I know what you're talking about." I drifted free and walked away.

"Hey," he asked.

I turned back around.

"How did your date go?"

"Ah, you heard about it?"

"Of course."

"Figures."

Luke chuckled and then leaned against the counter again.

"He invited me to the wedding of the summer."

"Sounds like it." I could tell Luke knew what I had told Kayla.

"Dodging his kisses became the hardest part of the afternoon."

"He's into PDA?"

Luke always made me laugh when I least expected it. "When he drove me home, silly."

"He drove you here?" He stood straight with concern on his face.

I nodded.

"Did he walk you up?"

"No. Just dropped me off."

"He doesn't know which apartment?"

"No. Well ..."

"What?"

"He put 319 Pinar in his GPS. Why?" I turned to read his face.

Luke stood there and ignored me. He became silent for the first time since the day I had arrived. "When do you see him again?"

"Tomorrow, for gelato."

"Okay."

"Is everything all right?"

"I'm sure it will be. Just let's always meet everyone out and always make sure you're not followed. I didn't think to tell you those things last week, but now that we know what this family is capable of, it's best we keep a distance."

I hugged my arms, feeling a chill. "You're scaring me."

Luke walked over. "I don't mean to." He sat and placed one hand on my back and used friction to warm me. "Hey, it's gonna be fine. He's a puppy dog. It's Primo I'll keep my eye on. You have fun with Merrico—not too much, though." He said, squinting at me.

I pushed his chest. "Stop it. You're nuts. You know that, right?"

"Yeah. You like it, though."

"Shut up." I laughed as quietly as I could.

"Yeah, I'm right." He walked off, nodding his head.

I pulled the covers to my chin, still picturing him nodding all the way up the stairs. He could be so cocky. That should have irritated me more than it did. Instead of thinking of the security issues that bothered Luke, I replayed the entire conversation from slippers to nods in my mind, analyzing what each sentence meant. I hated how he made me feel so uncertain, but at the same time, it was thrilling to see my body react that way to a man. It was crazy what I was thinking, and I barely could admit it to myself, but I was afraid and excited he might kiss me. After the thought of it, I then berated myself for even finding pleasure in such a thing. I squeezed my pillow and punished it all night long.

The next day being Monday, I was alone. The sky was empty of clouds, not one spot in its watery sky. The hottest day of summer yet, the weather report predicted. I helped myself to food, prepared coffee, and even did the dishes when Paul wasn't around. I felt a part of the family and the team. It still felt odd going upstairs to use their shower. Today, I used it until the hot water ran out, being more comfortable than normal. As I wrapped a towel around me and headed downstairs, I noticed the unmade bed. Impressions were left in the pillows where Luke slept with two pillows under his head and three down the middle of the bed causing me to imagine him asleep. Did he drool?

I twisted around and smacked my flip-flops down the floating stairs and through the kitchen to the corner of the living room where my suitcase sat, hidden behind the couch. I dropped the towel and stood naked. It felt free to stand there alone. My reflection moved in a mirror by the door. I went over to look at my wet hair and clean face, the freckles across my bridge, a scar over my left eyebrow, and the bright red of my natural lips. I usually toned them down with tinted lip-gloss. I saw my father in the slant of my eyes. When I stared long enough, I could see the little girl with hair like sea grass, dark skin like the wet sand, features as delicate as broken shells. I pictured a lighthouse peninsula from South Carolina vacations with my dad, reminding me of when he taught me how to build sandcastles. However, today, that little girl was hard to see. Here in Italy, I didn't resemble the sturdy, wet earth. I was swaying in the waves, floating out to sea, losing my bearings.

Later, preparing for my meeting with Merrico, I changed into my new dress. It was the one I'd bought with Luke, yellow like a daisy with elastic sleeves falling off my shoulders and onto my arms. I pulled skinny strands of hair away from my face and put on a halo headband. Then, I read my book and checked emails, posting pictures to Facebook.

Luke walked in with the heat of the day still on his skin. Paul was off on some date today, getting away from all the stress of the things he had no control over. I didn't ask but imagined Sammy. Kayla had been shopping, and went to lie down before work, so I headed downstairs.

Cookies cooled on the stove, and I took a deep breath. "Yum."

Luke looked at me with an intensity that made me weak, then over my shoulders, my hair. "You want one?"

"You made these?" I wondered why he didn't get on to me for dressing up for my so-called date with Merrico.

"Yes."

"Wow."

"I was hungry, so—"

"Homemade?" I asked, picking one and sniffing it.

"Of course. You touch it, you eat it."

"Is that a Marine rule?"

"Yep."

"Well, since it's homemade." Giving him a hard time came effortlessly. The morsels of chocolate melted on my tongue.

"You've got some on ..." Luke pointed and stared at my lip.

"Where?" My tongue searched for the chocolate.

His finger swiped the chocolate off my cheek and landed it in his mouth, making a kiss sound.

"That's mine," I teased.

His eyes dropped, and a crooked grin became mischievous. "Come and get it."

My gaze lingered too long on his lips in his hazelnut scruff. My stomach flopped, and it reminded me to breathe. His watchful eyes noticed me nervously lick my lips. I turned around and walked toward the couch to hide a flushed face. He knew I'd considered it.

Luke laughed and grabbed another cookie. "Didn't think you would."

I turned around, walked over to him, and hit his chest with both my fists. "Stop it!"

"Ow," Luke said but wasn't hurt. He kept laughing at me.

"I'm not joking. Just stop it. Stop making passes at me. Kayla's right upstairs, not that ... that matters. I mean."

"Oh, you want to be alone with me. I can arrange that."

"No. Luke, you're married, so stop acting like a jerk and actually act like you are."

I walked away, and he caught my wrist and pulled me toward him. His face closed in the gap. My neck leaned back until I couldn't move it anymore, and his lips were on mine. Every muscle warmed, sending a fire to my toes that moved straight to my head. My mouth responded. Like being dropped from a helicopter into a waterfall, I fell, not thinking, only responding. I draped in his arms like a cooked noodle, finally giving in to what I couldn't fight any longer.

"Well, I'm not surprised," Kayla said behind me.

Chapter 12
Kiss and Spin

I stood straight and whipped around to find Kayla's face. "Oh, Kayla, I'm so sorry. Nothing like this has ever happened, and it won't—ever again." Her face mortified me, her sweet face. I reacted with instinct and bolted out the door.

"Maggie?" Kayla yelled.

"Hey, Maggie. Stop!" Luke's voice followed me.

I ran and found the elevator open, jumped in, and watched the doors close, blocking out the rushed words Luke said as he tried to follow.

Alone, in silence, I heard the voices of right and wrong. I was guilty. I beat Luke to the street and just kept going. I fled from the disappointed faces. I felt free to run fast, but when I thought of why I wanted to be free, the shame stung me and chased me further like a swarm of bees. I ran until my lungs burned.

When I stopped, I noticed the street faces staring back at me. I walked with my head down until no one noticed me again. My mind raced with the implications of what I'd done. I should have been more careful. I should have left, knowing I was attracted to Luke. I should have learned by now not to play with fire. Why was he doing this? Why did I want him to? This had become my worst nightmare.

Remembering my plan to meet Merrico, I walked toward San Crispinios. I didn't want to go, but I didn't want Merrico showing up at the apartment. I slowed my heart and reordered my mind, focusing on the task at hand. I didn't see Luke chasing after me anymore. I walked in, and there sat cheerful Merrico like nothing had happened in his perfect little world.

"Oh, Poppy, you are so beautiful. In your dress, you look like a sunflower." The back of his hand grazed my bare shoulder. Everything felt as foreign as the country I had found myself in.

I smiled my appreciation and walked to the counter to view the flavors. The gelato chilled beneath stainless steel lids.

"*Stracciatella*." I picked a name at random, unwilling to take the time to ask.

"Another flavor?" Merrico asked me.

"One is enough. One at a time," I said and took a deep breath.

He stepped forward and ordered Spumoni, a Neapolitan type with dried fruit and nuts. My random pick resulted in chocolate chip. I secretly rolled my eyes. We sat outside where I enjoyed every bite of my cone. It soothed my beaten ego.

Merrico asked more questions about my life. I tried to return the rapid-fire query, asking why his sister wanted to get married, being so young. I could tell he had no idea his sister was pregnant. I tried to find out more about Primo, but I hit a huge wall. Despite the obvious friendship between the two, he admitted to hardly knowing him.

After sitting with bellies full of ice cream, we chose to walk off the sugar. We cut through side streets until we arrived at a park where we strolled more than walked.

"Poppy, come here, look at this."

I walked over to a tree where Merrico stood. I searched for what he wanted to show me, but instead he turned my chin to face him.

"Look here. At me."

I fidgeted and focused down at the ground, uncomfortable with his stare. "It's so hot today, isn't it?" I moved and dodged his face falling into mine.

"Maggie?"

I turned toward him, and a sad face stared back. I sighed deeply. I had to gain some kind of strength to get through this. The ice cream and walk had helped, but these sad eyes made me feel bad all over again.

"You don't like me?"

"Yes, I do." I said unconvincingly, I'm sure. Filled with pity, I stepped closer to reassure him. "I just move slower."

"I didn't know Americans were so shy. The ones I've met haven't been."

"Um, Southern girls are more so."

"Here in Italy, the northern girls are shyer, the southern ones are very friendly."

"Well, a Southern American is friendly, but not necessarily forward or loose like you're referring to." I wanted it to be true but knew it wasn't. Morals were not regional, national, or historical.

"All the better."

Merrico's words conveyed disappointment.

"What can I do to sweep a shy girl off her feet?"

I laughed, caught off guard at such a blunt question. I knew *off her feet* meant into a bed. I realized how unprepared I was to talk to an Italian. I giggled, and it glided me through all the rough parts. I didn't care if I resembled a blonde idiot.

My thoughts kept drifting to Luke. I had kissed Luke. I had to deal with that. I had forgotten the very agenda with Merrico. With no plan of action, I didn't know my next step. I needed to get out of there. I welcomed the distraction in the beginning, but now I wanted to think— alone.

I made my excuses and escaped, but not without giving him one more kiss. I only gave him a peck this time, probably disappointing him even more than its purpose of appeasing him. He kept making me promise to meet again, but I couldn't give it to him. He almost made it impossible to leave him, and Fear kept poking at me like he had something to tell me, but I was ignoring him.

To elude Merrico following me, I snuck through a store to the back street, getting lost in a party, and then I hid in a bathroom for a while. Once relieved I wasn't followed, I wandered without thinking, weaving through stores onto one street and out onto another. However, none of the streets had answers for me. I had exhausted my mind and body and looked up to find my whereabouts. There was nothing more to do, but face what I hadn't been able to three hours ago.

Intersection after light after turn, it took twenty minutes before I saw the white building. I ran across the street, hopped on the elevator, and pushed the button.

Rehearsing what I would say to Kayla, I walked out of the elevator and found the apartment door open. My heart beat faster. I pushed my fingers against the door to see more. The couch cushions were overturned, the glass table was in pieces, and the computer monitor's screen laid on the floor, cracked open. From one side of the room to the other, everything had been touched and thrown. Pages of my green journal sprinkled over the mess of ingredients like salt. A red X over one page stood out. I grabbed it.

Was it possible that Luke and Kayla had a horrendous fight? None of this made sense. Were they hurt? Where could they be? I walked through the room, picking up my stuff I had to have: my shoulder bag, passport, and debit card. Then, I remembered my necklace in the half bathroom. The cracked door revealed a dark room, and I walked toward it.

Then heard books fall to the ground upstairs. I froze to listen. Was someone still here? I ran to the floating stairs, and a man stood at the top with shadows covering his face. He spoke foreign words, but I couldn't tell if it was Italian, since the accent was so thick. My throat closed up and my heart hammered. I turned and grabbed the pearl. I ran but peeked over my shoulder and saw two men rounding the bottom of the stairs, coming after me. I slammed the door shut.

I flew down the stairs, two at a time, and then slid down six at one time, stopping at the landing on the second floor, my left shin having acted as a surfboard. This was becoming a habit. I could only hear steps, unable to differentiate between mine or someone else's. I burst through the final door and ran half speed with a limp until I caught a cab past the park. I kept checking to see if anyone came out of the building, but no one did. I told the cabbie to "just go" with no destination. Relief washed over me as my sweat cooled.

"Stay in San Lorenzo," I told him when his dark squinty eyes peered at me in the rearview mirror.

I slouched down to avoid any eyes gawking at me through the rolled down windows. The back of my shoulders touched the grimy leather. Leaning forward in response to the thought, I threw my head to my knees and tucked my chin. I could see my cleavage and the journal note I had stuffed there. Lifting my head, I searched the flying landscape through the windows and thought of the Iron Gate, Luke's safe place. I had to find it. I instructed the cabbie to turn on whims and intuition.

"Here. Stop." I paid the cab driver fifteen euros.

Even though I knew the villa had to be nearby, I wandered lost. I didn't know what to do. I gave the cabbie the last of my cash. I passed three pay phones, as if a sign to call someone for help. I bought a calling card with my debit card and stood in a booth, trying to make a decision. I didn't know any Italian numbers by heart. They were so long, and I hadn't been here long enough. Who at home could help me?

My mom had Paul's number or the embassy. She could get hold of him. I couldn't do it, though. I couldn't face her anger. When my mom was afraid, it always came out as anger. But, Shawn could get the number.

After five months of dating, I knew his number by heart. A voice mail answered.
"Shawn. I need you. I'm stranded. Something happened to the apartment, and I don't know what to do. I don't know where Paul's place is, and you know, just call me, please. I need Paul's number. Make something up and get it from my mom. Okay. Okay. I'll be here at the booth waiting. Okay." I left him the pay phone's number.

Shawn always had his phone with him, unlike me. The booth heated up. I recognized it when a bead of sweat ran down my temple and my back within seconds of each other. I stepped out and paced. I bought a bottle of water from a stand twenty feet away, keeping within earshot of a possible call. I stood at the booth and drank the water, thinking. If I could get Paul's number, he could come pick me up. If not, I guessed I could show up at the embassy, but that door led to home, and I had no plans of leaving yet.

Where was Luke? Was Kayla safe?

Twenty minutes later, I had to pee. I went in search of a clean place. Then, I saw the balcony with a yellow and black bike. After what must have been three hours, I found Luke's iron gate. Exhausted, sunburned, and sore from flip-flops blistering the tops of my feet, I rested against the familiar gate. Hidden inside the zipper of my wallet was the key Luke gave me. I took a deep breath and held it. I opened the gate along with the two doors to the house.

I found no one inside. Smothering air trying to escape masked my face. I turned on the air, lights, and TV—just to hear the noise. An Italian newscaster sounded grave, so I turned it to a game show. They rambled on in Italian but laughed in English. It calmed me. I sat and waited. With every inhale, I built up faith. With every exhale, I felt the weight of dirt shoveling over me.

After thirty minutes, the hourglass in my mind still appeared half-full when I heard the iron gate clank open. My breathing turned shallow. *Be Luke, Be Luke.* I forced a swallow. The wooden door creaked; the handle moved. I hid behind the chair next to the sofa.

"Maggie?" Luke's voice called out.

"I'm here." I popped up and met Luke half way.

"Oh, thank God." He grabbed me and pulled my body to his chest, rubbing his hands over my back. "I thought—" He stopped. I felt his heart thumping inside his ribcage. He pushed me to arm's length, holding me. "Are you okay?"

I glanced at the bruise throbbing on my shin. "I'm okay. I guess."
He turned me side to side, inspecting, "Oh, shit, Maggie, you're bleeding. Your knee."

"Oh, I didn't know. It's just a small cut from falling down the stairs. When I heard their voices, I just took off as fast as I could. I didn't know what to do but come here."

He held my face in his hands. "No, it's perfect. You are so smart.

So ..." He pulled me to himself again and kissed my forehead. "You're pretty good at running away," he said with a laugh.

"Kayla? Paul?" My voice cracked, but I fought back the tears with shallow breaths. When I could speak, the words tumbled out of my mouth as I explained to Luke what I had seen and heard. "The voices, Luke, who were they? Why did they do this?"

"Paul's at the embassy. Kayla is fine." He was the Luke I knew again. He rushed to the bedroom, pulling guns and ammunition out of a smaller door in the closet. "They took my gun. I had one under the bed at the apartment."

"Who, Luke?"

"I don't know." He locked his eyes on me this time and answered. "I told Kayla to leave work. I told them both not to go back to the apartment. She should be here soon."

I dreaded seeing her. "Maybe she doesn't want to see me right now, she must hate me. I'll go get a hotel or something."

"What? Are you nuts?" Luke stood, and his hands glided down my shoulders, to my wrists and back. His fingers over my sunburn chilled me. "There is something you should know."

I pulled my arms away and stepped backward. "Stop doing that! It's one thing to think I was dead, but don't act like we didn't just break Kayla's heart."

"There you go, talking when you should be listening."

"You drive me crazy!"

"Maggie. Sit down. Just listen."

I sat without a word or grunt uttered. My folded arms warmed me while I held in my tongue.

"Kayla is ..." He stopped. He began to pace.

My shoulders sank deeper in the chair. I imagined him telling me how devastated she was, how I'd hurt her. Her innocence, joy, and love she showed everyone made me feel despicable. Why is it easier hurting someone who deserves it? I couldn't rationalize this feeling away. Nor did I want to. Sometimes, facing the dark side of desire was the only way through it. But, just when I knew I needed to take the blame, own it, and deal with it, anger at Luke rose within me.

"It's your fault. You should have stopped pushing. I told you to stop. I—"

"No. I ..." He took a deep breath. "Ah, shit. What the hell? Listen.

You deserve to know the truth."

I sat straighter in the chair.

"Kayla is my ... my sister." He waved his arms as if saying, "There you have it."

"What?" I stood and paced the floor. Nothing he said made sense.

Silence filled the room for a few seconds while we both stared at each other.

He confirmed it in a calm voice.

"I don't understand. How is that possible?"

Luke gave me a look, as if I were stupid.

I realized my own words didn't make sense. Overwhelmed, my face filled with fear and shock.

"Does it terrify you now that you know I'm available? Did you only have feelings for me when you thought I wasn't?"

I sat confused and forgot the questions. They spun inside the answers I first heard, disappearing, making the answer larger and larger until *yes* became the only word I knew. I held it locked behind my teeth, threatening its very life with one chomp.

"Look at you. Petrified of the truth, aren't you?"

His words ricocheted to my forethoughts: *you only have feelings for me when ...* "You assume a lot."

"Yeah, after that kiss, I do. You kissed me back."

"I'm just a little confused right now." I pulled a chair out and sat at the kitchen table. The scenes of Kayla and Luke since I had arrived flashed through my mind. The verbal, the touch, and the lack of both. It made sense, yet I never saw it.

Luke came to sit by me. He placed his hand next to mine, not sure whether to touch it. "Kayla lived with my grandmother in Norfolk after my parents died—*our* parents died. Even though we changed Kayla's name, they found her. They blew up the house, presumed Kayla dead. My grandma died a day later from a heart attack. I knew Kayla had to be protected; they would find out she was still alive. So, I married her. That way she could be with me at all times in the military. She's seventeen, not twenty."

"You two *are* married?" My head spun like a CD.

"Officially, yes, but only to protect her. I'm not a weirdo. It's a long story—one I want to tell you completely one day."

"Why are you telling me this?"

Luke cupped his large hand over mine, engulfing my fingers. "I think you know why. I haven't known you long, Maggie, but I want you to know the truth. I choose to trust you. I just hope I haven't scared you off. From what I believe about you, I don't think I have." Luke dipped his head down to break my stare, resting on the grain in the wooden table.

    I stared into his face. I couldn't deny I had feelings for him, but I had been crushing them at every turn. I now had to see what they were, if I owned them. I knew I felt safe with him. Unlike Shawn, I saw Luke as a man, ready for a real relationship.

Chapter 13
A Night of Sunshine

Exhaustion set in my bones as my brain tried to grasp everything that had happened in the last few hours. My thoughts kept returning to the ransacked apartment. I had seen at least two men, and they weren't speaking Italian, so who were they? Luke seemed to know more than he told, and I wasn't sure if I should be angry or relieved. Was he protecting me the way he had protected Kayla all these years? He'd better not think I was too young to handle the truth. How did I get involved in this anyway? My brain kept circling, dipping from one thought to another, but always coming back to the one truth. Luke *did* trust me. He and Kayla were not husband and wife, but siblings. It all made sense to me now. Luke never had a problem being attracted to me, because Kayla wasn't his wife, and he wasn't cheating. My brain couldn't handle anymore and slipped into sleep.

The crackle of eggs and bacon woke me. I stretched shortened muscles. Luke had left me to myself, but now the smell of food filled the once-shadowed, stale villa.

"Good nap?" Luke asked.

"Uh huh," I said, still stretching and yawning. Outside the kitchen window, dusk had fallen. I walked over to him, peering from behind, watching him work the spatula. "Smells good. What time is it?"

Luke checked his watch. "8:11."

"No wonder I'm hungry." I took a piece of bacon off a grease-covered napkin.

He freed his hands and turned to face me. Brushing hair off my forehead and cupping my face with his hands, he kissed my eyebrow, the tip of my nose, cheek, and then pressed into my closed lips. I let him. I allowed myself to feel it—to receive it.

I smiled as big as my muscles could with a closed mouth. It made Luke laugh. He turned to flip the eggs. "Wanna get out some plates?"

"Sure." I opened cabinets until I became familiar with the kitchen's organization. "By the way, I love breakfast for dinner." I filled glasses with orange juice and set out the silverware. "Did you have the food here?"

"No, I went and got us a few things."

The lock at the door made a noise. My muscles tensed.

"Kayla," Luke said.

"Oh, okay."

"Hi." Kayla entered and relocked the door. "Are y'all doing okay?"

"Yeah," I said.

"Did you?" Luke asked her.

"Yes. Clear."

I could tell they were a good team. They had done this before.

"How many times have you two had to move and leave everything behind?"

Luke bit his lip and turned to Kayla. "Three?" The somber look between them revealed a shared pain. I turned to gaze out the window over the sink, where dark red roses climbed past.

"You told her, right?" Kayla asked.

"Yes, she knows."

"Can I hear it from you?" I asked. I knew they had to be talking about the last time I had seen Kayla.

"Uh, yeah. Luke's my big brother," Kayla said with a child's smile. "I'm so glad you know now. And y'all kissed. How cute." Kayla gushed like she had never had her first kiss.

He rolled his eyes, a signature look of his that said so much. I hid my blush in a laugh.

"She thought we wrecked the apartment," Luke mocked.

Kayla turned to me for answers.

"No, I didn't. I heard voices, so it was only a split second."

"O-Kay. I'll throw out some random thought to see what you would say next time. I'll make sure it's extra crazy with a paranoid cherry on top," Luke said.

I laughed at myself, and they both laughed with me.

Luke held a plate out for me to take, then handed one to Kayla. As we sat to eat, we were all quiet for a minute.

Luke's voice broke in. "I talked to Paul. He's going to stay at the embassy. He knows you're safe right now, but he wants you there tomorrow."

"This has something to do with Maggie?" Kayla asked.

"Yeah, I think so. Not sure yet. Travis couldn't be sure, but he thinks Rurik is dead. He'd be surprised if we had any more trouble."

"Travis? Rurik?" I hoped my confused face would encourage them to elaborate, not sure if I was privileged to this side of their life, but hoping.

"Travis is our uncle," Kayla said first.

"Rurik was an assassin. Travis killed the other man who got away the night of my parents' death. So, I'm afraid this is about Primo."

"Wow," Kayla said.

"I can't believe I was so careless."

"Don't beat yourself up; it was a matter of time. If you didn't tell Merrico where you lived, he would have followed you and found out anyway."

"I don't understand what they're looking for?"

"More of a scare tactic is my guess," Luke said.

"From what?" I asked.

"I don't know yet. I need to find out what Primo knows, what he assumes. Is this just territorial markings of 'leave my girl alone,' or does he think you are trying to investigate his family's business deals? How intertwined are Merrico and Primo?" Luke said.

"When I saw them together, they appeared closer than Merrico let on."

"I just don't understand why they would call attention to themselves by ransacking the apartment," Luke said.

I covered my face with both hands. "Oh God, none of this makes sense."

"That's why I gotta get some answers. Apparently, we were close to something we didn't even know. Listen, I'm going to go back over there. See who all's around."

"No, I don't want you to go," Kayla pleaded.

"I have to. I'll be back in an hour."

I nodded.

I cleaned up the dishes and went into the bedroom and found Luke hiding a pistol in his jeans. He handed another one to Kayla. My worried face gave away all my thoughts. Kayla walked over to the bedside table and closed the drawer on the gun.

"Now, you two don't do anything crazy."

"How about you?" I said.

He ignored me. "Come here. I want you to know how to use this."

"No. No. I'm fine."

"Just click here and the safety is off. The one in the drawer is loaded." He pulled something out of the handle that housed multiple bullets and slammed it back in with a click. "Put both hands on it, Maggie. It has a kick."

I watched him like a TV documentary, distant and removed, as if he was telling someone else how to use the gun, not me. I saw how smart and brave he could be. He knew what to do. As long as Luke was around, I felt safe.

I nodded.

After pulling on a gray lightweight jacket, he came up to me, hugging me so tight he stretched my spine and it popped. "Sorry."

"Don't be, it felt good." I smiled and kissed him. My lips stayed there, imprinting his taste on my mind, hoping it wasn't the last. "Come back, no matter what."

"I will." He left and locked everything behind him.

I went to the living room, turned on the TV, and sat with Kayla. I'm sure both of us were trying to think of something else. I just wanted to scream a prayer at the top of my lungs. I wanted to plead on my knees. I did neither, nothing to draw alarm or panic to Kayla. Were we in danger? Was Luke?

Fear had been a protective friend but he was hiding now. I could hear him mock me, like the mean girl in the lunchroom, laughing because I slipped on vegetable stew. I wanted to go find him—under the bed, behind the shower curtain, or in the closet. I wanted to find Fear, not to be surprised or overwhelmed, or play on his terms, revealed when he had the upper hand. I wanted control of Fear. Put our gloves on, throw us in the ring, and let me bloody his lip. I wanted to mangle his face until he couldn't talk, so he couldn't tell me I was about to lose it all just when I knew what I wanted.

"Maggie?"

I turned my focus away from the TV images.

"There wouldn't be anyone at the apartment? Would there?"

"Highly unlikely."

"What's he really going there for?"

It was the first time I thought Luke might not have told us the truth. He would lie to protect us.

"Maybe to salvage some of our things?"

"Maybe he didn't go there at all."

Her imagination flared in full color, but as I tried to downplay her suspicions, a new doubt flooded my mind. She knew him best. She thought him capable of doing something dangerous. Didn't all Marines run head-on into danger—thirst for it even? I hated being the little woman who waited. It wasn't me at all. Not being trained for danger, reason restored me to sanity.

"I'm sure that's exactly where he is. Hopefully, getting my journal." I gulped and took a deep breath, wide-eyed in panic.

"What?" Kayla asked.

"Oh, God, what if he sits and reads my journal?"

"Maggie, who cares? What do you not want him to see?"

"Just all of it, the thoughts of my whole life. No one should ever write a journal. I brought it with me to read it one last time before I destroyed it. Now, it's scattered all over your apartment."

He wouldn't have gone there just for that, would he? I realized how absurd my narcissistic train of thought sounded. "Like you said, who cares?"

"If he reads it, it's only because he cares about you. Luke usually doesn't let anyone in, not just into our world, but here." Kayla pointed to her chest. "He's so private."

"I know the type." They're a vault I fail to open.

"He's a good man, and for some reason, he has let you in."

"You don't act seventeen sometimes." I thought about it. "Then again, sometimes you do." We both laughed.

Kayla threw the clicker at me and then spoke again. "I'm so glad you're here—not just tonight with me, but in Italy. I never had a sister."

Kayla's mom came to my mind, I assume to her as well. Unspoken was that she'd missed having a female friend of any kind.

"I am, too."

"I hope you don't leave tomorrow."

The thought of leaving made me feel sick inside. I just couldn't. I had lost myself in Italy. It amazed me how much I had changed in two weeks. I had become a different person over here. This city had made me vulnerable. Relationships I would have never allowed had sprung forth quickly, like a Florida afternoon rain shower. Even fighting it on a daily basis, it happened. I saw more of Luke in two weeks than Shawn in five months. It still baffled me.

"I'm sure Paul will understand I need to stay awhile longer, soon as he knows about this place, that we're safe. Will you two stay here?"

"He's stationed here, for now. I know he can get reassigned whenever he wants by calling Travis, but I like it here. Scratch that, I *liked* it here. If we're not safe, we'll leave."

"I hope I've not messed that up."

"Maggie, you can't take all the responsibility. I think it all started when Paul met Eleana, not when you went on a date with Merrico."

"I don't know. There has to be a way to fix this. Primo wouldn't want to raise someone else's child, not a guy like that. Family is everything to a Catholic Italian."

I went into the bedroom and pulled the sheets back. Then, I thought to offer it to Kayla. She had already had a nap though and appeared ready to stay up all night, but Luke wanted her home, and so she took sick time. I sat back with her on the couch, grabbing the blanket I had used earlier to cover my chilled body. Inside the blanket, I found my journal page with the red X on it I had retrieved from the apartment. I was glad I grabbed it from the apartment. At least, Luke wouldn't see that one. I didn't have to read the scene to remember what I tried to write, to forget:

Through the door I heard him pleading. "Please, let me come and hold you. We will just fall asleep together. I want to make sure you're okay. I didn't hurt you. Did I?"

"No, I'm fine." It was true. He had not hit me too hard that time. I stood and unlocked the door. His face changed so fast, I knew I had to run. I shot up the stairs, using my hands to crawl faster. I turned the corner and ran to the end of the hall. He was on my heels. I locked the door just in time. The door shook, bulged and then burst open.

"You are mine! You will make love to me!"

My shirt tore from shoulder to waist, filleted open using his bare hands like a knife. My khakis peeled off like wrapping paper. I couldn't believe he was trying it against my will.

"Andy, please stop!" I screamed as loud as I could, but no one was home.

I remembered writing it the summer I turned fifteen, the last summer of my journal. I hated it: the font of a scared girl, the letters, and the lined paper it was written on. Maybe, I just hated Andy.

"What you got there?"

"One of my pages. Garbage now." I got up and went into the bedroom and hid it in the drawer below the gun, not able to ask myself why I couldn't throw it away. Only that I knew I wanted to burn it—burn them all.

As the night tapered, Kayla's stamina from her nap grew apparent. She had popped a bag of microwave popcorn while glued to the TV.

"Kayla? Is Luke dating anyone?"

She burst out laughing with a mouth full of popcorn. "No. He is ..."

She swallowed to prevent choking. "Maggie, Luke doesn't date. He isn't your everyday kind of guy."

"So you keep saying." We both giggled.

"Now, if I go and lie down, you won't leave without me or anything, will you?"

"No, I won't do that." Kayla's sincerity stood out like a witness on a court stand holding a Bible. I knew I could trust her. "I'm just gonna watch TV until I get tired."

"Okay, sounds good. I gotta shut my eyes."

Kayla nodded while she kept her eyes on the television.

I went into the bedroom after a pit stop to the bathroom and slipped out of my yellow dress. It and my underwear were the only clothes I now possessed. I handled it like a child, laying it down on the dresser, unwrinkled with my bra on top. I slid into the cotton sheets that felt like satin with an audible *ah* as my whole body relaxed against the pillow-top mattress. It had been a few days since I had enjoyed a bed. It reminded me of seeing Luke in his underwear. His long body standing in moonlit shadows with a lull to his voice that vibrated over my skin even now.

I curled up in the comfort of the luxurious sheets while Luke was out there, sneaking around in the dark, in danger. I said a prayer for his safety. It took my thoughts to the last time I saw my dad. I hadn't wanted to leave him with his wife. There was no way I could have known, but I feared something bad was going to happen. I never thought she was crazy enough to kill him, though. My heart raced, filling my ears with its drum. I had to calm down.

Losing Luke now would not be on my terms. I thought of Shawn. I would have reacted this same way, if one day while we were dating he just didn't come home, hit by a car or something and taken before I said goodbye. Death is the worst. When you love someone and they could die on you, that is the worst pain in the world. Better not to love, right? Not to need someone so bad, that if they weren't there you'd feel as if your breath was ripped from your throat?

I allowed the events of the day to roll out in my brain, initialing each one to keep or not to keep: The walk with Merrico, the images of the torn, strewn apartment, and the conversation when Luke told me Kayla was his sister. I would keep them all ingrained. But, it would be the kiss I loaded on a looped reel, to feel over and over again at a moment's recall. That was the only thing to silence my thoughts to sleep like a lullaby, taking me to a place where danger didn't exist: his soft lips.

I didn't know how much later it was, but the sun had yet to rise. The longest day had now turned into the longest night. I awoke to the soft kisses from my dreams on the back of one shoulder. Thank God Luke was okay.

I rolled over to face him, and he was already under the covers beside me. His upper body swooped over me, staring down. Light from the bathroom lit the room. The covers draped over Luke's back as he held a push-up above me. I lifted my neck to see what he saw. My breasts stood to attention and embarrassed me. My stomach stretched flat, and he could see down to my pink lace-trimmed underwear. I squirmed.

"Mmm, you look so good." His face changed. Thicker eyelids caused his eyes to open only halfway. His irises diminished as his pupils drank me in like through a straw, first with his eyes, then his mouth.

He grabbed my bottom lip in a kiss and plunged into my mouth. I followed his lead. My hands wrapped around his back, feeling skin, bone, and muscle. His contours excited me, and I pulled him down against me. When he relaxed his body against mine, I gasped for air from the sensation. Endorphins infused my muscles as they flexed, aware and awakened like tiny fireworks going off all over my body. My half-asleep stupor made me forget to even question if I should be doing this. Those thoughts should have entered my rational mind. There, in the middle of the night, with chemicals surging through my body, I felt nothing rational. I felt liquid fire in my veins. My speech was incomprehensible.

I warred with the guilt of pleasure inside of me. Andy's face popped into my mind. I wanted to think of anything else. Shawn's face then appeared, wanting me. I struggled with desire in my body and memories in my mind. I wanted to feel Luke touch me, wanted to know what he could do to me. As I tried to suppress images from the past, Luke moved from my neck to my breasts. Like from a defibrillator jolt, my whole body reacted, arching my back and wrapping my legs around his. I couldn't stop this.

He raked himself against me as he brought his face to mine. I opened my eyes and knew I wanted him, all of him. He rolled over to his side and stroked the hair from my face. He pulled me against his body and hugged me. "We need to get some sleep."

What? We were going to sleep? The tension cooked like hot coals; we both felt it. What kind of game was this? In his crescent, I folded. Resting against his warm, bare skin, I felt his hand skim my stomach, press on my rib, then run down the curve of my hip and thigh. He rested his arm there. My stomach ebbed away, and then toward his hand with every breath.

I thought he would continue, but he didn't ask anything of me. It only made me want him more. I didn't know anyone could have that kind of strength.

The next time I awoke, I squinted with one eye open to see the orange glow seep through the blinds. It made me remember all the mornings I ran from the sun at the apartment. Luke stretched at my moving, yawned with a moan, and finished with a smile, staring straight at me.

"Good morning, sunshine. Did you sleep well?"

"I don't think I've slept well since I arrived in Italy." I gave him a sleepy smile.

He sat up and put his feet on the floor but squinted back at me. "Yeah, can't say I slept all that well with this …" He pointed to my half-dressed body. "Lying next to me all night." We laughed.

I sat up, holding my pillow to my chest. "Sorry. I don't have any clothes. I thought you would have tried to …"

"No." He leaned over and gave me a sweet kiss and stood. "Not that I didn't want to." He walked across the room to the bathroom in his boxer briefs, flashing his eyes at me over his shoulder. He moaned, as if saying *my, my, my*. He shook his head all the way into the bathroom and closed the door, leaving me with an inerasable smile.

Chapter 14
Burning Secrets

During my turn in the bathroom, I slipped into a tub of shampoo bubbles. The warm water soothed me. I submerged my whole body under the water. Descending into my mind, I thought about last night, how close I had come to Luke and I doing it. Why did he stop? I didn't know but was glad he did. What was I thinking? Clearly, I wasn't, and I needed to watch myself with him. I couldn't trust my body alone with him like that. He looked incredible, and I wanted to know what his kisses all over me would feel like.

Luke knocked, and I told him I would be done in just a minute. I stood and patted down, then wrapped my body with a towel.

"Everything okay?" Luke asked when I walked into the bedroom in only my towel.

"Sure, why wouldn't it be?"

He reached into the pocket of his jeans, the only thing he wore at the time. A folded piece of paper dangled like a cigarette between his fingers. "Do you want to talk about this?"

"I don't ... what?" I took the paper and noticed the X written in red.

Luke dropped his head and took a deep breath.

"I just don't know how."

"Try—please?"

"I didn't tell you the truth earlier. I don't like sharing it with anyone." As I spoke, my eyes and nose burned. I walked over to the dresser and held my dress. "I was raped, not almost, but all the way. At fifteen." I opened my eyes wider and looked up to keep the tears from falling. They fell anyway. "An old boyfriend." Why did this have to be my story?

Luke walked over to me and reached for my hand. For a moment, we stared, watching the pain in each other's eyes. "Will you help me ... put it all behind?"

Luke nodded.

"I want to burn it. All of them. Can you get them from the apartment for me?"

Luke's eyebrows furled. "Depending on how you look at it, it's already done."

"What?"

"The apartment, I torched it."

"Oh my gosh. Why?"

"It's better that way." Luke stood with me. "We can destroy this one together."

"But the people?" I couldn't understand why Luke would do that.

"No worries, I pulled the fire alarm before it was lit and made everyone from the fifth floor get out. I made sure it was contained to our unit only, and it was out before I left."

"You know you're a little crazy?"

He laughed.

I didn't understand him, but I knew I didn't fear him. He would never turn on me like Andy.

After I dressed, we drank our coffee on the porch in the morning light under a dappled shade of a bougainvillea. Kayla took a shower inside. I sat there on the edge of a small wrought-iron bistro chair, waiting. Luke came and took the other chair, ready with a lighter in his hand. The journal paper sat on a plate.

"Here you go," he said, handing me the lighter. "A few words beforehand?"

"Sure." I sat and thought about what I wanted to say. "Goodbye. I don't ever want to think about you again. This ... will no longer control my life or my destiny. This day. It's done. Gone. I burn the words I wrote, the words spoken, the words I will no longer remember. I choose life, to be healthy." I clicked the lighter and its flame blazed with power. I held it to the edge of the paper. The fire consumed the handwriting, turning its edges black before it crumbled into ashes.

Luke squeezed my wrist that still held the lighter. I placed it down and took his hand. He raised mine, motioning to stand with him. His arms wrapped around my shoulders, heavy like a bear rug. A gust of wind came and blew my hair. I watched it take the ashes with it, falling to the brick-paved floor, rolling away into nothing. I smiled and gave him a long, closed-lip kiss. Luke pinched off a red flower from a vine over my head and placed it in my hair.

"You know, Miss Maggie, you're going to be just fine." My chest warmed as his hand tingled the hair on my arms.

Kayla opened the door behind me. "When are you two going to get anything done around here and stop kissing all the time?"

We pulled apart and faced her.

"Wasting no time, I see. Do I have to go to the market myself?"

"I'm afraid I have to go the embassy. You go with her, Luke."

"I need to go with you."

"Nah, I need to tell my brother myself that I'm staying. He might get you on his side, talking about danger or something."

Luke laughed. "Are you sure you want to stay?"

"Wild horses aren't getting me to leave."

"We have some pretty powerful stallions here."

This time, I laughed. "No Italian stallion can take me away from you. I've found my white horse."

"She's getting all cheesy on me." He ruffled my already messy hair, and we all walked inside.

"Okay, it's a done deal. We'll meet back here in a couple of hours," Kayla said.

"Sure. I'll pick up a few clothes. This one little dress just won't do."

"What a fine dress it is, though. I wouldn't mind seeing you in it every day."

"I don't think so. Hey, I need to call Paul. Can I use your phone?" I remembered I didn't call Shawn again yesterday. I needed to call him immediately.

"Well, I kind of forgot the charger before I torched the place. I'll pick up a new one today."

"Nice going. I guess he knows I'm coming, or I could call from a payphone on the way."

Luke turned to his sister. "Can you wait till I get back to go to the store?"

We both asked at the same time, "Where are you going?"

He turned to me. "With you. I don't feel good about you going alone."

"No problem," Kayla said.

After grabbing my IDs, Luke suggested we travel by cab, not wanting anyone to notice me in the yellow dress. The view outside the cab felt like a movie of the last two weeks of my life. The lemonade stand, the market where I strained to see Giuseppe, and the church where I lit the candle. I couldn't leave. There was too much left to do. Rehearsing the speech to counter Paul's overprotective rants made my heart beat faster as I approached *Via Vittorio Veneto* Street.

When we entered through the embassy's gates, I was glad to have been there before. I didn't see Paul for him to walk me through this time. However, being with Luke sped up the security process. Luke told me to wait next to a guard named McCord. He walked over to a tall, pale, dark-haired girl holding a notebook. After reading the paper, his face hardened and became serious.

I learned the guard had been there three years. I knew some McCords back home, and we started up a conversation, but I grew impatient. I almost asked him to call for Paul again when the door to the back opened.

Paul walked through, and I smiled with relief that my wait was over. Then, I saw Shawn and my mom appear from behind him. I stared at the Travertine floor, clenching my teeth together and feeling my gums pulse.

"Maggie, come with us," Paul said.

I cut my eyes over at Luke while I followed Paul. Luke saw me but still spoke to the dark haired woman. We entered another door and went down a long hallway to a boardroom filled with a table and a wall of windows hidden behind closed blinds. The room's electric sconces emitted a stark white light, and a wood panel hid a screen or board. The three of them stood in a row in front of me. I stared at the gold in the paisley swirled carpet with my back to the open door.

"Margaret Dulaney, I dropped you off at the airport to go home, and you got on a plane to Rome?"

My glare shifted from my mom to Shawn. I had realized at that moment what I had done. My phone call worried him so much he told my mom everything. I closed my eyes and tried to keep the anger from coming out of my mouth.

"Listen, I know you're nineteen, but how on earth was it you were going to help Paul?" I could see it in her eyes. The panic mode had set in. Her curly hair bounced while she talked. Even though she was shorter than I was, her voice shrilled as she stuck her bony fingers in my face. This wasn't her best moment.

"I thought it was important enough to try."

"Couldn't you have at least told me?" Hurt replaced the anger in her eyes.

"We didn't want to worry you," I said.

"You just wanted me to be scared to death from a phone call? Was that easier for me?"

We both turned to Shawn. "I ... no. That was never my intention," I told her.

"But when I couldn't get Paul on the phone, I had to make a decision, and I'm glad I did. Because now you've gotten yourself in so deep, dangerous people have destroyed the place you were staying. Paul tells me it burned last night, and they had to abandon the whole building. What if people weren't able to get out alive? These are the kind of people you are involved with? People that might want you dead?" She took a deep breath as her shoulders shuddered.

I didn't interrupt. I saw her fear. It made me want to cry. I would have done the same thing.

She started again. "I know Paul can take care of himself. He's a Marine, Maggie; you're not. Paul agrees that it's time for you to go home. They have heightened security at the embassy and are encouraging travelers to leave."

I looked at Paul, dumbfounded.

"Sis, she's right. I appreciate everything, but it's just too dangerous now. I don't think I could live with myself if something happened to you."

I turned to Shawn, waiting to hear him pipe in as well. His hair appeared as if he had just rolled out of bed, a shadow of scruff filled his jaw, and his eyes hung heavy with sadness.

He took his cue. "I was worried, Maggie, that something ... I called that number, and you never answered."

Barely above a whisper, I admitted, "The phones were lost in the fire." It was a lame excuse. When desperate, I used a payphone. When I forgot, I blamed it on a lack of cell phones. Shawn was hurt, but he was smarter than to fall for that excuse. Why was he here, though? Just standing next to him, I ran my fingers through my hair and realized my hands were shaking.

"Listen, Maggie," Mom started again. "We bought you a ticket at the airport. Where are your things?"

I held my hands up and let them fall against my thighs. "This is all I have."

My mom just shook her head.

"I don't want to go yet. Stay and we'll—"

"I'm not going to listen to this. You're coming home." She yelled now.

"Look who decided to be a parent, finally."

Paul grabbed my shoulder. "Don't go there, Maggie. You know you'll regret it."

Mom continued. "I'm not proud of some things I put you through, but–"

"Things you put me through? Are you kidding? You were a drunk. I had to get you up every day just so you would go to work, so we could eat. I had to be the parent! I'm grown now, and I'll do whatever the hell I want to do!"

"I'm sorry, Maggie. I've tried to show you just *how* sorry. I've been clean for over a year, and I'm the mom you had when you were a little girl again, the one that loves you more than you will ever know. I just can't leave you here. I won't abandon you again." Tears filled her eyes as she choked out her last words.

My nose stung as I tried to speak. "It's just not fair. You did abandon me. You left me with Dad and that crazy lady, and you only got me back because he died." I had to blink to see through the tears. "I was strong enough to survive that, and I don't need you to save me now."

I shook with sobs. I wiped the sides of my face, feeling no relief from the daggers I threw at her. Instead, I saw the pain in my mother's eyes as she broke down.

"Maggie, I'm so sorry. Please, let me be your mother again." In a whisper above her cries, she uttered, "I love you so much."

I cinched my eyes closed, trying to hold it all in, but it came out, along with the tears that slid down my face onto my neck. Her arms surrounded my hunched-over frame. I grabbed my mom and held onto her for the first time in a long time.

Paul handed us both a tissue. After fixing our faces, I stood silent. They talked arrangements between them.

"Can we just stay here? I want you to meet Luke and Kayla." I knew I couldn't tell them we were close to figuring this out; I couldn't tell them about Luke's background. Both things would convince them even more for me to leave. "Luke's here. You'll see he's a great guy."

I noticed everyone's attention changed, greeting someone behind me. I turned. Luke stood there waving.

"Luke." I grabbed his arm to pull him further into the room. "This is my mom, Karen, and this is … Shawn."

"Nice to meet you." He shook both their hands. Luke and Shawn never smiled but exchanged an expected greeting. "Maggie, I think your mom is right. You should leave Rome. Go somewhere safe."

I heard his words but couldn't respond. Why would he say this?

"Thank you, Luke. Maggie, I would love to stay and even spend time with Paul and get to know your new friends, but I just know we should leave."

I stood there exhausted, overwhelmed, and too sleep deprived to form a good argument. I was outnumbered. "Okay, when?"

"We have flights to London today. We should get back to the airport."

"Now?" My eyes pleaded with Luke in desperation. I searched for any sign on his face that he wanted me to stay, even one more day. I only saw his agreement. "Can I talk to you alone for a moment?"

He nodded. I followed him with no contest from anyone in the room. He went to the left and unlocked the last door on the right. The door opened to an office, Luke's, judging by the belongings. I scanned the walls and saw awards, commendations, and pictures of ceremonies. He chose not to sit in the green leather chair behind the desk, but instead, we stood in front of the desk without taking any of the seats to our side. I waited.

Luke grabbled both my arms and rubbed them. "I know you're upset."

I still waited. He had so much to explain.

"But, you have to trust me."

That was it? Just blind trust. They wanted me to leave because they thought Rome was dangerous, but that would not be why he would want me to leave. I shook my head. I didn't understand.

"Please, Maggie." He kissed my forehead.

I shook his hands off me. "This just doesn't make any sense." I stormed out of his office. I turned around. "I guess I was wrong about you—about us. I feel like an idiot." I walked off, saying under my breath but loud enough for him to hear, "I didn't see this coming." At the end of the hall, my eyes locked with my mom's.
Luke followed after me. "It's too dangerous, Maggie."

I threw the words over my shoulder while I kept walking, "That's just convenient for you, isn't it?" I walked up to Mom, and as I approached, I told them I was ready to leave. Luke held back ten feet and waved with a "nice to meet you" when Mom said, "goodbye."

I wrapped my arms around my big brother and told him I was glad we had this time together, that I would miss him. I reminded him we needed to talk about Eleana, the apartment, and everything. He promised we would.

Chapter 15
Accents, Money, and Silence

The ride to the airport, outside of Rome, was long and quiet. I used the car and plane trip to London to process what had just happened. I couldn't believe Luke wanted me to leave. It was like I'd never even mattered, some little girl he had to rescue from her past to entertain himself. Relief washed over me that I didn't do something stupid with him in his bed. Of course, that was all subjective. Some would say sleeping next to him all night was stupid, but then again, some would say not jumping his bones was stupid. I couldn't live my life for others. I knew where my morals had come from, and even though I wasn't living the life I wanted yet, I knew I would. Someday. Maybe soon.

I thought it would be safer to remain in Rome with Luke. Right there next to Kayla? Nothing made sense. Italy had not even had terrorist issues yet. And, wouldn't I be safer at his side than traveling through Europe? His reason for safety didn't hold up. He had to have other motives. Why did Luke really want me to leave?

Mom insisted she buy me a sweater at the airport, arguing the plane would be too cold for a sundress. I happily took it for the warmth and the opportunity to cover up the yellow dress that I must have been destined to wear all over Europe. When we got on the plane, I only had more time to think. Then, I remembered the journal paper with an X on it. I knew he read it, but did that somehow change his mind about me? Did he look at me now as damaged goods? I couldn't seem to break this cycle of how the rape made me think about myself. Fear sat there and helped me think of all the scenarios of Luke's behavior. Fear kept telling me I wasn't good enough, though more disturbing were his suggestions, accusing Luke of lying, selfishness, and betrayal. At this point, my emotions boiled to anger, and I had no counter argument and began believing Fear.

Only time could soften my anger, by coming in contact with everyday things and the strangers to whom we were forced to talk. Mom began to smile for the first time since I'd seen her, pointing out people's accents on the plane or unusual architecture on our descent.

"Oh, did I not tell you? If I had to fly half-way around the world to bring you home, we're going to stay in London a few days. Don't worry Shawn, it's on me." It looked like she brought Shawn as a pawn, thinking we were still together. I had no idea if he was dragged into it or if he cared. I wasn't asking either.

"Linda, I just don't think I should take such a generous offer. This is a time for the two of you," Shawn said, leaning over to talk to Mom from across the aisle. There was the answer: dragged into it.

With sincerity, Mom said, "I hope you will. I think you will be a much needed help." Her eyes fell on me.

Mom reclined her head back with her eyes closed and prepared for the plane to land. I had no idea what time it was to their bodies or when they had arrived in Rome. Now they were heading backward at least one time zone. I leaned against the window and watched a white floor of clouds and smooth, blue sky disappear below us as land became larger and larger. Shawn rested his hand over mine. The last five months came flooding into me with his touch. His hands were always so hot.

"It's good to see you," Shawn said.

I squinted my eyes at him, trying to figure out what his angle was.

"Things aren't the same without you," he said.

"I bet they're not, no one to wrestle with on the couch. It got so hard. Talking shouldn't be that hard."

"I know, I know. I didn't know what you wanted from me, then you dropped the Italy bomb."

I pulled my hand out from under his and placed it on top of his with a pat. I gave him a small smile. "Shh, not now, not here."

After we sat in silence, Shawn said, "I have to admit I didn't think your mom could get you to leave Rome. Just because she asked you to, you know? Considering how tense you left things with her in Texas."

"Sure, I could have stayed. I thought of that—since I'm nineteen and all. But, my family isn't all that large, and when Paul and my mom were there, telling me to leave out of worry, I just couldn't tell them to go screw off." I left out Luke's role in the whole thing. "They are the only family I have left."

"And his friend, Luke, you seemed surprised he agreed."

Surprised? Damn straight I was surprised. I nodded. Everything about Luke had been a surprise.

"I'm glad you're coming home." He leaned over and kissed my cheek. I couldn't pull away and hurt his feelings, so I closed my eyes, and of course, all I saw was Luke.

Mom was efficient. We hailed a cab to take us to the hotel. Instead of an interstate, a four-lane road twisted most of the way into London. The drive was long, but the cabs in London were nicer, with air freshener. It gave me time to formulate a plan. The first time I found out where we were going was when Mom told the driver. Hilton in Kensington. She sat up front, since it would be a forty-five minute drive, to keep us from being cramped in the back seat.

"Mom, you didn't need to spend a lot of money." Her generosity weighed on me.

"Believe it or not, I'm getting the place for one-sixty-six a night."

"Are you kidding? I could almost afford London," Shawn said.

"Why are we here?" I asked.

"Shopping, of course, and sightseeing." Mom said.

"What about the bridge and the clock?" I asked. I tried to be nice about it. I didn't want to be on her bad side.

"Big Ben cannot be referred to as 'the clock,'" Shawn said.

They laughed at me. "Uh, Ben, that's its name. Are we going to do all that, Mom?"

"Let's just get settled in and see, figure out the money."

"Where did you get the money?"

She didn't say anything right away and then turned to face the backseat. "I sold your grandmother's ring."

"What? No, Mom." I whined like a child, but I couldn't help it. She sold my grandmother's anniversary ring, ten diamonds, near perfect. My favorite grandmother. How could she be so unsentimental? But, she was. My mom was never attached to things. She could load up her possessions and move with a two-week notice. She once gave away a whole set of china because she was tired of packing it up every time. She only holds onto what she needs.

"But Mark ... couldn't he have given you the money?"

"I didn't want to ask. I didn't want him not to like you. I asked him for the four thousand I gave you for the summer, which I'm thinking is about gone?"

"I haven't had to spend too much while I've stayed at Luke and Kayla's. I have near three thousand left. You can have it back."

"No, what's done is done. You keep it. But you'll have to get a job when you get home."

"I knew that when I decided to go."

Mom stared out the window at a park we passed. I was glad we got some of that settled. I still felt sad about the ring, but now I didn't feel guilty about the trip anymore, since the ring would have been mine one day, so the trip was on me. I wanted her on my side. I wanted her to decide to go back to Italy and not return home. It felt like the beginning to compromises I hoped would heal us. I twirled my pearl between my fingers and stuck it in my mouth.

London was bigger, more stretched out than I could have imagined, but few buildings were over three stories high. The crosswalk lines were zigzagged, and people walked everywhere. We passed old brick buildings with white painted windows ten coats thick. Colorful advertising posters hung from every street-level window. The roads were skinny, along with the cars. After a congested roundabout, I saw newer, taller buildings.

We turned off the main road and found the Hilton nestled in what resembled an upscale New York residential neighborhood, like in the movies. The attached brick buildings with thick white window trim and doors sat in a row with wide, welcoming steps. Trees and cars lined the narrow road, and I thought it odd to put a hotel at the end of all these homes. London was older than anything I'd ever seen in America, but you could not slight it for that. The older buildings almost seemed to stick their nose up at the newer ones, as old money did to new.

We walked into the lobby, a tan and black spacious room. Black circles hung with dangling glass in the center for the chandeliers. The linear stripes in the carpet crossed white on black. Reservationists sat on tall stools behind green glass. Some spoke with American accents, some British. A man in a suit lounged on a round chair with his laptop. It was a working hotel made for the international travelers with expense accounts. It all seemed so modern to me, and although London was in vogue, I didn't think of it as modern. Regardless, I liked how it felt clean and organized.

We went to our room on the fifth floor and found two queen beds with chocolate chenille throws at the end of each and matching curtains around the large window. A flat screen, desk, and beige travertine in the bathroom appearing brand new. Shawn took the bed by the window and ogled a black and white rugby picture over his bed. Mom and I took the one closest to the bathroom. I had nothing to unpack, but I watched Mom lay her stuff out on the bathroom counter.

"I'll be back in a bit." Shawn told us as he left to pick up the dinner we ordered over the phone from the corner pub.

I kept watching Mom unpack.

"You can borrow most of my things, but I'll call down for a toothbrush," she offered.

"I can get my own toothbrush, Mom."

She inspected my dress and the new sweater. "You'll need a few more clothes, too."

I couldn't argue with that. "I'll buy some new ones while we're here."

"I would be happy to help," she said with a smile, trying to be nice.

I wanted her to understand why I went to Italy, why I wanted to go back. Every mile away from Rome, Fear kept trying to get me angry at Luke, but deep down I didn't want to be. I wanted to hold out for that small chance he still cared. "Sure. I need to check my email, too. Do you think they have computers in the business center?"

"You can do that in the morning. I'm going to call Mark and take a shower, okay?"

"Your phone works here?"

"Yeah, I called and bought an international package before I left. Something Mark told me to do so he could get hold of me."

"That's what I failed to do. I don't even have my phone now. It was in the apartment."

Mom laughed. "Oh, baby girl, you are not going to have a boring life, are you?"

"Could I check my email on your phone?"

"I only get to use one gig or something, so watch the data."

"I will." I logged onto Google mail while we waited for Shawn to return from the Plum Bar and Grill. I hoped Luke had sent me an email. I needed to know why he wanted me so far away where he wouldn't know if I was safe or not. I still tried to believe he cared and not the scenario Fear was selling me.

My finger flew through my password without thinking. The blue Gmail bar loaded, and my emails filled the screen. I scrolled through a list of friends and businesses offering coupons, but nothing from Luke or Paul.

I composed an email to Paul:

Hi. We are in London safe and sound. Mom and I are already making up. Would you give Luke my email or send me his? His phone number, something. I need to talk to him and Kayla. I hope you're all safe. Please let me know something as soon as you can. Mom's phone works over here, so just call when you get this!
Thanks,
Maggie

    I searched over my emails. At the bottom, I found Shawn's:
Maggie,
Why are you not even responding?
Shawn

    Another before that one:

Maggie, what happened? I tried that number like fifty times. Please call me ASAP. Very worried about you. If I don't hear from you, I don't know what else to do but call your mom. Please call me.
Miss you,
Shawn

    Miss you? I breathed a deep sigh as I realized Shawn wanted me back. He wasn't just worried. He had not been roped into this by my mom. He was trying to reconnect.
    After we all ate a bite, none of us finishing due to the late hour, we lay down like worn out basset hounds. The television kept us from conversation and put them to sleep. I wrestled with sleep as I tried to wrap my mind around the last forty-eight hours.
    "Hey, let's go downstairs while your mom sleeps," Shawn suggested.
    He startled me, thinking he was asleep, but I nodded. I threw on some of Mom's shorts under the oversized t-shirt she had given me for pajamas.
    After we slipped on our shoes, Shawn and I left the room and headed toward the garden at the corner of the hotel property.
    "Maggie?"
    "Huh?"

"Can we talk, yet? Are you up for it?"

"About what?" I pushed the elevator button.

"Us." We entered the elevator and the doors closed around us. Shawn continued in the wake of my silence. "I hope this is a good time."

"It's okay." We walked a long hall and turned right until we saw the glass doors to the garden. I sat on a wrought iron bench under the scent of various trees. "What's up?"

He stood and paced on the brick pavers with awkward pauses. "You seem like … you're slipping away and …" He leaned against a half wall of stacked stone after he said it. "You've wanted me to talk." He sighed. "I think of all the stupid stuff I've hidden from you, that I never should have. Things I should have said …"

He paused again and I listened. "I don't know many people like you. It took me some time, to know if I could trust you."

I sighed. I didn't know if I wanted him to trust me anymore. Wouldn't that mean I was saying I loved him? I would always care about him but if I let him tell me now, he might think he has my whole heart, and I knew I couldn't give that. "Shawn, you don't have to tell me."

"I want to, I want you to know me," Shawn said and sat next to me.

"A lot has happened since South Carolina. If we're being honest, I should tell you."

"Like what?"

I turned around and faced him. "I have feelings for Luke."

"Ah, Maggie, not a married man. I thought you were smarter than that."

I peeked around to make sure we were alone. "No. I mean he—" I realized I couldn't betray Luke's trust. I couldn't tell Shawn the truth. "It's not how it seems."

"Perfect. So who's the one that can't talk now?"

I took his hand. "Oh, Shawn. Every time I get around you, I just …"

His eyes waited for good news. It was true, as I stared at his face and heard his voice, I knew I could see myself with him. We had so much fun talking, but it was only about ideas, or values, never about him or his past. If he could be open and honest with me, I had once thought …

"Maggie, I've been able to deal with some things from my past, and it has allowed me to be able to forgive. For so long, my parents' screwed-up marriage distorted my view of it all. Of you know … love."

"How?"

"Ah shit, you don't want to hear that. I mean if you do I'll tell you but—"

"I do." I could tell Shawn had to get something off his chest.

If anyone couldn't love it would be me, a product of divorce. Then, I watched a second marriage end in death. Yes, if anyone had a reason to shy from love, it was me—but I didn't. I wanted someone to love me for all of me: the good intentions and the protective defenses. I should think it impossible, but I didn't, and what gave me that hope? I thought of my grandmother. She was good. She was love. Even when the world had been cruel to me, I could see the good even more. Even if at times I didn't feel it, I knew it.

"They ... liked to party, with other couples, and they didn't have their clothes on."

"They went skinny dipping?"

Shawn's hand rubbed almost every square inch of his face before he answered. "No, a lot more than that."

"Oh, I see."

Shawn let out a sigh of relief. There was no need to torture him with details I could tell he didn't want to share.

"When I let all that go, it did something to me, and now all I know is that I want to be with you. You *are* my future." He laughed. "I sound like a schmuck, don't I?"

"No," I told him. I never thought sharing what you felt for another person made them weak but instead courageous. I knew it was the hardest thing a human did, to become vulnerable, humble, and broken.

"I will risk anything now, and look like an idiot, not to lose you," Shawn blurted.

His declaration should have felt awkward, but instead, it was just sad. "I'm glad you told me." I placed my hand on his. "Timing is everything, though."

"What?"

I shook my head in disappointment.

"All I know is, only when you forgive can you love. And, I've done that," Shawn said.

I pictured my mom's face.

"I love you, Maggie."

I hung my head. "Then, I am unable to love."

I almost didn't know the person talking to me. Shawn no longer acted like a boy. He even appeared older, with a dark shadow cast on his chin by stubble. I kept staring at his face, while his lips moved toward me. I thought he was going to kiss me, but he hugged me, and it felt substantial.

I pulled away and stared at an indigo globe on a pedestal. Despite the hum of noise from people and cars, there was a slight peace found here, away from the electronics of the room.

Shawn stood, relaxed for the first time since I'd seen him at the embassy. I admired him. "I know you can't say it right now. It's okay. I'm a patient man."

Startled, I squinted at him, realizing his angle was not what I'd suspected.

Chapter 16
Longing in London

We returned to the room, and this time I couldn't fall asleep because of what Shawn told me. I turned my head and saw him trying to sleep in the next bed. How could two weeks have changed me so much? I used to love watching him sleep. I would imagine what lay behind his eyes. How did he see the world? My mind struggled with the familiar of Shawn and the desire for Luke.

I could still smell Luke on me, and I didn't want to shower. The strength that oozed from Luke's pores like sweat became what I wanted to touch, glide over, and absorb. But, had it all been an illusion?

The morning came, and despite their continued sleep, I couldn't anymore. I couldn't keep weighing the merits, feelings, and events of Shawn versus Luke. I went to the bathroom and cleaned up, slipping the yellow dress on once more. It made me laugh. At that moment, I thought it might be a good idea to get out of it as soon as I could. Another eventful day in this sundress might just send me into a catatonic state. After inquiring from the reservationist at the front desk, I found some shops four blocks away. On my trek, I grabbed a coffee and decided I would also have to buy a new pair of shoes.

I passed a phone store and went inside. The temptation to buy a new phone overwhelmed me. In the end, I told myself I could not drop three hundred dollars just to have a phone for three days. Desperation almost won. I bought clothes to wear just for the day with more haste than normal.

I returned to the room and found Mom in the shower. Shawn stirred when I came in.

"Where did you go?"

I held my bags up. "Clothes."

"I would have joined you."

"You were pretty out of it. You looked like you needed the rest." I placed my bags on the bed.

The bathroom door opened and steam escaped. A wet-haired Mom with fresh clothes came out. "Good morning. I see you've already been shopping."

"Just something to wear today."

"Is it okay if I jump in there for a second?" Shawn asked her.

"Absolutely, go right ahead."

"Mom, can I borrow your phone? I want to call Paul."

"It's in my purse over there," She said and brushed her hair at the mirror.

I walked out into the hall, anticipating his answer, but Paul didn't pick up. I left a voicemail and checked email again. I knocked on the door to reenter. A wet-haired Shawn answered. His black t-shirt hung on his long-waisted frame from two strong shoulders. His eyes stared at me, and he gave me his puckered bottom-lip sad face—the one he used as often as a tick, involuntary and ingrained. A quick flex of his chin and then back again. I walked into the room, patting the side of his waist.

He smiled at my gesture. "Hey. Come here." Shawn pulled me into a hug.

I could smell him again. Months of memories came rushing into my mind. I stayed there transfixed. I didn't want to remember, but I did.

The bathroom door opened behind me. We pulled out of our hug.

"I'm starving and I have to get some coffee. Who's joining me?" Mom asked.

I walked over to the window and pulled the drapes open. Even though I couldn't take a deep breath of fresh air, it still made me feel better. I stood there with my back to them, studying the cars passing below. I was almost too overwhelmed with wanting to be somewhere else I couldn't even speak.

"I will be," Shawn said. "Maggie?"

Controlling my emotions, I turned around and faced them both. "Sounds good."

A few minutes into breakfast, Mom's phone rang. "It's for me," I said and reached out for the phone.

Mom pulled the phone out and checked the name. "I don't think so." Speaking into the it, she said, "Hey, sweetheart."

She proceeded to have a non-eventful conversation with whom we assumed was Mark. I sipped from my coffee cup again, realizing it was my third of the morning. My leg bounced up and down while I played with a packet of Splenda.

"Why are you so antsy for a phone call?" Shawn asked.

I shrugged my shoulders.

"So, whatever happened with Paul and that girl?"

"We know she's pregnant and engaged to a dentist's son who might be connected with the Italian mafia." I bit my ring finger nail. When I realized it, I grabbed my pearl from my neck and sucked on the tip.

"That's awful. What in the world is Paul going to do?" Shawn asked after drinking half his orange juice in one gulp.

"I think Paul's given up, but that doesn't mean I have." I kept my gaze on the ice in my untouched water.

"Oh, yes it does!" Mom snapped at me as she laid her phone down. "I plan to get you home, and then we'll talk to Mark. Let the adults try to work this problem through the legal system. Okay?"

I gritted my teeth together, knowing speaking up would make things worse. I hated being here. I wanted to go live my life and not be sitting at a table, having to bite my tongue, like at so many dinners I'd had with Mom. The pictures of all the bad times we had could be triggered so easily. Every time they made me want to run, from her, and anyone who made me feel the way she could.

She broke the silence she created. "Listen, I'm sorry. I know you can see now this is way bigger than you, bigger than Paul, and maybe even more than Mark and I can help with. Before we tackle all that, I suggest we make the most out of being in London and try to have a good time. I just can't think about Paul's situation right now, or that I might never see my own grandchild. So, for me, please try to have fun today." She focused on Shawn. "You two should be ecstatic to see each other again."

Shawn and I turned toward one another.

"I'm thrilled to be here," he said.

"Fun it is then," I said with thick sarcasm. "Where to?" I was used to putting the shiny coat on things and pretending nothing was wrong, why should now be any different?

"I thought we could get a feel for the city if we went on an open-bus tour. It would let us see where to go shopping and which landmarks we want to see."

There were no disagreements with her logic. We paid the bill and spoke with the concierge. Within fifteen minutes, we had taken a cab to the location where the tours started. This was not the hop-on/hop-off type of tour. It showed much more of the entire city. There were twelve bridges over the Thames, and Mom wanted to see every one of them.

By noon it was hot. The chrome on the bus became untouchable. I sat on the edge of the baked seat. When the bus began to move, a breeze formed and I relaxed. The roar of the engine and wind through our hair kept us each in our own world as we viewed the building rows, monuments, and people. With ample room, we stretched out on both sides of the open-air bus to secure the best views, Mom and me on one side. Shawn squinted under his Dallas Cowboys hat to my right across the aisle. I watched the people on the bus as much as the ones we passed on the street.

I clung to my purse, remembering how cautious I had to be in Italy. I wondered if the same was true about London. I searched around for suspicious characters, for the gypsy type, an old man asking for change or a child with a dirty face hunting their parent. I didn't see the same people in London as I had in Rome. The people here were less colorful or, at least, their clothes were. But, there were still joggers and people waiting for the bus. Some with backpacks made me wonder about colleges nearby, or if it was just the British culture.

After the bridge tour, we walked around downtown. Mom pulled me aside while we strolled down the street to find a restaurant. "About Texas," she started, but I interrupted her, wanting to talk about the embassy. We both deferred to the other until she spoke and I listened.

"I understand why you've been so angry with me. I'm glad you finally let it all out."

I shook my head, relaying the regret I still had over some things I told her at the embassy.

"No, it was good and healthy. If you don't open up and let someone know you're hurting, then how can you ever put it behind you? How can we put it behind us, if you don't? Now, we can move past this." She put her fist to her chest. "And heal inside."

I nodded.

She told me only time would show she wasn't going to be the old person who wallowed in her pain. As she spoke of pain, about herself, I began to listen as if she were talking about me. My mind drifted through memories as I saw my past in clearer waters.

We walked up to an old pub, The White Hart. Upon entering, the sign read *Oldest licenses premises in London..* As I walked in, the air felt thicker, as if the light had not entered in a long time. Neon signs, small low-wattage sconces, and hanging lights casting yellow shadows illuminated the restaurant. It was the oldest pub, serving pints since 1300, but what marked the walls were newspaper clippings from 1888: the slayings of the unsolved murders of Jack the Ripper. A black chalkboard displayed a hand drawing of his well-known profile. The pub had been refurbished, but the years it had stood there could not be erased.

Even though my mind knew it was the middle of the day, eeriness settled all around us. I almost expected a lady of two hundred years to walk out and take our order, but a redheaded, ponytailed British girl with no smile did instead. There were no jolly faces to tame down the words on the wall. It was as if they had all been sucked up into this place. It seemed to breathe, and to do so, it took life from those who stayed here.

Surprisingly, the food was great and cost less than ten pounds per person.

The waitress walked up. "What else for ya?" She said in a British accent. "Want to try our house drink? Jack the Ripper?"

"Oh, no. I don't think so." My eyes grew large to take in even a twinge of movement from Mom to see if that bothered her.

"Don't worry about me. You two get a drink and have fun," Mom said.

"Two, then?" The waitress's pushiness irritated me.

Shawn nodded.

She walked away, and I felt a cold draft run across my feet. Daylight entered behind me like a crack in a wall. Two old guys came in with it and sat at the bar, despite struggling to sit on the high seats. They chatted about terrorism. I heard the President's name. Brits loved to talk about America, I had noticed. Like a parent interested in a child's job, kids, or wife, it mingled with some criticism and hope. And, like all parents, they weren't saying they had it all perfect; they just hoped America would get it right.

As I disappeared in my thoughts of the old timers, our drinks came. "By the way, what's in this?" I asked the waitress.

"Crown and butterscotch schnapps," she said and walked away.

"That's odd. I thought it would have Jack Daniels in it."

"Jack is an American whiskey, and I think Crown has something to do with the Monarchy. Remember, you're in England," Mom said.

"Yeah, it does. I think it was created for one of the kings after World War II," Shawn said.

I tasted the drink, and it was more sweet than caustic. I couldn't drink it, though. I glanced over at Mom reading the wall clippings.

"Did you know there was a barber here in the basement of this place who they think might have been Jack the Ripper?"

Shawn's drink was gone, so he finished mine. His eyes squinted and his smile grew as I looked at him. I couldn't help but smile back. His "sheepish" manners were charming.

His drink arrived with a mate, he laughed. Another one for me, yet I wasn't drinking. He tried hard. His pout came out, the *can you blame me* look, and a hint of a smile.

He was a guy, and we had a history. Could I blame him? He drank and I flew about the room looking at wall clippings. I turned my head as I heard a couple talking about Italy. Everywhere now, it stood out, calling me to come back, in the Gucci purses, Versace, and Prada, or the bottled water and olive oil.

I left to go to the bathroom. I wasn't the kind of girl who asked anyone to join me, but as I sat alone in the stall, with no other strangers even washing their hands, I felt as if I wasn't alone. Then, I stared at the wooden wall separating me from the rest of the room. White carved words stood out against the dark stain. I searched past that. I could feel Fear; he was hiding in the room—Fear, the friend who kept me from making mistakes. However, I was in no mood for a fight. I flushed and washed my hands, rushing to leave. I glared behind me as I charged out the door and ran into Shawn's chest.

I squeaked out a scream.

"Whoa, there. You okay?" he said with his arms around me, stopping my momentum. "Maggie?" His voice floated to me like in a dream.

I looked up, blinking several times before his lips heated up my own. My body went from cold to covered in goosebumps.

My body betrayed me. What had Luke awakened in me? I pulled my chin to my chest and waited for Shawn to back up.

"You okay? You taste so good. I can't wait to get you back to the hotel. Do you think we could find a way to be alone?"

"I don't know." What question was I even answering? "I have to go."

"Maggie? What's wrong?"

"Everything isn't the same."

He closed his eyes longer than a blink, leaning against the wall.

When I returned to the table, Mom pulled her vibrating phone out of her purse and handed it to me.

I gasped, "Hello?"

The unknown number displayed gave no hints as to whom was calling.

"Hey! Are you okay?" Luke's voice asked.

"Hi." I strained to hear above the noise. "I'm okay, I guess. Not where I want to be but making the best of it."

"I knew you would."

"But, I'm mad at you. I don't understand why you wanted me to leave."

"There is no other reason except that it's just too dangerous right now."

"I thought I would be safer there with you and Kayla."

"Some things you don't know yet. I promise, I'll tell you when I see you."

"I don't want to be left in the dark. Just tell me now."

"Why don't you understand you're going to have to trust me?"

I held the phone out and screamed into the dark air, "Arrr."

Shawn mouthed to me, "Everything okay?"

I nodded and turned toward the door, pressing the phone into my ear. "Trust, huh?"

"Have I ever proved you couldn't?"

"I don't know." I swung the door open and stepped out into the day. The man who shared all his secrets now had a lot of them. I hated guesswork. "I just want to know everything, whether it's good or bad. I need to know."

"Maggie, I will. Not over the phone. I just can't–"

Click. The phone went dead.

I waited for him to call back. There were three bars on Mom's phone. After a minute when Luke had not called, I tapped the number to redial it. It was a nonworking number, a number at the embassy for outgoing calls.

I tried for several minutes but couldn't get through. I even searched on the internet for the embassy's number and called it, but no one was answering. I walked back through the White Hart doors, and my eyes were blinded. I stood for a moment to adjust, blinking.

My ears were acute, and I heard the TV louder than before.

"Today at 1:26 p.m., a suicide bomber attacked the United States' embassy in Rome."

I stood with Fear hugging me, listening to the British accent deliver the matter-of-fact news. Shawn walked up beside me, but I couldn't look at him. I stood there trying to control my emotions, to stay quiet so I could listen. I clamped off my throat, squeezed my hands, and bent my knees to brace for the images. As my eyes adjusted, I could see the building I stood in yesterday morning was half destroyed. It appeared to have its face ripped off. Floors were exposed, cut like a cake revealing layers. Wires hung, sheetrock torn mid-wall, and rubble lay at its feet. I thought of the towers in New York when we watched a video of it in my fifth-grade class. This time, I knew two people who could be dead, two people I loved.

I fumbled for Mom's phone. I checked to see the time Luke's call ended. It was 1:26. I could no longer be a dam. I cracked. Falling into Mom and crying, I could not stop. I felt complete despair.

"Whoa, Maggie. Paul may not have been there."

Mom didn't jump to conclusions as I did. I cried loud to drown out anyone, because no matter what they told me, they wouldn't understand I knew Luke was there. They didn't even know who he was. I cried harder that he would never get to know my mom. Shawn assisted me outside as Mom hung onto me. Flashes of the future I would never have with him filled my cries. I didn't know where this came from.

As the doors opened, I took a deep breath of fresh air, squinting my eyes against the light of an overcast day. I kept taking deep breaths as I walked to the curb while Shawn hailed a taxi. With each breath, my clarity returned. I wanted to walk until I was exhausted, until I knew what to do. I flopped in the backseat of the taxi into a mind-numbing confusion with whimpers against my shoulder.

At our hotel room, Mom called Paul. With no answer, she left a voicemail. I heard her words as they quivered, but I could not move from my curled up position. I quieted, thinking of Paul. I didn't know he was there. He might be alive. I had to hold onto that. I sat up and wiped swollen eyes that felt submerged in saltwater. "Luke was inside."

"Are you sure?" Mom wiped her tears. She watched the screen that had already moved on to the continued earthquakes in Japan.

Shawn searched my face for answers, with worry and confusion.

I nodded. Then pictured Paul, Luke, and ... "Kayla! Oh, no. Poor Kayla." I turned to Mom. "We have to go back—"

Mom put her hands up for me to slow down. "Let's just wait a little bit, try to hear from Paul. Do you have Kayla's number?"

I shook my head *no*. "We have to go to her, to Paul—make sure they are okay. I have to know about Luke."

Mom asked, "Maggie? Were y'all close?"

Close. Did we get close? Images filled my mind of my fingers stopping over a mole or feathering his arm muscles as he held me. I could see the dimple that appeared on his left cheek, the same side his smile leaned toward. I even noticed his big toes had blond hair on them. I got real close. The weight of all the memories revealed how important Luke had become to me. I drew a deep breath to remember, and I remembered Mom's question.

"Yeah, we all did."

"Let me see if I can find out anything as a parent by calling the U.S. government." She went to get a pad of paper and a pen, returning with a phone to her ear. I turned toward Shawn as I continued wiping at tears that had streamed all the way to my neck.

Chapter 17
Gaping Holes

I was thirsty and rolled over for the bottle I always kept on a nightstand anywhere I slept. My muscles, sore from crying, spoke louder than my parched mouth, and I decided to take a long shower. I sat down in the shower and let its rain pelt me. I would have almost preferred a pressure-wash, though. I wanted to feel any other pain than the hole inside of me.

Coming out of the bathroom with a towel on my head, I watched Mom hang up the phone. Even as a parent, she couldn't find out anything regarding Paul. She spoke with Mark extensively, the final word was we were going back to Rome.

"Due to the bombing, there are no flights to Rome. We leave tonight by train."

"The trains are still working? All the way to Rome?" Shawn asked.

"We'll try to get as close as we can."

"Mrs. Johanson? I don't want to go home. I think now, more than ever, I need to be with Maggie. Is it okay if I go, if I pay you back any expenses incurred?"

"I was going to pay to send you home, but since the train to Rome is only a hundred pounds, it makes no difference to me."

"I'll get myself home." Shawn turned toward me. "Of course, only if all this is okay with Maggie."

I looked at Shawn and realized I didn't want to lose any more love. Right or wrong, I needed him. Being alone, I thought, could kill me. I had no declaration of feeling or thoughts to share, so I nodded.

Two hours later, we were at the train station going through customs. On the televisions, continual news coverage showed all flights were grounded. Masses of people were at the station. Even though it was my first visit, I could tell people were moving fast, frustrated, and more tired than usual. There were not enough seats for everyone to sit, some women and children stood with their husbands, while some without children sat in seats. They had issued a full security alert in all embassies worldwide, and our president would soon make a speech. It was real.

Shawn let Mom and me sit together, while he sat two rows over. He watched me and mouthed, "It's going to be okay." He tried to soothe me, so I tried to be strong.

With two train changes, we arrived in Rome just before four in the morning and we took a taxi to Hotel Caprice by five. No one had slept on the train very well, so when we arrived at the hotel, we all crashed into the beds.

I thought of Paul, Shawn, and Luke. I remembered my childhood running through sprinklers with Paul or play-wrestling during commercials. I dismissed the thoughts of never seeing him again. I couldn't even let my brain go there.

I tried to make sense of all Shawn had told me, but I didn't want to think about that either. Even as my head fell upon the overstuffed pillow at the Caprice, I returned to the images from when Luke tucked the flower in my hair, when he held me, when he kissed me in bed. He stared into my eyes and told me my blue eyes had gold flecks like a halo. He told me my touch electrocuted him, how he wanted to feel it every day, to feel alive. Thoughts of Luke pulled me back in time, but Shawn's presence kept reminding me of what I'd lost. I was split between the past and present, fantasy and reality, and if I cracked anymore, I feared I'd never be whole again.

I wasn't in a hurry to get up and find out the identities of the dead bodies. I wanted to melt into my covers and go back to a time when I felt safe, without pain.

"Maggie? Maggie, dear? She is out like a light. Maybe we should just leave her to sleep some more." I heard my mom talking, and I felt a hand on my back.

"No, she'll want to go with us."

I sat up. "Go? If y'all are leaving, so am I." I rubbed my eyes.

"It's almost lunch time, and we have a lot to check on," Mom said.

"I'm good. I'll be ready in fifteen." I jumped out of bed and forgot the flip-flops to protect my feet from the carpet's abyss of germs. I wore the same clothes I bought yesterday. Then, I used a few of Mom's make-up vials from the counter. I grabbed my shoulder satchel and double-checked for my passport.

"Ready." Ready for what? I couldn't go there. The day waited like a blank canvas. I couldn't imagine what it would bring, or I would go back to bed.

We walked toward the embassy, relieved we were staying so close, since Italian police had everything roped off, and a taxi couldn't get near it. We still had to walk a mile. At the edge of the barricade, police cars sat with armed men. Mom strained to see if Paul was one of them.

"Hello."

"Ma'am, you will have to stay behind the yellow line." A strip of plastic tied to sawhorses drew the line he referenced.

"Yes, that's fine, but I need to speak with Marine Corporal Paul Dulaney."

The officer glared at Mom. "What business do you have with him?"

"I'm his mother. I need to know he's alive." Her left hand dangled, shaking while her voice quivered. I felt sorry for her, not knowing if her son was alive.

"Can I see some identification, please?"

Mom reached into her jacket for her passport and came up empty handed. Panic struck her. She rummaged through her purse and found nothing but a copy.

"This says Johanson, ma'am," he said, returning the document to her.

"I've been remarried."

"What about mine? I'm a Dulaney. I've been here twice in the past week. Joey, he knows I'm Paul's sister. Ask Joey or Luke."

"I can't, ma'am," he said with anger held behind his clenched teeth. He inspected my passport. "Just a moment." He rattled off my passport number into the radio attached to his shoulder. He waited for a reply, and even though it came across garbled, it sounded positive. He turned to talk to a uniformed man ten feet away. "Tony? Escort these two—"

"Three."

"A brother?"

"No, but—"

He turned back to Tony. "These *two* to Officer Woods."

"I'll be right here," Shawn said. His dark eyebrows pushed into one.

"Follow me and stay close. Do not touch anything," Tony said. I forced the tears to stay locked up and continued through a maze of vehicles. Once we came closer, the horrific pictures on the news became larger, and a charred smell hung in the air. Rebar stuck out of jagged walls like teeth on a dinosaur, roaring its ugly mouth open. An ambulance sat with its doors open, waiting for the next dead body found under debris. On the second floor, a bathroom had been ripped in half, and I saw Fear sitting on that damn toilet, laughing.

"Paul's family," Tony said to who must have been Officer Woods.

My knees dipped from the weight of Fear on my back now, realizing Paul could be dead. *Oh no, not my big brother too. I can't handle this.*

"Easy there, girl," the officer said as he grabbed my arm, lifting me up, and preventing my fall at the same time. "Parker, get over here, got a pale one."

I saw Sammie's worried face. Mom had her hands around my waist, and I felt better just seeing Sammie.

"Listen up, girl. You're gonna be okay. Paul's fine."

"Paul's alive?" Mom must have been feeling similar to me. Her voice sounded like an eighty year old's.

I choked out the words, "Really? Paul's okay?"

She nodded at us and we hugged.

"Sammie, this is my mom—Paul's mom, Karen."

She spoke to Mom using a softer voice than her usual booming one. "It's so nice to meet you, Mrs. Dulaney. I have heard ..."

"Johanson."

"Sorry. Yes. Paul has told me so much about you."

"Where is he?" I asked, impatient.

"Investigating. Our Sarge ..."

Over Sammie's shoulder, I could see Kayla twenty feet away, watching the workers moving debris.

"Our sarge what? Did they find him?"

Sammie shook her head.

"Can I go to her?" I asked Sergeant Woods as I pointed to Kayla twenty feet away. "Kayla?" I yelled, but she didn't turn around.

He nodded.

Leaving Sammie in mid-sentence talking to Mom, I wove my way around a car, garbage cans, and five people until I grabbed her arm. "Kayla!"

She looked at me with red, swollen eyes and collapsed onto my shoulder. Quaking sobs shook us both. I held her under my chin and squeezed her tight, releasing my own pain.   As her crying subsided, she wiped her nose and eyes. "They can't find him."

I felt as though I'd been kicked in the stomach.

She sobbed again with new tears. "Ten bodies have been found .... None are him."

I sighed, but without relief, remembering the news said it would be hard to know just how many had died, since some bodies might never be found.

"He can't be there." She pointed to five stories of rubble. "Oh, Maggie." She dove into my arms again. "I just can't lose Luke, too. I'll be all alone."

I lifted my shoulder back and made her look at me. "No. You'll never be alone."

We both cried until there was nothing left. I wiped my tears. I matched eyes with Mom's through the multitude of people. "Let's go over here, Kayla. I have someone I want you to meet."

Moving with her under my arm, we walked back to Sammie and Mom. When I saw them, I took a deep breath. These women meant something to me. I could feel it, like I knew they would all be a part of my future. "Kayla, this is my Mom, Karen Johanson."

"Nice to meet you," Mom said.

"You, too."

Quick-talking Sammie jumped in, turning to Kayla. "Well, I know the Sarge very well, but haven't met you yet. I'm Sammie Jo Parker."

I smiled to myself; only my eyes would have given me away. I liked knowing the truth about Kayla and Luke, being privy to their special world.

"I work at the hospital, crazy shifts. Nice to meet you too, Sammie," Kayla said.

"I'm sorry about all this," Sammie said as she squinted at the building. "I hope we find out something soon."

I was relieved to hear her speak with optimism. I knew Kayla had plenty of time to face the possibility of Luke's death. For this small window, I wanted us both to concentrate on the possibility of his life.

"I tried Paul's phone again and got him when you went to talk to Kayla. He didn't want us to worry, but he said to tell you he got an email from Luke that brought him up to speed on a few things. He couldn't talk about it over the phone but will tell us in person," Mom explained.

"He knows about what?" I asked.

"He said he was very shocked about some new information and wanted to hear it from you," she said, turning to Kayla. "He's about an hour out and heading back this way. We are to meet him at .... " She held out a receipt where she'd scribbled in pen: *Checco er Carettiere in Trastever district.*

I realized now my brother may not have known about Kayla and Luke.

"Oh, that's just over there." Sammie pointed west. She walked to the edge of the walled off yellow ribbon, now flapping in the wind as clouds rolled in.

"Will you come, too?" I asked Kayla.

She looked behind her at the gaping building. "I don't know. I—"

"I'm sure we'll be coming back soon."

"I'll come for a while," Kayla said.

I lifted my eyes to the embassy, and chill bumps spread down my arms like a rain shower. I knew I had to get away from Fear's laughter. We walked back to the line of sawhorses and squeezed by the first Marine and two Italian guards.

"Shawn, Paul is alive. Mom talked to him." I tried to contain my excitement next to the long faces who waited to know if their loved one was safe yet or not. "We're going to go meet him now."

He followed in behind us as we all followed Sammie. I introduced Shawn as a friend. He double sniffed his nose, a tic of his, and his movements quickened. Why was he nervous?

"Taxi!" Sammie yelled.

The three of them piled in as I hugged Sammie goodbye. Mom handed Sammie a piece of paper with her number. She shouted after us, "I'll call with any news."

"Thanks," I yelled with a wave, then turned to face the driver, "*'Cheeco's* please, in the *Travestere* district."

The driver smiled. I knew I'd butchered it. I didn't care anymore. I wanted to get from Point A to B as fast as possible. I wanted this part of my life to fast-forward.

We arrived before Paul, so we ordered appetizers to munch on while we waited. None of us were up to talking about the events. Small talk filled the air about food in Italy, then people, then the language. It was the conversation people have to avoid another one. We talked with uncomfortable gaps, trying not to upset Kayla, but relieved about Paul. When Paul walked in, we were all sharing the only Italian words we knew. I jumped up first, then Mom, meeting him with a hug. He then went to the table and hugged Kayla. I watched it last longer than normal, and Paul held her while she sobbed. I watched his face soften.

When they separated, Kayla dismissed herself to the bathroom. I wanted someone to hold me and let me fall apart but rejected the thought, refusing to believe Luke was gone. I looked around the table. The only one here who knew how I felt was Kayla.

Paul greeted Shawn. "Glad you're okay, man."

"Yeah, off-duty saved me. But ..."

"Paul, sit down and eat. Tell me what you're investigating," Mom said, glancing at me, hoping I wouldn't notice she diverted the conversation away from Luke.

Paul's lips formed an inaudible question.

"Sammie said you had been reassigned—investigating something, and that's why you were not at the embassy?"

"Oh, I'm lucky they didn't ship me off like they did two hundred other people. They kept most of the Marines, though, to secure the building, but ..." He turned to Mom. "I can't tell you what I'm investigating. Confidential, Mom, sorry." He turned to me. "I can't believe y'all came back."

"If you had answered your phone last night, we wouldn't have."

I mouthed *thank you* to Paul.

He mouthed back to me, "I need to talk to you." Louder, he said, "I'm starving. Let's order," looking at his menu.

Later, Mom and I became too sappy for Paul, watching him eat. He was already making his exit.

We secured him for two hours at least, but then Mom wanted to go rest at the hotel. Shawn offered to escort her there while Paul orchestrated Kayla and me to accompany him back to the embassy.

When the three of us were alone in the taxi, Paul turned to Kayla and asked, "So you're Luke's sister?"

Kayla smiled—her first one since the bad news. They stared at each other with stuck smiles while I sat back and observed.

Chapter 18
Perspective

"He told you?" Kayla asked while looking forward as the taxi weaved through traffic.

"At the embassy yesterday. I'm a little shocked. I had no idea. Luke's my best friend, and he'd never told me," Paul said.

"He's pretty adamant about security. I mean, you guys have no idea what the last two years have been like. Sometimes I thought I was a captive, but the older I got, he loosened up a bit." Her expression sobered, remembering him. "Before the bombing, Luke said he would be going out of town, not to worry. I half thought he was going after you," Kayla said and smiled at me.

"The email he sent me talked about going out of town too," Paul said.

My nose burned. "What does any of that matter now? I was talking to him when—" I stopped talking. I couldn't tell her.

"What?"

I shook my head.

"What are you not telling me?" Kayla asked.

I let out a sigh as I collapsed back into the taxi seat. "I think we just need to wait and see." I didn't want to tell them that Luke was dead. That he was at the embassy. I couldn't break her heart and steal all her hope. Could I?

"What do you know?" Paul asked.

They both looked at me. Trapped in a corner, I heard the words coming out of my mouth, hoping Paul would help me console Kayla. "He was at work when we were talking and got cut off. At … 1:26." My nose stung and my eyes filled with tears, despite opening them wide. I didn't want to cry, not in front of Kayla again.

"I see," Paul said in an odd way. "You're sure your phone showed the call end at 1:26?"

"Yes, when the bombing occurred."

He clicked open his email on his phone. "Hmm."

"What is it?"

"In his email, he said he took care of the two guys at the apartment. The Italian police picked them up at Primo's family restaurant, Cavour or Caviar, something like that. That email was sent at 1:21."

"Do you think Primo's men had anything to do with the bombing?" Kayla said the word like it was fragile and could blow up.

"The Italian mob doesn't want to go to war with a government, much less America. I know it's easy to put a string of bad events together and think they are related, but sometimes they just aren't." Paul eyed his phone as if waiting for it to ring.

"What is it, Paul?"

"I had a second email from Luke."

Kayla and I sat up straighter in the taxi, listening to him. We waited for the rest of his words, hoping.

Paul continued. "It was sent incomplete at one-thirty. It said that he would see us tomorrow, but didn't say where."

"What does that mean?"

"I don't know," Paul said, and we all sat back thinking of the possibilities.

Was Luke alive? Did he type that message when he was talking to me? Was it sent delayed, or did he really send it after the bombing? I was afraid to hope, but the alternative would wreck me.

After the taxi dropped us off, we cut through the roundabout circle, the same as I had when I first walked to the embassy two weeks ago. Walking past the fountain, I stared at their nakedness and the motion of water flowing seductively over them.

We walked down another street with our backs to the fountain. I strained to see the embassy. With the images of the chipped stone faces of the fountain fresh in my mind, I imagined the death within the embassy's crumbling walls. The linear street revealed the torn building before we were close. It no longer bled out destruction as it did on TV, but sat there in a quiet death with dust at its feet. It, too, was frozen. Would this also become a monument?

I wanted so much to believe Luke was alive, but when I looked at this building, with all its beauty sliced open, it reminded me that sometimes beautiful things die. Sometimes when you think you have control, you have none.

Paul walked over to a group of Marines. I stayed back with Kayla as we both watched the workers remove debris on the other side of orange construction barricades. I felt the heaviness in my face; it drooped as I stood there. If Luke was gone, would my love die with him? Had I known him long enough? Was it love at all? Tears rolled down my cheeks like a signature on a dotted line. I remembered the feeling of him lying beside me, and I knew he would always be a part of me. We would always have our night of sunshine. I wrapped my arms around myself. I hugged Luke, the part of him I would always carry with me.

Enough time passed for a bead of sweat to fall down my spine. I suggested to Kayla that we go down the street for some waters at a gelato shop. After returning, we sat in the shade and waited. The other families were scattered around waiting for news—news no one wanted. However, we needed answers, and this was the only likely place to find them.

Another hour passed before Paul came and sat near us, a consoling presence more than anything. He left in a hurry after a phone call, an investigative lead he said he had to follow.

A stone in the mulch made a good seat while the tree's trunk gave us something to lean against. We rested there from the draining sun. My eyes dropped to the pavers below my feet. I saw what appeared to be faces in the smooth rocks, people at the embassy: Joey the Marine from Oklahoma, the guard who stood with me in the hall, and the American-Italian behind the counter who always watched me from afar. Another stone resembled Luke's profile. I kicked some mulch onto it and made it disappear.

Kayla brought up London, and I welcomed the change to my thoughts. She wanted to know all about London and Shawn. It was awkward telling her about him. I found myself trying to explain him but then realized she understood better than I thought she would.

"I love the idea of someone coming across an ocean to tell someone they love them, so rare." Kayla said but then wrinkled her forehead.

"What's wrong?"

"I know you've known Shawn longer, and his affection for you is obvious but ..." She paused. "I just hope my brother has a chance with that history. Shawn's a great guy, but I think my brother really likes you."

She used present tense. I was glad she was being positive, but Luke was writing that email—at the embassy—while we were talking. I feared we would never find his body. What would Kayla do? I teetered between optimism and despair, like a keep away game. I held onto her optimism while fighting Fear's rants and images of a torn body under the rumble. Neither concept was beneficial.

"Well, I kinda like him, too." We smiled, but I wiped a tear without her seeing it. I sat and pondered her responses, watching the clouds thicken and separate. Then, I said aloud, "Timing is everything." The clouds moved, and the sun glared through the sky, causing me to drop my eyes to the grass beneath us.

"What?" Kayla asked.

"Oh, just about love, Shawn and Luke." I ran my fingers through my hair and turned my face with my eyes closed to the sky, feeling it warm my bones.

"Yes, I guess time does dictate who we love," Kayla said after taking a sip of water.

"How much of all this is chance or fate?"

"I think we are surrounded every day with things that influence our lives," Kayla said.

"Fate?" I stared at her.

"Like the spirit world."

"Spirits? You mean ghosts?" I wiped sweat from the back of my neck.

"No, like angels and demons."

"Like in the Bible?" I scratched above my ear.

"Yeah. You believe in the Bible, don't you?"

"I do. I think so." What I knew of it influenced my morals, no doubt.

"What do you mean you think so?"

"Well, I guess I need to read it all first, before I know completely."

"Sure! Don't want the President only reading half the Constitution."

I laughed. "You aren't a normal seventeen-year-old girl."

"I think I like that."

"What was it like for you growing up?" I asked her.

"I grew up with so much heartache but so many other amazing things, too. I have learned to take the good with the bad. My parents dying was awful, to lose them at the same time like that."

I knew I had not felt a pain that deep. I had lost my dad, but at least I still had my mom. She was an emotional cripple, but she was alive and here wanting to love me. Kayla would never have that. I didn't understand how Kayla could be so strong at such a young age, having lived through so much tragedy. I admired her but felt sorry for her as well. Then it hit me. Is this how others see me?

"But then, I went to live with my grandma, and that was wonderful. She taught me so many things about God and how to get through the hard times." Her words reminded me of my own grandmother.

"That's cool." I smiled. "Did she tell you about angels and demons, or did you just read it?"

"Once, when she went through chemo treatments for breast cancer, she was sitting in her chair, and she felt this hand on her shoulder while she was reading the Bible. She said an overwhelming peace came upon her. She was afraid the peace would leave, so she didn't want to move her head to look. But she did, and she saw a hand with a circular scar on the back of it."

"Wow." Cold chills covered my arms.

"I know, but my grandma wasn't a whack, just a little Baptist girl. She didn't grow up believing in some of those far-out crazy things like snake-handling. Still, she told me, whether I believed it or not, the spirit world existed. She said, 'Be on the good side, honey,' and smiled at me. That's what I'm trying to do," Kayla said.

"That's an amazing story. I wouldn't mind that happening to me."

"You might want to read the Bible first, girl," Kayla poked in fun.

I knew what she meant. Kayla looked radiant. Right here in the midst of this tragedy, she sat with the most beautiful and peaceful look on her face. Kayla had a strength I did not have yet.

"What do you think's going to happen?" I nodded toward the building.

She stopped to think, squinting at me, and then back at the embassy. "I don't think he's there."

I sat up from leaning against the bark. "What are you saying?" What did she know? Did God tell her something? I sat on the edge of the stone, holding on.

"I don't know, but I've had time to think, to pray, and I don't think he's here. I just know it but don't know why I do. Ever happen to you?"

"I would like that to happen to me, but no, I couldn't say it had. Where do you think he is?"

I knew this sounded crazy. I was going down a road where committed people lie in beds with drool on their faces. However, sitting under a tree in ninety-five-degree weather, waiting for a corpse sounded pretty insane, too. I wanted to do something, to run straight into the future. I wanted to catch Time, and when I did, he would have to tell us if Luke was alive.

"Let's go to Merrico's restaurant," Kayla said.

Had she also decided sitting here was futile? I moaned at the thought of Merrico. "I don't want to see him."

"Why, because you think he tore apart the apartment?"

"No, he wouldn't have done that. I know that was Primo, but he is too close to Primo."

"Exactly why we are going to go see him." Kayla laughed. She stared at me, saying "come on" without words.

"You like to walk the wild side or something?"

"It's in my blood, but seriously, I can't sit here while Luke may be in trouble."

"Why do you think he might be in trouble? You know he also might be …" I couldn't finish the sentence. I couldn't say he was dead. It felt too wrong—or it would hurt too much.

"I told you, I don't know. I follow my gut. I *am* my brother's sister."

I sighed. What did that mean? I realized she knew far more about him than I did.

"Plus, Luke had said, 'Merrico was harmless enough,'" she added.

"Oh hell, I suppose you're right. It's the only place to start."

A smile spread across her face as she jumped up and offered her hand.

I grabbed it and pulled up to my feet. "Are we really doing this?"

"What else do we have to lose?"

I cocked my head to the side. "Did you have to ask that?"

She laughed. "Besides the obvious."

"Does your phone work?"

"Yeah."

"Okay, good." I walked around until I found Sammie. She confirmed Kayla's cell number on a clipboard. We didn't tell her any of our plans, only that we were tired and wouldn't be back until tomorrow. She agreed to call us with any news. We walked a mile before we could hail a cab. As we slid into one, a different cab, already carrying a passenger, honked at us. For a minute, my heart leaped, hoping it was Luke rushing to tell us he was okay. It followed us. I squinted enough to know it wasn't Luke, but a man with a hat and a slender face.

We went to Alla Rampa, and Kayla loved the atmosphere of the place. The room smelled of marinara sauce, as if our noses were over the pot for a tasting. Then a tray of bread floated by smelling of garlic. My mouth filled with saliva, and I had to swallow.

We sat in a booth farthest from the bar. When the waiter came to our table, we ordered drinks and asked if Merrico was around. He wasn't, but was due to arrive any moment. *Ahh*, I thought, *Time has given us a bone, and it must like the game we were about to play.* I wondered then if Time picked sides, and I hoped that maybe, just maybe, he would be our friend.

We had eaten four hours ago and neither of us was hungry, but we ordered an appetizer and two wines. A half-empty glass later, my stomach rolled over, reminding me this was not a normal meal. I glimpsed back at the door, as I had done twelve times already.

After the food arrived, Kayla sat straight up against the booth's back cushion, looking at the door with widened eyes. "Is that him? He looks important, and he's talking to the waiters."

When I looked, three waiters scurried away to reveal all of Merrico. He was the epitome of Italian. His wore a skinny tie that matched his skinny belt that matched his skinny shoes. Black leather, not biker leather, it was smooth, just like the words that rolled off his tongue. His eyes met mine, and his lips parted into a smile. He walked a straight line that led right to me. I broke eye contact and asked Kayla, "What do I say?"

"My Poppy. I thought I had lost you." He stood at the end of the table with one foot propped on the booth's elevated floor, bending his knee and reaching to hold my hand. My hand obliged, as always.

A nervous smile erupted. Damn, I wished I could control those things. "No, still here."

"I saw your building, part of it burnt, the top floors. The paper said no one was hurt, but the building's abandoned for repairs, and I had not known where to find you."

"Well, I was on the top floor, so ..."

"Oh no, you were not there when it went aflame, were you?"

"No, no. I'm fine."

"I am relieved. You do look very fine, indeed. But I've lost my manners." He looked at Kayla. "Her beauty blinds a man. I apologize. I am Merrico."

"Kayla. Nice to meet you."

"Beautiful women do like to run in packs, don't they?"

Kayla blushed.

"Merrico, I need some help."

He sat down next to me, wrapping his left arm up behind me on the booth. "Anything for you." His other hand reached inside his jacket.

"Oh, no, nothing like that."

"What is it?"

"Kayla's husband is ... missing."

"And who is your husband?"

"Luke Seager."

Nothing moved on Merrico's face except a squint of his eyes and a flare of his nostrils. I sat so close I could see it in his profile. He turned to me. "And how is it you know this Luke?"

Fear had been hiding under the table. He used to be nice and whispered things in my ear. At times, he became rude and made fun of me, but lately he had become physical. He punched me in the stomach, and then came out like a gremlin and started dancing. Kayla sensed him, too, from the look on her face, but I knew no one saw him like I did.

"I just met him. I'm trying to help Kayla. She's a friend of mine." My lack of truth was a signal for Kayla to choose carefully every word that came out of her mouth. I could tell by her widened eyes that she heard me loud and clear.

"Oh, sweet Maggie, that could be a dangerous adventure for two pretty girls in Rome. You're better off going back to the embassy and waiting there."

"How ..." I didn't mean to say it out loud. How did he know we had been there? That meant he knew Luke was a Marine.

"Maggie." He took my hand again. "I say this only to protect you, to keep you safe. You do not want to know."

"But I do. We have to find him!"

"Why do you not believe him to be under all that rubble?"

Kayla jumped in. "I refuse to believe it."

"Yes, a woman's denial, wide as the ocean." He paused and turned to me. "I do not say this to be a heartless, callous man, but men like Luke belong at the bottom of the rubble. He does not deserve a woman like you wasting one tear for him," Merrico said.

Confusion ran across my forehead, and I rubbed the lines into submission. "What are you talking about, Merrico? Luke's a Marine. A good guy."

"Yes, the Marine, I know. The good, I don't."

"Why do you think he's no good?"

"You know the night we ate here?"

I nodded.

"Primo, my future brother-in-law, the ice-cream?"

"Yeah, yeah. I know Primo. What about him?"

He squinted at Kayla, then returned his intense stare to me. "Luke works for Primo's father."

No! What? Lies. They were lies. Why would he say that? Did he kill Luke? That's it. He knows that I love Luke, so he's threatened. "Don't lie to me, please."

Merrico turned to Kayla. "I am so sorry to have to tell you. I don't know where he is but I …" He paused to think. "You know, you are right. That was horrible of me to defame your husband, upon his death of all moments. I am ashamed of my behavior.   Please, forgive me." He turned back to me. "Please, forgive me."

Anger rose inside of me. "How do we find Primo?"

"Maggie, no. Let this go. There are dangerous men in this city. You don't want to get involved with them."

I clenched my teeth and raised my voice, asking, "Have you? Are you involved with them?"

"More than I want to be." He sighed.

"Did you tell them where I lived, where we lived?"

He hung his head and stared at the table. "It was not my desire to."

"You owe me, then. You can find out where Luke is."

"No, Maggie. You don't understand. I pay. That's all I do. When Eleana marries Primo, I won't have to anymore, but for now, our family still pays."

I understood what he meant. I had watched *The Godfather* with Shawn one night. I knew what he warned. The dead horse's head in the bed from the first *Godfather* movie flashed in my mind. I understood everything except Luke.

"How do you know Luke works for him? What did you see?"

"I know what you're doing. I won't tell you anymore. I won't give you leads to follow."

"Then you force me to go straight to Primo."

"Maggie, I hope you don't, but know if you do, I cannot save you." He shook his head, defeated in his attempts to talk us out of anything. Upon standing again, he added, "I hope you will think about what I've said and let this go. I would like very much to take you out on another date." His grave face ended with a small smile, an olive branch.

"I'll think about it."

He kissed my hand and left us, disappearing into the kitchen.

"You don't believe that slime ball, do you?"

"No, Kayla. Something doesn't add up here."

"Thank God, with all his kissy-kissy crap, I just didn't know if you were buying into that."

I dropped twenty euros on the table. "Come on, it's time to go." I couldn't tell Kayla, but something in Merrico's eyes told me he wasn't lying.

We stepped out into a beautiful evening, one less humid, just right for strolling without becoming hot and sweaty.

"Still hungry?" I asked.

"No. Why?" Just as she said it, she changed her mind. "Actually, I'm famished."

"Glad to see nothing spooks you."

"I've been living with my brother for two years; he rubs off. In a good way." We smiled as we both thought of that statement.

Chapter 19
Piping Detail

I could have sworn a cab was following us again. Fear kept watch in the rear window, flicking me in the head to keep looking. This one had a passenger, too, but no hat on his head. The odds it could be coincidence were low. Merrico's tail, or Primo's? Was there any difference? I hoped so. Of course, it could just be my cabbie's friend. I was getting paranoid and had to shake it off. I shook my head at Fear, and he quieted down. Thanks to Paul telling us the name of Primo's restaurant, we had our cab driver take us to 313 Cavour, the oldest wine bar in Rome.

The taxi dropped us off in front of an inconspicuous red-trimmed door with stickers all over the outside, similar to a convenience store's door. A scripted menu in its side window hinted at the true gem inside. Upon opening the door, wood filled every corner and covered nearly every surface. My eyes struggled to delineate the difference in structures. Long wooden slats on the floor ran the length of the restaurant front to back. Wooden booths, a rarity in Rome, were large and tall with pieces of wood meeting the ceiling like a four-poster bed. The ceiling housed the wine cellar. Hundreds of wine bottles hung over us, their dark liquids also blending into the wood.

We walked in and were seated across from the granite bar with a chalkboard of specials. It wasn't long before we had waters and an appetizer. Glancing around the room, we finally found Primo, standing behind Eleana, stroking her neck and back. She sat at the bar, eating a bowl of pasta perfectly, like all Italians knew how to do, twirling the pasta around a fork. Next to her, a couple ate their pasta with a spoon.

"Look, Kayla. First time I've seen that, using a spoon to eat their pasta. Sicilians."

I continued watching Primo. The food at Merrico's had settled my stomach, but here—with Primo in plain view and Merrico's words on my mind—I couldn't help wanting to vomit. There was no way Merrico could be right about Luke.

A thick-necked dirty-blond man walked up to our table. "We need you to come with us. Now." His Russian accent sounded odd. What was a Russian doing in Rome? It confused me for a moment, causing me to doubt my own whereabouts. I was still in Rome, judging from the room and the patrons.

"What?" I asked.

"I said, *now*! Come with us." He pointed to a guy who stood off to his right ten feet away. He frowned at me. Their stern eyes held no humor, and their faces, smooth like statues, spoke loud and clear, but I didn't move until he revealed a black gun tucked behind his belt.

We both slid out and stood, leaving everything but my purse. I clutched the flat leather against my chest. We followed the man who stood farthest away. The Russian followed behind me. As we walked through the bar area, Primo lifted his head, making eye contact with me. One side of his face smiled.

I looked around and saw a Dallas Cowboys cap. The same annoying hat Shawn wore on his visit to see me in Texas. Could it be him? Before the kitchen door closed behind us, I yelled his name. I hoped the man in the cap would turn his head, but he didn't. The Russian squeezed the back of my neck, clamping my scream.

They shoved us through the kitchen, where I searched for knives but only saw stainless steel counters and lettuce. Kayla groped for my hand. She looked terrified, but I was waiting. I wasn't convinced we were in serious trouble. I had waited to have the conversation with Primo for weeks and now was ready for it. It wasn't until we were ushered out the back door and shoved into a car with rough bags over our heads that I knew. We were in trouble. Fear danced all over me, while I strained to see through a burlap cloth. I breathed harder and faster until I realized I was going to pass out.

"Wake up, bitch!"

I felt a kick to my left shin, another to my right forearm. If I could have spoken quicker, maybe I could have spared myself the bruises. "What?" I forced the words out with all my strength to prevent any more pain. Breathing hard, I strained to regain enough strength to open my eyes. A moment later, they opened. Difficult to sustain, but I had to look again. Primo's face filled my entire view. I blinked.

"There you are. What the hell is your problem?"

"I don't understand."

"I know, 'cause you're a stupid *lit-tle* bitch." When angry, his accent rolled out thick.

I scrambled to sit up. My bones ached. How long had I been out? The stiffness in my joints told me at least four hours, maybe more. I looked around and saw Kayla. She was maybe twenty feet away curled up on the concrete floor next to some barrel drums. Her legs moved, but her eyes were still closed. I scanned the warehouse and noticed rows of industrial equipment. Garbage trucks in front of massive roll-up doors spanned the length of the building. The same two muscle guys were there. I noticed shadows of people on the other side of a glass wall that resembled an office. I could sit up now, unbound, but I knew that didn't mean I was free.

"What are you doing, Primo? Why would you bring us here? We just wanted to talk to you." I pulled my knees to my chest and wrapped my arms around them.

"Why are you two even here? You should have gone back to America."

"How much do you know?" My eyes darted everywhere. My heart raced, and my head felt each beat. Nothing made any sense.

"I know everything." He peered at me with hate.

"Oh, you know your future wife is carrying my brother's child?"

He slapped me. It stung my face so hard and fast, I had no time to pull away even a centimeter.

"You lying bitch! How dare you say that? That is my child. My heir."

I soothed my pain with the touch of my hand. I saw Fear hiding under a garbage truck.   Terror filled his eyes.

"What are you going to do? Kill me?"

He took out his gun and bent down, holding it to my face while his right hand stroked my hair. "Why would I want to do something like that when you will go for such a nice price?" He laughed as if it was a private joke, and the Russians joined him. His walk reminded me of a Brooklyn Italian, a bounce that aired confidence. One of the guys handcuffed my ankle to a pipe. The three left and disappeared behind a door next to the office window.

Price? What a psycho. Would he actually sell us to someone? When they were gone, I tried to shimmy the cuff free, finally aware of the quiver in my hands, my dry mouth, and the tears running down my face. I didn't even remember crying.

Kayla still wasn't responding, and I was afraid to be louder. I leaned my shoulder against a bag of limestone and considered all the possibilities for escape. I searched around for anything to use as a weapon or a lock pick. After a while, my eyelids became heavy as night had fallen. Kayla's unconsciousness worried me. I didn't understand what they could have done to her, and my stomach twisted. I was worse than tired from lack of sleep. I struggled to stay awake. After hours of not being able to move, I rested my eyes.

"Are you okay?" The soft, gentle voice nudged at me, as if I were six years old and it was time for school. My ears awakened.

My body shook, and I responded by negotiating more sleep, "Okay, okay, in a minute." My left side felt numb, my neck stiff, and my feet cold. Being so uncomfortable alarmed me.

"Maggie!"

I opened my eyes. The light came in through windows near the roof. The dark shadows only appeared darker as my eyes opened, and the light revealed the room as if it were a shattered mirror. Even the face above me, half darkened, seemed a menacing clown in the Hall of Mirrors at a carnival.

"Are you hurt?" A voice soothed me.

"I'm, oh—Shawn? Is that you?" I sat up. "My lips feel funny." I puckered and pressed, as if I had just applied lipstick.

"Maggie? Are you okay? Are you hurt? It's me, Shawn." He propped me against a hard bag. My senses awakened as I took in his voice and the numbness in my lips. "Am I hurt?" I moved my leg and my shin hurt. Shin splints? How did I get? Then, I remembered. Primo. I really despised that guy, and it was hard for me to hate anyone.

"Brace yourself."

I watched Shawn kick at the pipe to which I was connected. It bounced, and noise traveled but didn't ricochet and return. I remembered the room with men and rechecked it, but no one came through the door. He kept kicking at the pipe's joint until he stood on it. It gave way, and an old silver pipe revealed a rusted center. Chips of brick-colored metal scattered on the floor like pennies. I did my part and ran my leg down to the opening in the pipe to slip the handcuff off. I was free.

"Thank you! Thank you so much." I hugged him upon standing. His arms always found my hips, wrapping around me, sealing off any air between us. It unsettled me how his body fit next to me like a puzzle piece.

"Shawn? How are you here?"

He returned a tight hug, as he revealed his relief I was still alive.

I pulled away, looking at him, waiting for understanding.

"I've been following you both, by cab." The suspicious cab came to my mind. I sighed as things became clearer. I turned and looked at Kayla.

I had heard nothing from her, but the noise must have awakened her. When I looked over, she was sitting up, rubbing her eyes. Her ankle was attached to a pipe, just as mine was.

"Kayla, are you okay?" I knelt down beside her and checked her body for bruises or cuts. No marks were visible.

"What happened?"

"Primo kidnapped us—threatened me. I'm sure he's not far away."

"We have to hurry. Can you move?" Shawn asked.

She picked up her leg, but it clanged back against the pipe. "Um, sorta."

"That's okay." I turned my head to Shawn. "Do you think that will work again?"

He gazed over his shoulder at shadows moving through the muted glass, but the door didn't open. "Whatever we do, we need to do it now." He jumped onto the pipe.

I prayed for rust. With slow breaths in, then out, I watched the shadows in the room, praying they didn't come out. I watched Shawn's fifth attempt to break the pipe with his weight. *Please. Oh, Please. Lord, God. Please.* I stared at the metal pipe, then the joint. My breathing quickened.

A loud clank scared me. My shoulders shuddered as I blinked. I watched the pipe gush its red watery contents. My hands moved fast, sliding Kayla's handcuff to the opening until loosened. I helped her stand. A long sigh released into the stale air as we hugged.

Shawn touched my shoulder. "We better go."

I grabbed Kayla's hand, and we raced after Shawn. The metal from the dangling handcuff slapped against my leg. I leaned down to try to hold the unclasped cuff to keep it from banging against the floor. Kayla and I ran more like monkeys, half bent over. Adrenaline empowered me now. We ran across the large room to the only door. We heard voices through a window left of the door. I stopped.

"Whoa, are you sure we should go this way?" I whispered.

"It's the way I came through. There's a hallway. We can sneak past the room they're all in, if we hurry." Shawn searched around. "I don't think there's another way out without opening those large doors, and they will definitely hear that sound."

I took a deep breath. "Okay, let's just get out of here." My voice quivered from my heart beating in my throat.

Shawn opened the door. We crouched low like ducks to avoid being seen through another window. The hallway's previous traffic had thrown dirt to the wall's sides one inch thick. The pathway stained with unknown liquids repulsed me. I waddled a few more feet, but then the doorknob jiggled. We all hit the dirt, literally. My own exhale moved the grit along the wall as my cheek touched the cold cement floor. I looked up and saw the ice black eyes of Primo.

"Hmm, another American crime fighter? I'm beginning to hate Americans." His eyes looked like black holes.

Another man appeared, and my mouth dropped as I exhaled with disbelief. Luke's blue eyes leered down at me—whether in disgust or horror, I couldn't tell.

I dropped my mouth open for words to come, but nothing did.
He turned to Kayla. I dropped my head to try to breathe deeper. The hallway shrunk.

"There's been a terrible misunderstanding, sweetheart. Come, we must clean up. It's time to get you ready for the party." Whom was Luke talking to?

"What?" Kayla stood, and the two of them looked at each other. They were talking, but it was nonverbal. She nodded in sweet submission.

"Oh, so this is your little lady? Didn't know. You are lucky, Luke. This one is special. Yes, I can see it in her eyes. Your wife, you say?" His eyes rolled up and down her and landed with an aim at Kayla's eyes that made her turn away, popping out tendons from her neck.

Luke shot Primo a steel gaze. "Do I have to remind you about—"

"No!" Primo said. "Listen, I can drop her off. You take care of this." Primo pointed to me and Shawn.

Kayla shook her head but was ignored.
Luke turned back to Kayla. "I'll be at the apartment later to pick you up."

Kayla looked confused.

"Oh, sorry, sweetheart. They moved us down to the first floor until the repairs are finished—122," Luke said, but he wouldn't look at me.

She nodded. Whatever was going on, Luke wasn't revealing the villa's location to Primo, which told me he didn't trust Primo. But, in that game, I supposed none of them did.

I looked at Kayla for any understanding. She kept her eyes on Luke. I tried to see her expression but couldn't. What was going on? I wanted to shout, but Fear propped open the door to the warehouse and sent his heinous laugh through the corridor. He put his spiny finger over his mouth and sent a *shh* through the hallway.

Shawn rose to his feet, but I sat confused, staring at the floor, trying to find the answers. A hand reached for me to stand. I placed mine in Shawn's.

"We'll be leaving too," Shawn said.

"You've got balls for a twenty-one-year-old," Luke said.

I squinted my eyes at Luke, so he would know how disgusted with him I felt. How could he be doing this? How could he be working with Primo?

"You're taking care of the little problem then?" Primo turned from the end of the hall and asked Luke.

Luke snapped out of whatever he was thinking and turned back into the prick I found him to be. "I have the perfect place," he told Primo, and they shared a grin.

"Nothing around here. And, that one has a big mouth. You'd better duct tape her now."

Luke rolled his eyes and took a deep breath. "I got this."

Primo waved his hand and walked out with Kayla, leaving Luke, the Russians, Shawn, and me. Now, I could find out what the hell was going on. I knew not to ask in front of Primo. But, Thick-Neck grabbed my arm and threw me into the room where the men had their meeting. He shoved me onto a metal industrial chair. A loose screw in the chair tore through my thin shirt and skin. It stung like needles, but I ignored it as anger raged through me.

How could Luke, a man I loved, treat me this way? He was out in the hall with Shawn. I wanted to see them. What were they talking about? I tried to slip free, but Thick-Neck had his arm around my deltoids like a tourniquet.

"Hey! Luke, are you frickin' kidding me?" I yelled, wanting him to hear me.

Fat, sweaty fingers overpowered the duct tape's glue odor as it covered my lips. He pushed my cheeks into my teeth.

"Hey, take it easy with her!" Luke yelled as he entered but avoided eye contact with me.

Thick-Neck had my arms pulled abnormally far behind me. It caused me to arch my back against the chair.

"Do as you're told." Luke bowed out his chest. "Primo has plans for her."

While Thick-Neck held me, my left shoulder pushed against ligaments and tried to roll out of the socket. Before it did, the two Russians obeyed Luke and lightened their grip. Thick-Neck lowered my arms. My butt could sit its full weight in the chair as my shoulders came forward, but I still couldn't relax.

Fat–fingered Thick–Neck stood with pride and uttered in his broken English, "Let us see her talk now." He laughed like a deep-throated Santa Claus, eerie and wicked.

I thought of *Superman*, the movie, and him fighting his alter ego. Could Luke be this bad? How could I not have seen it? I imagined our night together. They were not the same man.

The Russians finished taping Shawn. Luke only taped his hands. Then they left us. I sat upright in a steel chair with duct tape around my wrists and wrestled against the tape until every muscle in my body had collapsed from exhaustion. There was little exchange between Shawn and me, since only our eyes could talk. Mine said I was sorry so many times, redundancy forced me to move on.

The door opened thirty minutes later according to the clock over Shawn's head. Thick-Neck pulled out a big knife attached to his belt. He held it and smiled then kissed the blade. I shook my head as tears filled my eyes. I scooted my chair backward until it hit the wall and had nowhere else to go. He laughed at me and walked closer. I could hear Shawn banging his chair against the floor and trying to talk through the tape. When Thick-Neck hovered over me, he squatted down and pulled out a key unlocking the cuffs on my ankles. He smiled with pleasure.

The other Russian cut Shawn's tape so he could walk. "Oops. Pulled da skin off." His Fs all sounded like Vs, and a smile revealed a rotten molar. I thought they were going to kill us. It was difficult to swallow with a dry mouth, and my muscles felt as if I had run a marathon. I had nothing left.

They left our wrists and mouths bound. My Russian pulled me through the door, down the hall, and outside by my elbow. The sun's brightness pained my eyes. I held them closed and stumbled as I walked. Thick-Neck lifted my shoulder to hold me up as I fell. I could feel ligaments rip in my shoulder. Sharp, searing pain filled my left arm, radiating to my thumb. I couldn't believe this imbecile. I moaned through the tape with the last of my energy.

I couldn't see. The light kept me in a squint that widened by a sliver. A large hand pushed me down and forced me to slide onto a hot leather seat. Luke sat in the front of a black, four-door SUV, much like the one that brought us here the night before. Yakov joined Shawn and me in the back seat, and Thick-Neck drove. My chest jutted out toward Shawn's as we faced each other, wrists bound behind us.

"Yakov, sit between them and keep them apart."

"I not like hump. My legs not—"

"I don't care," Luke insisted.

Before he separated us, Shawn and I stared at one another. I took a deep breath, wondering if things were getting worse. Yak repositioned me to face the window, and I squinted until my eyes adjusted. Through the tinted windows, I scanned dilapidated buildings and a wide parking lot. I could hear trains, possibly from both sides of the car. I let them sink in without connection and turned my attention inside the car. I strained my neck to see if I could catch a glimpse of Luke's face in the outside mirror. His head turned from the driver to the road in front of him, but he never looked out the window.   We ramped up onto the interstate almost within a minute. My only view then became a wall of concrete. It flew by at speeds that produced nausea, so I closed my eyes.

I was no longer angry, but a sadness washed over me. I felt too young to die. I felt too stupid to be executed. I no longer felt frozen, waiting for something, but was now a traveler being carried away. Maybe out to sea.

I scratched at the tape on my hand, for no other reason but to be able to move. I swayed with the turns of the car in and out of traffic, leaning against Yakov, then the window, back and forth. The rocking, along with the heat from the sun, bobbled me to a stupor. I drifted back in time to car rides with Paul on the road to Florida.

Chapter 20
Blowing Wind

"*Da? Cevo-nich-ium?*" Thick-Neck's voice startled me back to the present. We were still driving, and he was on the phone. I kept still, mimicking sleep.

"What?" Luke asked Thick-Neck after he hung up.

"Arman says es-change must be to-night." His accent grew thicker and harder to understand. "He has leave for Argentine."

"He's here, now?"

"*Da*," the driver said.

Luke let out a long sigh and ran his fingers through his hair. Short strands flared out and stuck up straight.

"If your boss wants crates, is now. Or, Arman will move on," Thick-Neck said.

"Oh, Primo wants them all right. He's just dying to break up the families of Italy."

"We like his ambition. This not enough, but will get him started."

"The start of WWIII." Luke's sarcasm seared the end of their conversation.

Who is Arman? The four families of Italy? I lay with my eyes closed, processing. Oh hell, what have I gotten myself into? I went through scenarios on how we could survive. I imagined kneeing Luke in the balls, biting Thick-Neck (Could I even penetrate that skin?), or wrapping the seat belt around Yak's head. They all had guns. Maybe I could steal one off them without him even feeling it. Of course, I had to get my hands free first. I decided to start there and peeled a piece a tape away from my skin. I just needed to cut it with a fingernail.

"What are you doing?" Yak turned and inspected my hands, pushing me up against the window. The pain in my shoulder flared again, and he laughed. "She thinks she can free herself. Women are *too-poy*." The driver joined in the laugh at their private Russian word.

He irked me, and now I wanted to bite him in the neck.

"Leave her alone. Don't make me say it again," Luke said over his shoulder.

"Albano?" the driver asked.

"Yeah, Gandolfo will be fine, save us another hour of driving."

The driver nodded. Was Luke giving or taking orders? I wished this tape wasn't on my mouth. I would give him a piece of my mind. I tried to stretch my mouth but it didn't rip the tape clear from my skin. I stuck my tongue out and tasted puke-inducing glue. Then, I imagined puking and decided it might kill me. I never had a good view of Shawn because of Yak in the way with his two-foot-thick stomach—not from sheer fatness, but from being one hell of a huge man. I shifted for comfort and stared out the window, always trying to catch a glimpse of Luke's face.

Perhaps thirty minutes had passed when we pulled up to a restaurant on a lake. I could see to the other side, but it was far away. A few boats were tied at wooden docks, and two floated on the water in the distance, not making waves. The outdoor patio had few patrons.

Thick-Neck spoke. "A lit-tle crowded."

"We'll untape them and they'll cooperate." Luke turned and looked at me, then at Yak.

"They wouldn't want us to kill innocent people." Yak threatened.

Doubt rushed in, imagining the Russians would open fire like crazy men, and I decided to nix any plan of escaping, for now. They parked the car across the street. Luke stood and got out of the car first and opened my door. The driver opened Shawn's door and helped him to his feet, and then Yak got out of the car. Luke leaned down and took my knees into his hands. He swung my legs around to face him, treating them like porcelain. He moved with caution and glided his fingers across my skin as he released his touch. "No yelling, Maggie. I'm going to remove the tape. Trust me."

Trust me? I would have to be insane to do that, but something in his eyes made me keep my voice.

He peeled the tape with care, then wrapped his arms around my waist and helped me stand. When steady on my feet, he reached behind me and tugged on the tape, leaning into my ear. "It's going to be okay, Maggie." He pulled back and made eye contact.

My forehead wrinkled with worry. "I thought you were dead."

He shook his head and mouthed *shhh*. His eyes turned away, and he spoke to Yak. "Get the kid free and act normal; we're going for a boat ride."

He laced his fingers through mine and walked toward the water, acting like we were on a date. Thick-Neck followed and started asking Luke questions.

"Shut up. This part of the country isn't fond of Russians." Whether he made it up or not, I liked it. I didn't know what he was about to do, but

Fear wasn't here. In fact, I hadn't seen him since the warehouse. Why did Luke always disarm me? I pulled my hand free of his. Even if I didn't fear him, I wasn't about to trust him.

Luke looked at my hand with a surprised look. I had not seen him pout, ever. He grabbed my upper arm gently and escorted me to the docks. After talking to a guy at the docks—a fisherman by his attire—Luke pulled out some money and paid him. The man began untying the small boat, only large enough for us, and more equipped for small fishing. Luke assisted me as I stepped down into it. I made sure Shawn followed us. He was untaped as well, escorted by Thick-Neck. He looked wretched. I hoped he wouldn't do anything to get us killed.

I waited for a moment to be able to talk to Luke, but once the old motor started and we were moving through the water, noise prevented any conversation. The lacquered lake resembled a tar pit, waiting to suck life from the tiny boat that dared to tread it. The wind blew through my hair, reminding me I was still alive. In the boat, I stared at the faces of each man who shared in this day's fate with me. What situations had brought them to this moment in time?

The lake reminded me of the time my dad took me to the Bahamas. We had snorkels in our mouths when we saw it, a black eye against reflecting mirrored scales. I almost missed the row of white teeth before Daddy pushed me behind him. I knew to swim as fast as I could to shore. Twenty feet away, I stood in ankle-deep water and watched. The barracuda's shadow spanned longer than my dad's body. I stood there watching them stare each other down, neither of them moved. Its mouth could take my dad's arm in one bite. He had saved me, but I was powerless to save him.

My dad backed up to shore without taking his eyes off the barracuda. I saw the shadow leave, and my dad stood in knee-deep water and walked over to me.

"Did you see that? He couldn't take his eyes off my watch. Probably thought I was a fish, but then decided I wasn't and left."

I grabbed him and held him tight. I couldn't survive, I thought, if something happened to him.

When I did lose him at nine years old, I thought for a long time life *was* over. But, another day came, even though I asked it not to. My stomach growled, even though I told it to shut up. I woke, went to school, met new people, and time changed me.

The boat bobbed up and down to a rhythm in my head. I grabbed the pearl on my neck and smiled, one that no one could see but I felt. A peace fell on me, surrounding me with my father, or the tangible thought of him. The peace stayed while the wind blew.

Hours later, the boat pulled up to a dock in the middle of nowhere; only trees were visible on land. I noticed Fear sitting on the gray planks, playing the card game Concentration, as if he had been waiting for hours. I ignored him.

Our silence gave way to nature's voice. The waves still whisked against the dock, the wind danced with the leaves in the trees, and a bird somewhere up ahead sounded an alarm. Our arrival disturbed nature, as our feet clapped against the wooden dock.

Does one always walk toward certain death? It wasn't certain, I argued with myself. Struggling for freedom had one-to-one odds, but going with the flow fared better. There was still a chance Luke might help us get away. Even in that hope, I worried the Russians would succeed in killing us all. I might think back and regret it, but a part of me thought I would know when it was time to act. It would well up in my belly like before public speaking. My heart would race, and there would be no turning back.

Through the trees, beyond Luke, I could see a dark shadow of a building, a cabin. We walked toward a screened-in porch. Luke pushed aside a rusted-out watering can and retrieved a key from underneath. He slipped it into the keyhole and unlocked the door. This guy had more hideaways than a prohibitionist.

"We should take care of kid outside. No mess," Yak said.

"Da, close to docks. Not far to dump," Thick-Neck agreed.

"What? Are you frickin' kidding me? You brought us all the way out here to kill us?" I screamed at Luke.

Luke appeared angry, holding the door open. "Everyone get inside!"

Shawn and I walked inside while the Russians followed holding their guns out. Luke led the way, turning on lights. An overhead loft bedroom peeked at the top of the vaulted living room. Dark wood covered the walls and floors, aged with time. Large trees overhung outside, giving the appearance of dusk. Dirty dishes sat on a counter over in the kitchen to the right. I expected cobwebs or some sign the rugged outside had made its way inside, but instead it appeared lived in. A blanket and pillow draped the long couch as if someone had slept there.

"Secure them, and then I want to talk to both of you outside," Luke said.

Of course, that meant the duct tape went back on. Yak placed two kitchen chairs in the middle of the living room on an old spiral woven rug. I stared at it under my feet while they re-taped us. I found a red thread to fixate on while he pulled my shoulder back. Tape muffled my scream as I tried to endure it.

"Easy there, muscle head!" Shawn said.

"Shut up, mouse," Yak said. He slapped the back of Shawn's head.

"I mean it. You don't have to be so rough with her." Shawn reached for Yak's hand pulling on my shoulder.

Yak lifted his hand and popped Shawn in the face. His lip bled. "Sit down, or you'll be bleeding everywhere." Luke returned from the porch. "Let me take care of this mouse now," Yak said to Luke as he finished wrapping my wrists and grabbed Shawn by the shoulder, ready to drag him outside.

"Tape him up," Luke said. The Russians were large but Luke carried authority. I could sense neither wanted to go head-to-head with him, but it was more than that, like they knew if they rebutted him they would be killed. I tried to make sense of it all, but the pain in my shoulder stole my mental strength.

Luke's phone rang. He spoke short *okay* and *yeah* responses. Yak and Thick-Neck had already walked out on the porch. After he put his phone back into his jean's pocket, he came over and dropped a kiss on my cheek. He whispered in my ear, "Did you replace me so soon?"

I grunted through my taped mouth with peering eyes.

He stood and spoke. "Sit for a minute. Then, get far away from this place." He cut half my tape around my wrists and placed a small knife in my cupped hand. He didn't remove the tape, though. He then put something in Shawn's hand and walked away without turning back.

Before exiting, he turned off the living room lights and flipped on the porch fanlight. I knew he was giving us a chance to get out of there. Whatever agenda he had, he wanted us safe. I saw a glimmer of the Luke I knew.

Shawn sat and waited. I assumed Luke had also given him a knife. I struggled with the tape and took longer than I wanted. Hearing the Russians' voices climb louder, I knew I had to hurry. I pulled my wrists apart, and the tape ripped the rest of the way. My shoulder burned, but I tried to be tough. I dropped the knife. I pulled the tape off my mouth with my right hand and picked the knife back up. I went to Shawn's tape and freed him while my left shoulder dangled beside me, unable to lift it through the pain.

I double checked over my shoulder, but Luke had kept the Russians away from the door, facing the water.

"To the boat?" Shawn held up the key.

"Let's go," I said.

We darted out the back door, and when the first step creaked, we walked slower with stealth. We were aware of the Russians so much more, as their voices boomed through the serene setting from the screened porch. As we crept around the house, we caught a glimpse of their profiles, their faces still pointing toward the water. We leaned against the house and listened.

"Primo talked to Arman? He changed drop place?" Thick-Neck asked.

"Your phone wasn't working. He got spooked about something. Said there have been some stripes sniffing," Luke said.

"Americans? I thought their hands full. They not need bother here."

"Thanks," Luke said with sarcasm. "Tripoli Square, CSM dock. At four."

"We finish this business, get back to car, and to Tripoli by four?"

"Yeah, which one of you is staying with the girl?"

"Ya. Yakov will take care of boy."

"I got a better idea. Follow me," Luke said. The three walked down the steps from the porch. The door slammed against the house. Their voices trailed off around the other side of the house. I hoped Luke would be okay.

When I heard a plane overhead, Shawn said, "Let's go."

We took off running toward the boat. I ran, trying to hold my shoulder still, but the movement caused a pain that slowed my pace. We arrived at the boat, and Shawn put the key in the ignition and began pulling the cord. The effort rocked the boat and ripples began to travel.

"Hey! Stop!" Yak ran toward us while pulling a black gun out of his pants. Thick-Neck followed. There was nowhere to run.

Shots ricocheted from the woods. Thick-Neck fell from a bullet first, as if someone had caught him on a fish line and pulled him to the ground by his shoulder. His gun flew through the air, lost in leaves. Yak bent at the knees and fired his gun before he slid on his belly. His gun pointed in a straight line at me. Luke jumped through the air and fell to the ground as I threw myself out of the boat, landing on the dock. I stood and ran to Luke.

Shawn followed me, yelling to come back to the boat. He followed me as I kept running to Luke. Just as we were about to step off the dock and onto the ground, a flash of light caught my eye. When I had planted a foot on the grass, the entire cabin blew up. The blast threw us down the embankment, half in the grass and half in soggy dirt. My ears drummed out all other noise. My face burned against the ground. For a moment, I couldn't move. I felt moisture seeping into me, or maybe it seeped out of me. For all I knew, it was blood oozing from some fatal injury I had sustained. I tried to clear the boom from the explosion still ricocheting in my head. I remembered Luke lying like a ragdoll, me jumping out of the boat to go to him, the gunman—oh shit! There was a gunman. The thought that he might still be out there made me push off the dark rich earth. My fingers sank into the mud, and I thrust my toes down and managed to force myself to my knees.

I saw Shawn's head bleeding as it lay on a rock pillow. I heard someone running on the dock behind me. The boat cranked, and its noise dissipated as I stood. I turned around, and the boat, the size of my thumbnail, shrank smaller and smaller.

Chapter 21
Drilling Blood

I watched the boat leave a trail of white water as I wondered who drove it. I turned to Shawn, hoping he was okay, the blood on the rock worrying me. I sensed a figure standing above me on the grass. I turned and found Paul, dressed in all black, holding a long gun with a scope. Worn out and exhausted, I almost collapsed at the sight of him. He rushed forward and side-stepped down the bank to me.

"Are you okay?" Paul asked.

"I'll be fine. You? How are you even here?"

"I'm with the CIA. I'll fill you in later."

"Luke?"

"That was him in the boat."

I rolled Shawn over, searching for any sign of consciousness. I raised his eyelid, and his pupils appeared normal. But, what did I know.

When I glared at Paul, worried, he responded, "I called for a med-flight so we can get him to the hospital as soon as possible."

"Okay," I said, still stunned but glad someone was making decisions.

"I'll be back. I gotta check on Dee and Dumb."

"I hope they're dead."

Paul laughed. "No, they'll live. I already cuffed them. They're just dining on mud pies right now."

In the flurry of my emotions about Shawn and Luke, I almost forgot about the Russians. I couldn't believe what had just happened. I watched the house pop and crackle, engulfing the trees that used to shade it. As the fire rose, the wood collapsed with the sound of a branch falling. I wiped the blood off Shawn's lip from Yak's slap, then ran my fingers through his hair, feeling for other damage.

Shawn woke before the helicopter arrived.

"Oh, Shawn, I'm so glad you're awake. You scared me to death."

"Maggie? Where are we? What happened?" He had no recent memory.

The paramedics suggested it could be temporary. It was odd, but I almost didn't mind if it wasn't. What if this whole ordeal could be wiped from our minds?

"You going with him?" Paul asked.

I nodded.

Paul pointed to a black helicopter landing in the distance. "I've got to go.

"I have a million questions for you." I watched them put Shawn on a stretcher, knowing we didn't have much time.

"They will have to wait. I need to know what happened over the last twenty-four hours, and if perhaps, you have any idea where a meeting will be tonight. I could get it out of those idiots, but it might take a while. I thought if you knew something—"

"I don't know if it will help, but I heard something changed to Tribecca Square, CSM dock at four a.m."

"That's perfect, Sis. By the way, you can't tell anyone, even Mom." He grabbed my face and kissed my forehead before turning to run.

"Hey, Paul!"

He turned and faced me.

"Luke is CIA, too, right?"

"No, Maggie." He shook his head with furrowed brows.

"I don't think Luke is all bad. I just don't know. He helped us escape, you know."

"Thanks. I think I have an idea what he's up to."

I shook my head in disbelief and yelled, "Why is no one who they say they are?" I threw my hands down, and he left me there with a big question mark on my forehead and a *what?* on the tip of my tongue.

I watched him disappear into a black, unmarked helicopter until the paramedic broke my concentration. "It's time to go, Miss," he yelled over the roar of the blades.

He helped pull me up into the helicopter. The wind whipped through my wet clothes and hair. The medic wrapped a blanket around my shoulders and then turned to Shawn. The pilot spoke into his headset, and we lifted off the ground. Paul's black fly-eye helicopter disappeared in the opposite direction of a deep, watery sky, and the fire's blaze could be seen for miles, with black smoke carrying the news even farther.

A twenty-minute ride in the sky with deafening hums prevented talking as much as the duct-tape. When we were on the ground, the medical team asked a flurry of questions which I tried to answer as best I could. They began working on Shawn as soon as we arrived, taking blood and asking him questions he couldn't answer.

"Why are you moving so fast? Is he going to be okay?" He was conscious and not bleeding to death. Their urgency scared me. When he was taken to CT, I asked to be shown how to make a phone call from his ER cubicle. I called my Mom's cell.

I had to tell her I was at the hospital. Relieved it wasn't me in need of medical attention, she tried to mask her anger. I left out the part about my shoulder. Some sort of pain medicine sounded good, though.

I then followed up with a call to Shawn's mom. She was able to fill in the blanks that Shawn was unable to tell the staff. She asked for details, which we had little of so far. She took it very hard and ended our conversation in tears. I promised to call again after I spoke with the doctor.

The nurse walked in with a clipboard.

"I need to get you to sign a few papers, Miss Dulaney." The tired nurse instructed.

Puzzled, I told her, "I'm not related to him. I'm just—"

"This is for you. The doctor said he wants your shoulder x-rayed."

"I don't think that's necessary. I could use some pain medicine, though."

She shoved the clipboard under my nose without a word. I tried to write with my one good hand, but I couldn't hold the clipboard steady, so it was messier than the nurse was willing to accept. She took the clipboard away and began firing questions at me. I answered with all my biographical information. The nurse held the clipboard while I took the pen with my right hand and signed in three spots.

"That'll be fine," the nurse said. She made English sound as beautiful as Italian, but her dark circles aided her haunted look.

Shawn slept in the ER stretcher with a pale, dirty face wiped with my spit. Some blood from his lip had dried on his shirt.

They didn't put us in separate triage rooms. They came and took me to x-ray anyway. When I returned, my mom sat in a chair, biting her thumbnail.

"Maggie." She stood and grabbed a hug. "You look awful. What is this?" She thumbed her fingers through my hair, squinting for clarity. "It's singed. Why is your hair singed?"

As I ran my fingers up to my forehead to feel the spiked hair, I thought of an answer. "That's kind of a long story. I better start from the beginning."

While I told her a made-up story, she took a washcloth, wet it in the sink, and then wiped my face clean. The nurse brought in silver cream to sooth my first-degree facial burns. Mom brushed my hair and put it in a ponytail. When I told her about a building exploding, she pulled a little harder on my hair, but I was sure she didn't realize she had done it. Like clenching teeth, the brush dug deeper into my scalp. I left out most details and tried to give her a less dramatic version, leaving out Russians, Luke, and Paul being CIA. She glared at me, as if she knew I was withholding more. She had no suspicions about Paul. It was true moms didn't need to know some things about their sons, but believing we were a part of a terrorist attack was more plausible. Even to me.

Shawn's x-rays revealed a subdural hematoma. I had missed the doctor's explanation when I went to x-ray, so the nurse filled me in on the details. They took him to surgery to drill a hole and remove the pressure from his brain in a mad attempt to prevent brain damage. When no blood was visible, the damage could be worse. I had no idea. I felt bad that I thought it was nothing and almost a good thing he had lost his memory. I wondered if he would be the same. I welcomed spending the next few hours waiting and curled up on painkillers. After surgery, they took him to a private room and plugged him into multiple machines with lit numbers and beeping sounds. When he woke four hours later, he spoke to me.

"You okay?"

"You know me?" I asked.

"Yeah," he said.

I let out the breath I had been holding.

"You're not hurt?" he asked.

"You shouldn't be worrying about me. I'm fine."

"What's that?" His eyes stared at my left shoulder in a sling.

"They think I tore my rotator cuff a little, so they put a shot of cortisone in it. I'll have it checked out when I get home."

"What time ... is it?"

"Three in the morning."

"You look tired. You should leave," Shawn said.

"I needed to see you. I needed to know you were going to be okay. Your mom is kind of freaking, though."

"She coming?"

"Not if you're going to be okay. I guess. I don't know. Probably."

He sighed. "What exactly happened?" He pointed to his head.

I told him the diagnosis and about the surgery, but he meant how did he get hurt. I told him about the cabin blowing up, the rock I found him on, and how long he lay unconscious.

"Who blew up the house?"

"I don't know. I haven't talked to Paul, though. I hope that doesn't mean something bad."

"Paul is involved?" He shook his head. His IV-strapped hand reached out and grabbed my fingers.

I had to shut up. I pursed my lips together. I couldn't say any more. I shook my head, like I didn't understand anything.

"I'm so glad you're okay. Otherwise, I would sit here and contemplate how I could kill them," Shawn said.

I smiled. "A little bit crazy, wasn't it? By the way, how on earth did you find me and Kayla in the warehouse?"

He pushed a laugh out. "Thought you'd never ask." His voice vibrated with weakness but still held enthusiasm.

Shawn had been following us after seeing us get into a cab at the embassy on his return from escorting Mom to the hotel. He said he had just missed us and called to us, but we didn't hear, so he jumped into a cab. After finding out where we went, he decided to hang back, thinking two beautiful women could find out more on their own. He had been seated in the restaurant soon after Kayla and me. The NFL ball cap came to my mind. "Dallas?"

"Some disguise, huh?"

"Your disguise? That's a billboard screaming *American here*." I couldn't help but laugh at how crazy he was. "I guess now you'll need a whole wardrobe of hats." I ruffled his bangs and gazed at the large bandage on the right side of his head.

He took my fingers in his hand and a smile spread across his face.

I waited. In silence, I paused. It felt awkward. His long dark eyelashes and full eyebrows, both matching his thick head of short curls, contrasted against his smooth, light skin, except for the hair growing on his chin and upper lip. His top lip was thin, but his bottom full, and I remembered soft bites from his mouth that became larger as he kissed, threatening to devour. He was quiet in words but intense with action. Even now, as he held my hand to his face, closing his eyes to feel it and taking in a slow inhale through his nose, I dropped my eyes to heighten my other senses and felt his lips against my fingers.

Kayla's face emerged from the blackness of my eyes. I couldn't shake the thought of her for the twenty-seventh time since I'd arrived at the hospital. "I guess since you're stable, I'll go get some rest."

"Okay. I'll see you tomorrow?"

"You bet." I leaned in and kissed his cheek like a butterfly.

I walked out and nodded to the military guard that I assumed Paul had arranged. However he had been assigned here, it made me feel better about leaving Shawn.

"Miss, I am under orders for you to stay as well."

"What? Who told you that? Did my brother? 'Cause our mom is expecting me at the hotel, and I don't think Paul wants my mom worried."

"Well, um. No, but—"

"But nothing. I'll take responsibility. My brother knows me well enough. I'm going to do what I want. I'll text him and tell him now." I walked away fake texting, hoping he wouldn't stop me.

Mom gave me sixty euros and her phone before she left to return to the hotel for sleep, but not without cautioning me to stay put in the hospital. I wondered now if Paul told her that as well. But, I couldn't stay. I wanted to find out if Kayla was safe. Primo had her. Did she ever get away from him? I planned to return to the villa. I needed to talk to her. I needed to find out what was going on with Luke and how he had gotten involved with Primo. However, when I passed the nurse's station, I couldn't help but ask a nurse how far to Tribeca Square. She told me seven blocks. I stood at a crossroad.

I tried to call Paul with no answer. Neither Kayla's nor Luke's numbers had been saved to Mom's phone. I could have gone to the villa, as it weighed as the most logical place to find Kayla, but as I walked through the hospital halls, every clock I passed beamed three-thirty. The meeting would start soon, and Paul would be there. Luke could be there, too. I could just check it out from a distance, make sure another place didn't go up in flames like the last.

No. I couldn't do it. I had to be responsible. I had to stay out of danger. I had almost died. No. I needed to get some rest.

Chapter 22
Raw Oyster

At this hour, one taxi sat outside the hospital. I stood there mentally listing every reason I needed to stay away from Tribecca Square. I didn't want to see any more Russians, much less Primo. I'd had enough guns for one night. I just wanted a nice place to sleep, but I was too awake. Wired. My mind racing.

I leaned into the window. "San Lorenzo." I looked at the clear night and noticed a tiny twinkle. I sat in the back of the cab and leaned forward. "Make that Tribecca Square."

I needed to know what was happening, then I would go on to the villa. Just a tiny peek. The driver flew through seven blocks in no time.

"Don't pull too close. Just show me which street and then drop me a road past."

The driver didn't understand English and stopped too close. I paid the fare with a tip and slid out, closing the door without noise. The building's windows could have been painted black, and the streets loomed with emptiness as the taxi drove away with the last of the noise and light. As I walked toward the road, my eyes acclimated to the darkness. I crept close to the buildings. I knew this was crazy, stupid, and dangerous, but somehow, this was easier than waiting for the news. Waking up the next day and finding out something bad had happened to some of the most important people in my life was far worse.

I turned down a street onto an industrial boulevard. It resembled a grid of horizontal roads to each side, evenly spaced by design. A long building paralleled the road with large creased metal doors every fifty, or so feet, signifying a new loading dock. Some docks near the main street bore names, and trucks parked at others. I saw no lights until I noticed a car coming from behind me. I slunk up next to a building and hid in a shadow until it passed and turned right. I picked up the pace and followed, hoping I wasn't going to find anyone I knew dead.

By the time I met up with the car, men covered in black all the way to their heads were doing their own slinking around and snuck up on skinny Italians in white shirts. Every white shirt fell without a noise. I wondered if they used some Japanese grip hold, or if they had silencers on guns. From this distance, neither was discernible. It was impossible to get closer, and I decided to leave. This was over my head. I didn't know what I was thinking. Did I have a head injury, too?

    I then heard footsteps coming from around the other side of the building. I couldn't go forward, or I would run right into the mysterious black-clad men, and I couldn't go the way I came without being seen. I prepared to creep into the recess of the building, until I realized right over my head was a fire escape ladder. Even though I wanted to leave, this was now my only choice. My heart pounded in my throat. I grabbed the ladder and hoped it didn't make much noise. It moved so slowly, but it was better that way, and I could control the noise. Inch by inch, I pulled it down until it clinked into place. I waited and didn't hear anything coming my way. I used my one good hand to hoist myself and my other hand in the sling to steady my balance. The black cars had parked five docks down. As I walked on the roof toward the docking bay, Fear failed to deter me this time.

    When I stood to oversee the lit-up dock, I walked lighter on the pebble stones. I saw more cars on the other side of the building, four to be exact. From one vented fan to the next, I tried to listen to the room below. The men weren't loud enough, or maybe the roof was too thick. I needed to hear what they were saying. Near the front edge of the building, I noticed a metal lever and fewer pebbles. I pulled it up as slow as a bad internet connection. My hand began to shake. Pebbles slid off the lid in slow motion. I could see a few people through the rafters, but not well. Their voices boomed louder.

    "It's right here," an Italian said.

    The muscles in my good arm began to quiver and ache. I searched around for something to wedge the lid open. Something shimmered on the north side of the roof. I set the lid down softly not to be noticed and went to inspect the item. When I stood above their heads, crunching pebbles under my shoes, the noise echoed in the dark. I took off each shoe, being careful not to fall, and tucked them under my arm like a purse. I forced my feet to curve over the smooth pebbles, hoping it would unsettle them less. It forced me to walk even slower. When I came to the object, I sighed. It wasn't what I wanted, but it would have to do. Lurking back to the roof hatch, I placed the empty liquor bottle at the opening, letting the lid and the roof sandwich it.

    Laying my ear and one eye as close to the opening as I could, I listened while I noticed Luke's arms. He took hold of a black bag. After a few minutes of hearing men's muffled voices, I heard Luke speak. "It's all there, Primo."

"And the shipment?" an Italian, I assumed Primo, said.

"Four crates, and they're all full," Luke said.

"Well then, Arman, we've got a deal. I have your word more will be here next week?"

"Going to Argentina to get them. Sooner than that," a Russian said.

I heard footsteps and men moving crates. "Just a second, Arman," Luke said.

"Yes?"

Luke asked, "Do I look like someone you know?"

"What? What is this, Primo?"

"Luke?" Primo asked.

Luke said nothing. He looked in the direction of Primo voice, near the back door.

"I have nothing to do with this," Primo said. I heard steps walk toward the door and then it closed.

At the same time, Arman said, "I must leave. Now!" The word "now" boomed loud, and the liquor bottle next to me moved. That little rat, Fear, showed up and began picking up rocks and throwing them at me. Arman turned toward the front loading dock.

"You don't remember my parents?"

"What are you doing? This place is surrounded with my guys. Whatever it is, it's suicidal."

"I don't care, as long as I take you out." Luke had a gun to Arman's head. Other guys-- maybe three--in the room cocked their guns.

No, no, no. This wasn't happening. I changed my mind. I didn't want to see Luke killed. I couldn't handle it. I wanted out of there. "Now," echoed in my mind, just as it did when Arman said it. Something--but what?--had to happen now. Now. *Now! Shit! Do something, Maggie.* Nausea spread through my stomach.

"Let me refresh your mind. Erika and Markus Seager, New Bern, North Carolina. You shouldn't have left me in the closet, Arman."

"Ten years ago?"

"It takes a while, but it always catches up with you."

"I've lived hard, but I'm old. Are you sure you want to die tonight as a young man?"

"It ends tonight so others are safe."

"Others? I had no intention of wiping out your entire family."

"You're a liar. You've tried multiple times."

Arman's voice began to rise. His impatience grew obvious. "I never knew Primo hired you, or you would already be dead."

This time, I jumped, startled by the anger and the bottle's rattle. It didn't help that Fear kept flinging more pebbles at me. The bottle fell inward, and the lid slammed shut. I heard gunshots hitting the steel floor beneath my stomach. I rolled over until the shots stopped firing. I stood, wincing with shoulder pain and ran barefoot across the top of the building toward the opposite end I'd climbed. I watched the men in black on Arman's side all disappear into the building. I ran until I stopped short of breath from adrenaline.

I came to the end of the building where I found another ladder. My bare feet helped me hold on better, compensating for the one-handed grip. The pain in my sore feet became evident when I found flat asphalt. I stopped for a moment on the darker side of the building and caught my breath. I held onto the metal railing with one arm until I could stand straight again. The burning in my chest subsided, and all I could think of was Luke. Had I killed him? I shouldn't have been here.

I went to the north side and peered around the building. A hundred feet or so from me sat only three black cars. Men lay on the ground, handcuffed by the ski-masked men standing over them with guns. I ran back to the south side and peered around, but I saw no movement. I crossed over and to the next building, searching down each row until I found the main road again. I walked fast, hugging the shadows from the buildings, hoping and praying for a cab to show and not a street thug. Toward the city lights, I walked. Black cars with a blue light came barreling down the empty streets toward me, then past. Ambulances followed.

My bare feet moved slower as the pain in my body and my heart weighed me down. I walked and cried at the same time until I couldn't walk anymore. Bent over with snot in my hands, trying to be quiet, I shook. I leaned against a building to keep from falling. No matter how mad I was at Luke for the last twenty-four hours, I could never want him dead. I knew he went in there and created an impossible situation, but he didn't need to be distracted by me, getting him killed. He might have been able to get out of it. I felt horrible. Guilt made me want to die right there on the street. I could roll up into a little ball and let some creep come by and kill me.

After crying until I couldn't see, I settled down and wiped my eyes. I wiped my nose on my sleeve, and didn't care. I heard the quiet again. No more sirens, no more sobs, but a hum of life in the distance. In my deep breaths, I regained a sense of the larger world. I remembered Kayla, and it sent me into another unbearable moment of tears, but I choked them back and became determined to find her. Just like I had promised, I would be her family now.

I had to walk another two miles until I was able to hail a cab. I didn't even want to think of my feet that had to be bleeding by now. I collapsed into the cab, thankful I was still alive.

This time, I knew the crossroads of Luke and Kayla's villa. I gave the driver the rest of the cash I had from Mom. At 5:23 in the morning, I opened the iron courtyard gate with the key I had kept hidden in my bra, relieved the Russians never found it when I was unconscious. The thoughts of their paws all over me, their dirty thick fingers patting me, made my arms shiver. I felt dirty all over. Maybe Luke kept them from touching me. That thought made me feel better.

I wanted to walk through the door and find Kayla asleep or see her smiling face. No lights were on inside, but I wasn't expecting any. Walking in, I held my breath, turning on lights. No noise, no movement, and no Kayla. Not even a sign she had been there. Not even the gray sweater she wore, thrown over a chair, or water droplets in the sink. It had the same feeling as the first time I had walked into the villa, lonely, waiting for a mistress that never arrived.

I sat down on the couch and thought of it all. Italy, this villa, walking into 313, every mistake, where it had led me: to tears and bleeding, and people dead or hurt. Images of Shawn and Luke overwhelmed me as I faced the impact of my decisions. I bent over and rubbed my right ankle, bruised from the handcuff, then my left shoulder, still motionless in the sling. I swung my legs up and curled on my side, gripping a pillow.

I stared at the ceiling, and the dark-stained wooden rafters's swirl design. Knotted wood with lines and lines of years revealed its life. Even dead, the tree had something to say. With every layer, it grew, became thicker, wiser, and more resistant to the bacteria and the wind.

The layers of the pearl around my neck came into my mind. The strength it acquired through time had brought beauty. I took off my necklace and laid it on the coffee table. As I lay there alone, I heard the voice of my father in my head.

"You will always be my Margaret, my pearl. You will weather

through all the waves, sand, and filth to become a beautiful treasure."

Such a beautiful thought, vision. I wanted it to be true. But here, I sat covered with all the mess and grime of my decisions. I rolled over and turned my back to the coffee table. The mix of shame, guilt, and sadness made me feel more like a piece of grit than a pearl. Maybe I was just the slimy animal that lived near a pearl.

Chapter 23
Bursting Bubbles

I woke, still on the couch with a crick in my neck, catching light rays tanning the wooden floor. I pulled my aching body to the bathroom and ran the tub water. I slipped my feet under the forceful water, rubbing blood and black grime from my soles. I opened the hand-held shower nozzle and finished washing my face, hair, and body as best I could with my dangling arm. My hand rubbed the darkness down the drain.

I found Vaseline and smothered it on my feet before slipping white tube socks over them. Kayla's shirt wouldn't fit, but I found one of Luke's oversized white ones. Hunger overpowered my need for sleep, so I started cooking some eggs. Stopping right there with the spatula in my hand, I cried —silent, shaking sobs, like on the street, but then they changed to loud, open-mouthed, angry cries. My head began to hurt, and I settled back down. When my dad died, I would cry at random moments, in the middle of doing something. Knowing I would never talk to him again, smell him, or hug him. I shook my head at the insanity of life, my chest heavy with it all. But, just as I thought that, the bright, sunny eggs brought back the powerful moment in Luke's arms and then his smiling face when he was in here cooking eggs at night. That was Luke: sunny side up at midnight. I smiled while I finished wiping one last tear from my eye. I turned the coffee pot on and took Mom's phone in hand.

I heard a clink at the door. My breath seized for a moment. The handle turned. I couldn't move. All I could do was watch, like in a horror movie. My heart pounded while my chest froze. The door opened, and Paul rushed through it. I gasped for my breath then jumped up and hugged him.

"Thank God, you're okay," Paul said and twirled me around before setting me down with my back to the door. "I didn't find you at the hospital or the hotel."

"I … I went to the warehouse." My face pulsed as tears filled my eyes. "I'm so sorry."

"What?"

"I was on the roof. That bottle—"

"Was you?" His two hands cupped my face and kissed my forehead. "You're wonderful."

I wiped my eyes in confusion.

"I can't believe that was you. That was perfect, Maggie. You distracted Arman's guys. They started shooting at the roof instead of Luke. I shot the other three guys as Luke took out Arman."

"What? Luke isn't dead?"

"No. They were shooting at you? Are you hurt?" Paul started patting me and scanned my arms and legs. I pushed his hands away. Good thing he hadn't seen me before my shower. "So many bruises, Mags." He patted my head.

"Luke is okay?"

"Yeah, he gave me this key so I could come get Kayla."

"I did the same, but it doesn't look like she ever came here."

"Then Primo must still have her. I gotta go."

"Primo? Didn't you get him at the warehouse?"

"He got away. We got all his men, but he got away," Paul said.

"Oh, no. Where would he have her?"

I grabbed two cups and poured black coffee into them.

"You need to go to the hotel. I told Mom I would check on you at the hospital. You know she still thinks you're there with Shawn."

"Okay." I went and threw my jeans back on and grabbed my things.

Paul led the way out, and I locked up behind us. In the courtyard, the morning sun beat down, illuminating it with rays and spearing through the overhanging blooms. On our drive, I asked him about the CIA. He told me things I wouldn't be able to tell anyone.

Chapter 24
Victims

Paul pulled up to Hotel Caprice. "Let Mom know I'll be calling soon." I nodded and waved goodbye. I took the elevator up to our floor.

Mom opened the hotel door before my fist made contact for the second time.

"Wow, you've been standing there, waiting?"

"You have no idea. Where did you go?" She asked.

"Shawn got out of surgery and I—"

"I went there." She snapped at me. "Couldn't sleep after Paul woke me, and you weren't there. Came here to see if I missed you. I called the phone. Why didn't you pick up?"

I hadn't even checked it since before my bath. I planned to, but then Paul came through the door. "I'm sorry. I must have been in the shower."

Mom shook her head. "Where did you shower?"

I told her about the villa for the first time. I pulled the comforter back and sat on the empty bed while Mom leaned against her pillow.

"You have interesting friends, Maggie."

I wanted to drop it. She was hinting at something. Talking about it would be dangerous. "Did you not get much sleep?" I noticed the shadows under her eyes.

"No. I seriously don't know how long I can stay in Rome. It's killing me. I haven't slept this little since I was in my twenties."

The fact that Mom was a sleeper—a long sleeper—and still woke tired dawned on me. "How about we get a few more hours of shut-eye and then go see Shawn at the hospital?"

"Sounds good." After we were both under our covers, each in our own bed, she said, "I'm so thankful you're all right, Maggie. I love you."

I opened my eyes. "Thanks, Mom." It was hard to manage my mom's emotions sometimes, but I knew she was over here out of love. And, right now, not having to sleep alone was just the kind of help I needed. I closed my eyes, squeezed my cottony pillow, and relaxed all my muscles. Luke was alive. My body didn't have any trouble resting out of sheer exhaustion, but my dreams danced to a weird *Dumbo* march of worry for Kayla.

The alarm woke us at three-thirty in the afternoon. While Mom showered, I called Paul. He didn't answer. I ran down to the café next door and retrieved biscotti and coffees. Mom thanked me more than once. She awakened stiff and sore, which she blamed on poor sleep, tossing too much. I also woke sore and kept forgetting where I was bruised. I would lean on a counter, and my elbows reminded me. I would sit on my leg, and then my ankles reminded me. When I walked, I could feel the cuts on my knee and feet. While I slept, my shoulder ached more than when I stood. I never knew lying flat could hurt. But, I could, at least, hide most of it from Mom with a little extra clothing, capris, and short sleeves. The few bruises she noticed only made her worry more, repeating the fact we should both get home.

Mom dealt with her pain more verbally than I did. She walked on the side of her foot and complained about her hip, a pulled hamstring and plantar fasciitis—old injuries flaring up again. We arrived at the hospital an hour later to find they had moved Shawn to another room. When we found the correct one, he lay asleep with a nurse hanging an IV bag.

After explaining who we were, I asked, "How is he today?"

"We have him sedated. He had a seizure early this morning."

"Is that ...?"

"Normal, yes." She smiled. "He's fortunate to have arrived here in time. They took the pressure off his brain, but there is always rebound swelling after surgery. The doctor increased his medicine to compensate."

My mom jumped into the conversation. "What is his long-term prognosis?" In those moments, I was reminded that my mom was in the medical field. She knew a lot but never came off as pompous. She didn't have to work now, but she had been an ultrasonographer for twenty-five years.

"Let me get Dr. Albanese for you." The nurse left us alone.

I walked over to Shawn's bedside. The bandage, still on his head, was clean and white. I picked up his fingers and placed mine under them, trying not to disturb the IV farther up on his arm. My eyes watered.

"Oh, Mom, he has to be okay. I just talked to him last night. I told him what happened to his head." I took a deep breath and let out a sigh. "He was more concerned with whether I was all right."

A white-coated Italian who spoke very fast English with an accent entered with a solemn look. "Hello? Can I help you?"

Mom spoke. "We were wondering about his prognosis?"

"Yes. You are—"

"I'm Karen Johanson, and this is my daughter, Maggie. She is his girlfriend. He came over to Italy with us."

"Yes. I've just spoken with his mother in the U.S. She said you were here."

"Did you tell her to come? Is it that bad? Is he going to die?" I asked, looking at the veins in Shawn's closed eyelids.

"Subdural Hematoma is very serious. We relieved the pressure off the brain with the surgery, and the shunt will keep the swelling under control. About a third of patients will develop seizures from the trauma itself or swelling. Thus, I've increased his dosage to prevent seizures and swelling of the brain."

"When will he wake up?" I asked.

"We've sedated him to let his brain rest. He needs to heal right now. Last time he woke, he had a seizure. We will allow him to wake up in twelve hours to check his neuro status."

"Okay."

"Thank you, doctor, for your time."

"Lisa will keep you updated."

"Thank you," I said.

The doctor nodded and left. I sat down in the chair next to the window and threw my head into my hands. "I can't believe this. This is a big deal. A really big deal." I looked up. "He didn't say if Shawn's mom was coming."

Mom handed me her phone. "Only one way."

I took the phone and stared at the Foley bag hanging with Shawn's urine. I flipped open the phone and called the same number I'd found last night via information. With the weight of the doctor's words and the call I had to make, knowing Shawn's mom hated me, I dreaded what she might say.

Shawn's mom was now fully aware of what had happened to him medically but was more concerned with how it happened in the first place. She fired questions at me over and over, her anger incessant and her blame obvious. Her voice rose with each minute. Mom grabbed the phone from my ear and walked away.

Her first words were, "Wait just a minute, Ms. Richards. This is Maggie's mom, Karen." Her voice trailed as she left the room. I was once again glad my mom came. She had changed. In the past, she would have left me to deal with the difficult situations alone.

I sat down again, stared at the urine bag, then Shawn's right hand, and watched the rise and fall of his chest. I swallowed hard to prevent tears.

The memories of all my tears streamed together on a timeline—the first ones as Shawn and I broke up, then in the tub, in the kitchen, and all the way to now. My thick shell was gone. This—this here, in front of me—was my fault. Shawn came to get me out of the trouble into which I had gotten myself. I never knew throwing caution to the wind, not caring about myself, could hurt others. *Collateral Damage.* Was that a movie with Tom Cruise? I never saw it, but maybe I should have.

I hated being weak. In the middle of this trip, I let my mom come back into my life. But, I had also opened up my heart to be pierced by Luke. Was the only guy who loved me fighting to stay alive in a hospital bed? I remembered our long walks back home, curling up on the couch to watch TV, and all the food we cooked together.

Fear sat in a rocking chair and creaked it back and forth, waiting. I became aware of the myriad of problems within me. As much as I wanted to turn my feelings off for Luke, it felt impossible. I tried to twist and turn until I could hate him—hate him for sending me away, hate him for lying to me, hate him for working for Primo. I wanted to feel it so bad, but all I did was turn the anger inside of me onto myself.

My mom returned from talking to Shawn's mom. "She understands better now. She's on her way."

We sat in the room and waited, falling asleep in between nurse checks. A trip to the cafeteria around five fed us. By seven, we were awake and *Battlestar Galactica* came on for the third time. At this point, it was just something to distract us. Both our brains needed a break. I chuckled, because that's what Shawn was doing. I thought to myself, "Hey everyone, come on in here, where the brains have beachside loungers and sip on fruity drinks." I knew I was losing it. A delirium of mental exhaustion had set in.

I fell asleep again to wake up in a dark room. The sun had set. I found Mom drooling on her purse. Shawn's legs moved. I stood and held his hand, watching his eyes. The dim room hid the translucent eyelids he had earlier, and he appeared more normal. I touched his dark curls. They felt like silk from lack of washing.

"Shawn," I whispered.

He kept sleeping but appeared to be dreaming. I watched him. From his expressions, I thought he must have been replaying the events before his accident.

The next morning, when the nurse made rounds, we folded the blankets of our hospital beds and tidied the room. Mom left to retrieve coffee from downstairs. I sat back down to call Paul.

"This is Paul. Leave a message," I heard after four rings.

"Just checking to see if you found Kayla. Let me know you're okay. Love you."

Medicine bags hung over Shawn with Italian writing. His skin welted where the IV entered. When the nurse came in, I showed it to her. Before long, she had brought new supplies and found a vein in his right arm. Shawn first moaned when the nurse punctured his skin. The nurse kept her head bent and flashed her eyes at me while holding her hands steady and attaching the fluids to the IV catheter.

"Shawn? Hey, it's me, Maggie. Wake up. Wake up, Shawn."

Mom walked in with two cups of coffee. "Is he up?"

"Keep talking to him," the nurse encouraged while she taped tubing to his arm.

"You gotta stop being so lazy, big guy, sleeping all day like this. Time to get up." I felt stupid and didn't know what to say on the spot, but I continued rubbing his hand. "You gotta talk to me, Shawn. Please. It's Maggie and Karen. Your mom is on her way. She's worried about you. Wake up before she gets here, okay?"

He kept moaning and picking his knee up after it fell back down.

"I think it's working," the nurse said. "He knows your voice. Talk to him for real, between the two of you." She left the room to tell the doctor.

His eyes furrowed, as he appeared frustrated.

"It's okay, Shawn. You talk when you can. I'm here. You're going to get through this." His eyes relaxed but never opened.

I puffed out my cheeks in a sigh. I looked over at him and regretted ever leaving him in Texas. He wouldn't be lying here if I had stayed put. If I had just given him more time, he might have talked, felt safe to share his heart with me. I realized my impulsiveness and its consequences. I put my right hand in my pocket and found my necklace. I pulled it out.

"What's wrong, Maggie?"

"Feeling all this is my fault. I can't believe I did this to him."

"Wait a minute. I'm the first person to say you shouldn't have come to Italy, but you didn't hurt Shawn. I'm sure he doesn't blame you. You were both victims in this."

"I'm tired of being a victim. That's why I try to rescue other people." I blurted it out without thinking. I put the necklace back in my pocket.

"What are you talking about?"

"I'm talking about Andy, you for failing me, Dad for dying. Do you know how many things have happened to me, and I've had no control over them? I'm sick of it—sick of being a victim."

"The only way you can stop being a victim is to take responsibility for your life. It's not by tricking yourself that you're less needy than others."

"What does that even mean, Mom?" I threw my hands up and went to the window to stare at the security patrolman talking to an illegally parked visitor. Shawn had settled into another mini-nap.

"It means … to stop blaming everyone else and realize you make yourself the victim."

I turned around and huffed. "I don't blame everyone else; I blame myself. Isn't that taking responsibility for it?"

"I used to do the same thing, but just blaming yourself doesn't change anything. You have to decide you have the power to change things. When we blame others or ourselves, we say we are powerless—"

"I am!"

"For years, I would blame—your father—and myself, but nothing changed. It wasn't until I did something about it that change happened. I got into rehab. I learned things about myself and how to live healthily. I started applying what I had learned. I stopped blaming everyone, which only gave me the excuses to stay there and wallow. I used what I had been through to become a stronger person."

I stood there speechless. When she said it that way, it made sense. Why did we always see someone else's problem as easier than our own? The room went silent as we stared at each other. For the first time, I thought I could forgive her.

"Mom?" Shawn said.

I rushed to his side. "She'll be here soon. It's Maggie. Can you open your eyes?"

"Mam, mag, mom, mmm," he tried to say my name. Then he did. He opened his eyes.

"Nurse!" Mom yelled as she opened the door and jetted down the hallway.

I smiled. "Hey there, big guy. Look at you. Such beautiful, caramel eyes."

His eyes smiled, he gasped for more air, and then spoke. "Don't blame yourself. Rather ... it ... be ... me ... here, than you." It took a lot of energy for him to talk.

My eyes burned as they filled with tears. "It's so hard not to. I hate seeing you like this."

He shook his head, almost unnoticeably. "Shh, no. No cry."

He made me smile. I wiped my tears. At that moment the nurse, doctor, and Mom flooded into the room. The doctor went through a series of neurological tests on Shawn's face, hands, feet and even his speech. We all stood quiet and watched with our interpretations of what each reaction from Shawn meant. Test after test showed him to be slow but good, weak but present.

The doctor smiled. "I couldn't have asked for a better response. I don't see the need to sedate him any longer. Continue with current rates and wean him off the catheter."

"Sì," the nurse said. After the doctor left she added, "You can visit with him for a few minutes." She left the room.

Shawn was too groggy to talk, so we left him to rest. We went downstairs for lunch and returned to find him sitting up, scratches on his cheek, wet hair parted to the side, and in a clean hospital gown.

"So good to see you awake. You clean up good for a guy in a coma," I said.

"Even this crazy hair?"

"Especially this crazy hair. You know you scared me."

"Ah, I'm too stubborn to get taken out by a rock." He grabbed my hand I had near him.

"You're a tall guy. I didn't know if maybe the whole Goliath thing was happening."

He managed a smile, more genuine than the one he gave the doctor during the neurological tests. His breathing continued laboriously as he spoke, but he was more alert.

Mom said hello and replaced the existing flowers with fresh ones in the vase at the windowsill. In Italy, flowers were cheap from street vendors, and we took full advantage.

"Is my mom coming?"

"Yes," I said.

"What is it, Maggie?"

"Just sad."

"I'm going to be fine. You should be happy."

"I ... I am."

"Not entirely convincing. There's something you're not saying."

I shook my head. "No, this has been a lot, that's all." I paused. "I've come to know how losing you would affect me. It surprised me." I paused, but he didn't say a word so I continued. "I had a dream you were talking on the phone. I fell asleep to your voice, and it was six years in the future. We were good—best friends and happy."

His eyes smiled at me first, then his mouth. What he didn't say sometimes in words, he said instead with his eyes, more so than he could ever verbalize. I still wanted him to try.

"What? What is that grin? Why do you make me do all the talking?"

"You're so good at it. I love just watching you go on and on until—"

"I go right over a cliff?"

"Sometimes." He smiled bigger. "That's my favorite."

"You're so mean." I laughed and pulled my hand out of his, but he pulled harder and took my hand and placed it on his chest. I leaned in, releasing my arm to him. I stared into his eyes. In that second, I wanted to kiss him. Even with scruffy hair, even with a bandage on the side of his head, he could be so sexy, and I wanted to jump in and crawl up next to him—breathe him in.

"I think you should rest. We'll come back when you've had some more sleep. Get stronger so you can talk my ear off." I had to pull away. When I was with him, I could see myself at his side. As much as that was real, though, I couldn't shake what I had started with Luke.

"That is usually your job," he said.

"How is it you can lie here with a hole in your skull and still make me smile? Your wit might actually have improved."

He smiled and shook his head no.

"Well, get some rest." I kissed his cheek, close to his lips. "I'm wondering if that guy in London is coming back?"

"London?"

"The garden, our talk."

He shook his head.

That he doesn't remember? Of course. He looked at me with a question. "I'll fill you in later. Get some rest." I knew I wouldn't tell him, though. I tried to hide my worry as I wondered if he would ever be whole again.

Mom said her goodbye, and we left after informing the nurse. I stood in the elevator and let out a deep sigh so that my shoulders slumped. "I am so glad he's going to be okay."

"Me, too, honey. Me, too."

We took the elevators down and then hailed a cab. A car pulled up to the curb in a hurry, making its tires screech.

"It's time to go. Get in," Paul said through a half-rolled-down window.

Mom took the front, and I slipped into the backseat. My smile faded when Paul announced, "You have to leave the country, now."

"What? Where?"

"Home. I'm trying to figure out who bombed the embassy, and I'm saving you and Kayla more than getting any answers. So, I need you to take her back to the U.S." He glanced from me to Mom. "With you."

"Paul, can't we get our stuff at the hotel at least?" she asked.

"I'll send them later."

"What about Shawn?"

"He's fine. I'll make sure he flies as soon as he's able. I'll never allow the mistake again of bringing my family where the job is."

"Where *is* Kayla?" I asked.

"Luke will bring Kayla to the airport."

Mom gave me a dirty look at the mention of his name. "Kayla is okay. Thank God." I would see him again. My stomach flipped. I had told myself I would say what I needed over the phone. In person, my resolve wavered.

He swerved around a corner so fast, Mom couldn't brace herself. "Can't you slow down? You don't want us all to die in the car."

He gave her a stern look. "Mom, just let me do this."

She didn't say another word. When we got to the airport, he rushed us inside.

"You have your passports, don't you?"

"Always." I turned and faced Mom. She dug our passports out of her purse.

"Good." He smiled at me through his tough face and two days of stubble. He dropped us off and told us to get in line. When he had parked the car, he rejoined us.

"When does the plane leave?" I searched for the answer in the monitors of alphabetized cities above us.

"I've got the three of you on flight 2090. It goes to London, Atlanta, then on to Dallas-Fort Worth."

"Okay. Where is ..." As I asked, I turned around and saw Kayla at the curb and Luke driving away.

Kayla screamed and jumped up and down as she ran to me. "I was so scared they were going to kill you."

"Shh," Paul said, as he made sure no one heard her. It wasn't whether anyone did, but more like did anyone care? Paul whispered to me, "This is why you have to leave now," He peered over at Mom talking to the airline attendant, worrying if she overheard.

Kayla hugged and kissed my cheek. "We have so much to catch up on. My brother, the walking stone wall, hasn't told me anything since he rescued me from a car with Primo's creeps."

"They didn't hurt you, did they?"

"No, not really."

After Paul hugged Mom, he came over to us. "Y'all can finish this on the plane. We have to go."

"But when will we see you?" This all felt too rushed. We needed to talk. I still didn't understand everything.

He hugged me and whispered in my ear, "I actually have to find out who bombed the embassy. Remember, don't tell Mom about my real job." Finishing our hug, he added louder, "Luke and I have to report back to work."

"We'll call you as soon as we land. You'll answer your phone, right?" I said.

"Of course." Paul's phone rang. He placed his hand over it and mouthed, "Eleana."

I nodded as he turned and disappeared into the mass of travelers. The weight of their quick goodbyes left me with an elephant on my chest. I prayed they would be okay as much for me as for them.

Chapter 25
Flying

Waiting to board the plane, I called Shawn's mom to explain we would not be there when she arrived. The boarding call prevented me from blathering on with remorse and apologies that would only make her angrier. It ate at me while I stood there, imagining Shawn waking to the news from his mom. I could tell she didn't care for me, and she knew how to show it.

Kayla and I sat in the same aisle. She took the window, while I followed in behind her to the middle seat, and Mom sat across the aisle.

When the pilot turned off the "fasten seat belt" sign, we all relaxed from the takeoff and the talking began.

"Okay, what happened?" I asked.

"I'm still shaken up about the whole thing. I'm used to packing up in a day and moving to a new place, but nothing like this. I've never been held against my will, threatened, or thought I might die." Kayla held out her hand and tried to steady it but revealed a slight quiver. "See what I mean?"

I nodded and told her about the Russian as I rubbed my left shoulder. The injection had calmed the inflammation, but I could still only raise my arm ten inches. Then, I told her about the cabin on the lake while the stewardess gave us a Coke and Sprite.

"At least, you had Luke with you."

"At that point, I was still thinking he was Primo's idiot."

"What? You had to know."

I shook my head. "I was scared to death."

"How did you not know?" Kayla took a sip of her drink with widened eyes.

"When Luke said, *Going to a party,* I thought he was insane. I didn't know that was some code phrase."

"Oh, Maggie, what code? I just know when Luke is saying, 'trust me, and just go with this.' You thought the man you loved would hurt you?"

I winced. Why not? It wouldn't have been the first time a girl had delusions about how a guy felt about her. "We were chained to a pipe in a warehouse. You missed Primo's guys kicking the hell out of me. I wondered how on earth Luke could allow that to happen."

"I'm so sorry they hurt you, Maggie. I'm sure Luke didn't know, or he would have killed them." She crunched on a piece of ice from her drink.

"But, you don't have to worry about Primo anymore."

"Because of Luke?"

"No! He said more than likely, it was one of the four families. Luke said he may have let it slip to the Florence brothers what Primo was up to."

"Wow."

"Of course, it could have been me in the car with Primo. Luke was so mad about that possibility, he wouldn't even talk to me on the ride to the airport." Her anime eyes defended him.

I filled her in on why I thought I had killed Luke: the slipped liquor bottle crashing to the floor, the guns going off and me making a run for it, only to have Paul tell me later it saved Luke's life. "But I've yet to talk to him about it. He took off quite fast at the curb when he dropped you off."

"Luke can be ... intense, but I don't think he knows you were on the roof."

I took a deep sigh and scratched my eyebrow. It was difficult talking to Kayla about her brother. I wanted to tell her how mad I was at him, how betrayed I felt. She, of course, only wanted to defend him.

"I think he's crazy about you, though." Kayla smiled like a used car salesman, then laughed at herself.

"I hope Shawn's okay."

"Oh, yeah, Shawn. How's he doing?"

"That was his mom I called before we got on the plane. He's doing great. I just hope he doesn't have any more seizures." I realized by her puzzled face she didn't understand. "I'm sorry. When the cabin blew up, it threw him onto a rock, and he got a subdural hematoma."

"How serious is that?"

Mom was sound asleep. "It could have killed him. Paul got him to the hospital in time. Then, Shawn had surgery, a drill to his skull to relieve pressure. I just hate leaving him there."

"His mom is there now, though, right?"

"She's on her way."

We both sat there in silence while we finished our drinks.

"You feel something for this Shawn, too, don't you?"

I nodded.

"The question is—how much?"

"He almost died to save my life."

His quiet demeanor, his closed lips, his nonverbal clues, his hesitancy to share himself, but when he finally did ... made me feel wonderful.

She took a deep breath, as if she had discovered something.

"What?"

"You feel obligated to stay with him and guilty to be with my brother."

"What? I don't know about that. That's, that's ..."

The flight attendant walked by and took our trash. Mom opened her eyes and closed them again as she readjusted in her seat. After we were alone again, we settled back into our curled-shoulder space of low talking.

"You're insightful, but I think it goes deeper than that. What if it's more about lust versus friendship?"

"Maybe. I'll think about it." Kayla turned more solemn and gazed out the window.

We were chasing the sun. Rays of light scattered in a kaleidoscope of color. I reached across the aisle into Mom's purse and pulled out a book. I read to replace the dead end of my thoughts. Perhaps these pages held nuggets of wisdom. I needed something to speak to me. Hadn't someone else been through this before? Couldn't they tell me what they had learned on the other side of time?

I placed Luke in the book I read. What if he were a rogue agent of some sort and had lied to me and killed me in the end? Oh, the things my mother would have said!

I glanced over at Mom. It made me smile to look at her, peaceful in her sleep, and not the kind from drinking a half-gallon of wine. She had finally become a mother to me, instead of the other way around. She gave me advice. She listened to my emotional confusion and didn't judge me. She told me the truth, and most of all she was reliable. At nineteen, my mom might have also become my friend.

After a few chapters, I threw the book in her purse. I had read too much into it. There were no similarities. I wanted all this to be over. I wanted Luke, Shawn, and Paul to be back in America. Until that happened, nothing would feel right.

I didn't want to think about Merrico and his pursuits, Primo screaming at me, or the Russian pulling my shoulder out of socket—or worse—my confusion over Luke, if Shawn would live or die, or if my life had purpose. My brain wouldn't stop. It couldn't go to sleep. So, I thought of the future and the *what ifs* it could bring. It made that little shit, Fear, shut up. It made me feel warm inside again, and I took a deep breath, closed my eyes, and tried to go to the place I had created in my mind.

I slept until the captain's voice announced our descent into London. Mom and Kayla were already awake. We landed with a small hop after the plane touched down, but the jolt was over before I could respond. After finding our next flight on the prompter, we arrived at the gate with time to spare for a bathroom stop. After boarding, Mom sat behind me, and Kayla across the aisle.

I settled in and used my sweater Mom had bought me. An arm over the seat held out a phone.

"You need to hear this voicemail," Mom said.

I took the phone and held it to my ear, hiding it from the flight attendant. Paul had already said *hello* and was explaining the reason for his call.

"… are safe and the flights are going well. I have a huge favor to ask of you all. When you land in Atlanta, I need you to go to Concourse D and look for flight 3473. Pick up Eleana. She will be boarding the flight to Dallas with you. I need her to stay at the house for a while until I figure things out. Get to know her, and make her feel welcomed. For me, Mom? She isn't safe in Italy anymore, and I think I have her persuaded to raise the child in the States, and that we would help her. I wanted to ask you this in person, but there was no time. I hope you'll be there for her. I love you, Mom. Thanks!"

Since I was still unbuckled, I turned around in my seat. I shook my head in disbelief. "Oh, my gosh."

Mom sat there with an *I know* look on her face. She was calm but chewing on her thumb in thought. There was nothing to say, so I sat back down with shock still written on my face.

"What?" Kayla asked.

"We are meeting Eleana in Atlanta and taking her home with us," I said and almost couldn't believe it as I heard it from my own lips.

The two of us talked for the next hour about Paul and Eleana, but I left out the CIA. Kayla was protective of Paul, something of Luke rubbing off on her, I imagined. We ate, watched a movie, and slept for four hours, then the captain's lights came on. The stewardess began her safety speech.

After landing in Atlanta, we found Eleana's flight arriving in thirty minutes.

"Let's go eat at the Chili's we passed," Mom suggested.

"Okay," Kayla said.

I nodded.

We found a seat in the back, so it took a while before a waitress noticed us.

"We're in a hurry. Can we go ahead and order?"

"Sure." The waitress seemed pleased.

We ordered burgers for some reason. The meal I tried not to eat, I now had to have. It said America all over it. They might as well have stamped it in the bread with sesame seeds. We had not left the airport, but we could feel it. We were home and surrounded by so many Southern accents I felt safe again.

I knew it was time to talk about it. "So?"

Mom sighed.

Kayla blurted out. "Look at you two. You are twenty minutes away from meeting the mother of your grandchild or niece/nephew, maybe even a daughter or sister-in-law. Long faces with no words? Really?"

Kayla had the rare guts to say what she saw.

"The way you handle this may very well determine the next eighteen years you have to deal with her."

Mom smiled at me.

I told them, "You're right. We don't have to make this awful. It could very well, quite possibly be ... a good thing?"

"I agree. We need to be positive. Thanks, Kayla, for the reminder," Mom said.

We paid and waited at the gate for Eleana. I ran through the possible scenarios of what if she wasn't pregnant, what if she had been followed, or what if we were all in danger. I never believed any scenario, but I felt better just being prepared as I carried the thoughts to their possible conclusions. Still, every time I did that, I was never prepared. That's when I saw him, Fear, walking on the back of the plane taxiing to the gate.

I watched the door and blew out a long exhale. Nervous jitters took over my stomach. Five excruciating minutes later, the announcement came for the arrival of her plane. Thirty-five people came off before her dark eyes, pale skin, and long, auburn hair walked over the threshold. Her hair flowed behind her as she walked in high heels and skinny jeans. A long pink top with tiny sequins covered her stomach with no apparent bulge. She rolled her suitcase behind her and then stopped, glancing around the room until she noticed the three of us staring at her. A smile came to her face as she walked over. She was more confident and beautiful than I remembered. She stood out over here, unlike in Italy.

Remembering Kayla's words, I stepped forward to reassure her with a smile.

"Hello, I'm Eleana. I'm hoping you three are ..." She paused to think. "Karen, Kayla, and Maggie," she said, her English sounding romantic.

We all nodded to our names as she spoke them. I also extended my hand and shook hers.

Mom stepped forward. "It's so nice to finally meet you. We've heard so much about you."

I furrowed my brow at her, but Eleana just laughed, which made us all join her.

"I suppose you have. I will try to change some of that." When she spoke, an odd dimple on the right corner of her mouth caused her to look as if she were smiling every time she said something. Her accent reminded me of Merrico's, but less formal.

She threw me off guard. I could see why Paul would fall for her. I could understand it all finally. She had an American confidence to her but was full of Italian style. She stood out but didn't know it. Her first impression, I mean her first introduction, went well.

We walked and talked as we led her to Concourse C, to our gate. She spoke of simple things, maybe more like safe things: the plane ride, her luggage, and then she asked about Dallas. She admitted to not being in the States since she was five with her mother. She told us about her deceased American mother, and I saw my mom's reservations melt. Mom was open, if not already adopting her before we even boarded the plane.

Chapter 26
Oh Baby

The next flight into Dallas-Fort Worth airport was short in comparison. We were all separated by our seat assignments. Being alone gave me time to think, as if I had not already been doing that until I could puke. I leaned against the right armrest and stared at the men loading the luggage. It was strange to be back in America, as much as I loved it. I knew this was my real life, but it didn't feel entirely right. Italy felt real, as if I should still be there. Home, here, felt like a place and time, a part of me that I once knew. Now that I was home, I could tell how much Italy had changed me.

During takeoff, the man next to me held onto both armrests. I leaned farther away and into the window. I protected my shoulder without thinking now, but it was more than that. A smile was work, or a deep breath, smothering. As for talking, it was impossible. I wanted to hide away where no one could find me, at least not until I had found myself first.

When we landed, I dismissed myself to the bathroom. When I came out, Mom stood there with her phone, talking to someone, and then handed it to me.

"Hello? Maggie?" Shawn asked.

"It's me. We just landed at DFW." I walked back into the bathroom for privacy.

"I'm so glad you're safe. I was afraid that your call was a hoax and a kidnapper had put you up to it. Mom was confused, too. It just didn't make sense that you would leave."

"Paul thought it was best to get out of town. Safer and all. I'm not sure what he knew, but he was adamant."

"I'm glad you left then. Mom is making arrangements for us to fly back on one of those air ambulances."

"Oh, wow, Shawn, that's great. I had no idea you were that stable."

"My blood work came back with the medicine at the right levels and no bleeding on the CT scan. As long as I continue to feel great, no dizziness or seizures, they'll agree to transfer me to America in a few days."

"That's great."

"Mom's going to have to take me to South Carolina, you know."

"I figured."

"Will you be coming home soon? I mean, to Christina's?"

I thought of the my best friend's house and how I never brought her anything from Italy like she'd asked me to. "I haven't thought that far yet. I know I will at some point. I just don't know how soon." Shawn sounded so good, like his old self.

"I want to see you." His voice resonated, sexy and deep.

"I know. I just ...we'll talk and ..." I dropped my face into my left hand and rubbed my eyes.

"What does a guy have to do to tell you he loves you? After everything that's happened, I still want to be with you. More than ever. I love you. That's why I went to Italy in the first place. I was too scared to tell you before you left. But, I'm not afraid anymore. My love for you is greater than any fear. I hope I've proven that."

His words struck chords, and a song played in my mind. His memory had fully returned. A lady tried to get by me with a stroller in one hand and her baby tucked under the other. "I see the London guy has returned."

"Please, tell me you see what kind of guy Luke is. He's all about him."

"I just can't do this right now. I'm in the bathroom and with all these people. I can't think." I moved out of the way and walked through the exit door. "I'll see you when you get back."

"I'll let you know when I arrive."

"Okay."

"I love you."

"Thanks." I hung up the phone. I couldn't say it back to him. I walked over to Mom.

"Is he okay?"

"He feels great and will be allowed to fly in a few more days if all goes well. It was just awkward. He told me he loved me."

"I like him, Maggie. He's a good kid."

"Yeah." We hung outside the bathroom door, waiting for Eleana and Kayla.

After getting their things from baggage claim, we walked outside to the curb. Mark had been kept up-to-date on our plans and pulled up in his fancy, black Chrysler 300. After introductions, he took the bags and placed them in the trunk. Mom and her new husband, Mark hugged for a long time. The three of us girls squeezed into the back seat while Mom sat in the front and held Mark's hand.

Mom couldn't wait to tell him all that had happened, since their calls were so brief. Eleana and Kayla were all smiles and small talk after they both admitted to a nap on the plane. I sat in the hum of voices, unnoticed.

Returning to their house, I felt numb. Eleana and Kayla remarked with *oohs* and *ahhs* over the massive house.

When they asked for my agreement to their adulation, I nodded. My head felt spacey. I couldn't concentrate. I couldn't make connections to anything.

I was exhausted. I went to my room. I stepped out of my jeans, unbuttoning with one hand, shook off my cardigan with the other hand, and slid under the covers. I had hit a wall, and I couldn't say another word or do another thing. In my dreams, I re-lived the danger, but I also lived out the next time I would see Luke.

Over the next day, we got to know Eleana better. Mom fired off questions without sounding like a detective, a secret medical skill she had acquired. Eleana confessed she hadn't seen a doctor yet. Mom was not too excited about her lack of medical care.

"Is there even a baby?" she asked me later in confidence. I could tell she wanted there to be one.

Our luggage arrived from Italy, as Paul promised, shortly before dinner. Chicken, leeks, and olive oil simmered in a pan, keeping Mom busy. I took my bags to my room and went through them. There were things I wanted to see again. As I unpacked, Eleana came through my open door.

"Do you have a minute?" I never tired of her accent.

"Sure." I closed the lid on my suitcase.

Eleana closed the door behind her.

"This is nice." She picked up my grandmother's jewelry holder. I knew she hadn't come in here out of boredom.

"Thanks." I waited.

She wasted more time with questions about my thoughts on Italy and Merrico. I laughed, thinking of him. She looked at me funny, and I explained how he caught me off guard every time I saw him. He was nothing I was used to and nothing I had expected.

She smiled, but it was weak.

"Are you doing all right? Concerning Primo?"

The mention of his name turned her face pale. She didn't want to talk about him. I suspected she would never want to talk about him with me, but she had something on her mind. I hoped she had not changed her mind about confiding in me, whatever it was. Not knowing how to proceed, I was about to offer condolences, but then she blurted out, "I feel so bad. Your mother is the most generous person I have ever met." Still holding the ceramic box, she opened it. "She reminds me of my own mother. I cannot be ..." She stopped.

I wasn't sure if she would continue. "My mom wants to be a part of your life. I know she can come off a little strong—"

"No. It's not her. I cannot be dishonest. I need to know what to do."

The bad feeling I had about Eleana resurfaced. I glanced around my room.

Fear said, "I told you so" in the melody of a child's nursery song, over and over from behind my sheer drapes.

"I was scared for my life. I had to get out of Italy fast. I knew Paul could do that." She spoke fast. She put down the box and walked toward me.

"What are you trying to say?"

"I saw you that night—in the bathroom. Well, I knew Kayla. I told my friend to play along. I didn't like Luke at all. He broke Paul and me up. It was a dirty joke. I'm sorry."

"Joke?"

"I did miscarry. I didn't go to the hospital, but the doctor confirmed. He saw it."

"*It*? A baby?"

She nodded. "Two months." She cupped her hand. "It was so tiny, but it was a baby." She sat down on the bed next to me and began to cry.

"I'm sorry." Those words were lame. I had no idea what to say, but I wanted to be mad at her.

"I wanted it. I wanted to be a mother."

Speechless didn't even begin to describe my reaction. I think I was even thoughtless. I could only feel what she was feeling, so there was no room for anything else. When I finally did think, it was my mother's face that came to my mind. I understood now why Eleana was confessing. She had to find a way to tell my mom.

"What does Paul think?"

"That I'm ... pregnant. It was awful, I know, but I had to get—"

"Listen, you need to tell Paul immediately, but don't tell our mom yet. Let's sleep on it, okay?"

She nodded, wiped her tears, and smiled. "You are as lovely as Merrico said." She left me to my thoughts.

Yeah, yeah. Always with the damn manners. I wanted to smack her, but then again, she was trying to stay alive. I wondered about Luke's initial description of her as a *lying bitch*. Was he right?

As if the day needed any more drama, later Kayla borrowed my phone to call Luke. I took Mom's car to the store. I made up an excuse to pick up milk and some cough drops. My throat had worsened since the last leg of our flight home, from a dry tickle to swollen, red tonsils. I wasn't interested in talking, but I knew my throat was not why I dodged talking to Luke. I returned to a surprised Kayla.

"Where did you go? I went to hand you the phone, and your mom said you'd left,"

My stomach turned nauseous at the thought of talking to Luke. I didn't want to talk to him. I buried the words he could say in my mind, my stomach, and I realized Fear was holding my hand.

"The store, for some medicine," I said.

"I just thought you would want to talk to him. He ..." She beamed with joy. "He's returning to Quantico."

I said nothing but squinted, then took a deep breath. It made me cough.

"He needs to talk to you." Her eyes widened. "It's important." When I didn't move, she narrowed her eyes at me. "Why are you so afraid to talk to him?" She walked right past me, into the kitchen, returned with my phone, and held it out for me. It still had power.

I took the phone and stared at the last number shown. I walked away and into my room and closed the door behind me. It felt as if I'd swallowed acid. Before I chickened out, I pressed the call button.

"Hello?" Luke's voice said, strong and wishful.

"Hi." My heartbeat pounded from my neck, and my voice croaked.

"It is you. I'm so glad to hear your voice. You sound awful, are you okay?

"Just a little jet throat. I'll be fine."

"Good. We've not had any time to talk, and so much has happened."

"Yeah." The word hung there. "Last thing I remember, you were pulling away in a boat as I was picking myself out of the mud."
"I'm ..." He paused. "I—"

"That's what I thought. Talking isn't such a great idea, after all, is it?"

He took a deep breath, and his exhale vibrated through the phone.

"I'm coming home. To Quantico."

Where in the hell was Quantico? I thought Kayla meant another country.

He continued as if he could read my thoughts. "It's in the northeast part of Virginia."

"Kayla's thrilled."

"Thank you for all you've done for her."

My jaw clenched. "No problem. She's a great girl."

"She said she doesn't want to get on another airplane unless she has someone with her. Are you going back to South Carolina soon?"

"Yep." Every word became difficult. My mind raced with what I wanted to say, but tight lips and a flexed jaw held back the words.

"I appreciate that. You have been great with her. She really likes you, Maggie, looks up to you. If you could travel with her back to Columbia, I'll drive down and get her. Maybe hang out for the weekend?"

"That's not a good idea. I live with someone el … There's no room, and it would just be awkward."

"I meant in a hotel."

In shock, I protested. "Why on earth would you think I'd stay in one with you? You have a lot of nerve, Luke."

"I meant a hotel for Kayla and me," he said without raising his voice.

I plopped onto my bed and buried a scream under one of my pillows. It was followed by coughing before I could return the phone to my ear.

I heard him say, "Listen, it's no secret we need to talk. I just don't want to do it over the phone."

I found softer words. "That's fine. I'll talk to my mom and Kayla. How about the day after tomorrow?"

"Sounds good. I have a few days before I report to full duty."

I stood at the mirror and rubbed my flushed face. I searched for my own thoughts in the eyes looking back at me, but then I didn't want to know them. I walked back out to the living room and found Kayla waiting on the couch. She was smiling, though I was not.

"He said to use the credit card he gave you before you left Italy." Kayla did the clicking around on the internet, while I spent most of my time in the bathroom blowing my nose.

Later at dinner, I told Mom, Mark, and Eleana about our plan to return to Columbia, South Carolina so Kayla could meet up with her brother. Mom gave me another disapproving look when she heard Luke's name. She wasn't happy about me leaving but accepted it with Eleana giving her plenty to focus on.

Mom and I spent our last day together in doctors' offices. She forced me to see an orthopedic doctor who arranged a same-day MRI.

Shawn had left a message on my phone that he had arrived safely in Columbia and couldn't wait to see me. On a return call, he was sleeping but I told his mom I would be in town tomorrow. From her gruff response, I wasn't sure if she would tell him.

Eleana slept in. She had not rested well since we had arrived. I wondered if Mom would have to buy her a new bed. She had tried three already and none felt right, even Mom's own bed, which she gave up despite Mark's grumblings. I made a few jokes as we drove back home about her new Goldilocks guest.

Mom handled all the new changes to her life with such grace. She knew Eleana would not be easy, but it was her new project. She joked to me about getting her hands around Paul's neck. Her threats were hollow. She did better with projects, but this one might not last as long as she thought.

Mom didn't waste any time getting Eleana in to see her gynecologist, and I persuaded Eleana to go. Maybe the doctor could give Mom the bad news. If the opportunity had arisen, I would have told her—or had Eleana tell her—but no such opportunities arose.

In the exam room Eleana began to sweat. Dr. Hodges came in and acted normal, extending our agony. She came in with due dates and blood work to be drawn, firing off more questions. It would be a Christmas baby if it was on time, but only three percent of babies were born on their due date. This was all interesting, but I waited for the part where the doctor told us there wasn't a baby. Eleana furrowed her brows but didn't ask any questions. The doctor picked up on it and dismissed Mom and me. We waited in a mini waiting room.

I had read an article in *People* by the time we were asked by the nurse to follow her. We weren't going back to Eleana's room but down a different hallway. It reminded me of going to the principal's office to be lectured.

We walked into the ultrasound room. Was a dog digging in the pit of my stomach, burying a jalapeno? I half smiled at Eleana, and she returned the same weak smile. Mom walked in with nothing short of exuberance.

Taking Eleana's hand, she asked the sonographer, "What do you think we will see?"

Nothing, I said to myself. I couldn't help my pessimism. I didn't want a front row seat to my mom's disappointment. I held my breath, even though I knew the outcome.

The lights were turned down low and a towel tucked into Eleana's shorts. The tech squirted the warm gel over the lowest part of her stomach. The black screen revealed a white kidney shape.

"There it is."

"There *what* is?" I blurted out.

Eleana and I caught each other's shocked expressions and searched again at the screen, waiting for the tech to explain.

"Right there. That is the head, the spine, and you can see right here, this movement is the heart." She flipped a switch on the machine and a loud, fast heartbeat echoed through the room.

Mom grinned at our surprised faces. "It's amazing, isn't it? The heartbeat makes it all so real, doesn't it?"

"That's not Eleana's heartbeat?" I asked

"No, honey. That is way too fast for her heart. Babies usually run 120 to 160 beats a minute," Mom explained.

I ran my hand through my hair, rubbed my eyes, and tried to understand. The doctor entered and congratulated us. After the excitement settled down, we were sent to the exit waiting room. This time, I didn't read anything. Mom talked my head off about her relief. Until she saw it with her own eyes, she just didn't know if it was real. I knew exactly how she felt.

It wasn't until I got Eleana back to the house and alone that I got the full story. She was pregnant with twins and lost one a month ago. The doctor felt certain this one was safe but would be watching her closely with multiple ultrasounds. Eleana bounced around as if she was on the high school dance team, full of joy.

I made an excuse to go shopping with her. I wanted to get her something before I left, but more than that, I needed to know what happened between my brother and her. Not good at side-stepping a topic I want to discuss, I finally blurted it out in the breast/bottle-feeding aisle.

"So, you and Primo were high school sweethearts?"

Her eyes widened at the change of conversation. "We did date when I was fifteen. He was the boy every girl wanted."

"Is that what broke up you and Paul?"

She sighed. "Paul was wonderful. Spun my head around, you know?"

I smiled, relieved it was real between them at least.

"He was everything I wanted to find—what a little girl dreams."

I nodded.

She dropped her smile. "But, Luke didn't like it, wouldn't have it. He said Primo wanted me. He said I should be with an Italian boy."

"Luke?"

She nodded. "I don't think he ever liked me."

"Then, Luke knew Primo before I ever got there."

"I guess."

I wanted to see him, confront him about all the things he never told me. I wanted to tell him what I thought, what he did wrong. The anger welled up in me, and I didn't know what to do with it. I wasn't used to being angry. I didn't live in a world where I was pushed over the edges of my comfort zone. The only thing I knew to do was walk it off. When we arrived back at Mom's house, I went on a four-mile walk for over an hour and thought about everything: the past, the present, and my next move.

Chapter 27
Raining

The thunderstorms caused the plane to fall from the sky, losing our stomach three times worse than any roller coaster I'd been on. There were two to three seconds where no one was sure if the plane would stop falling. Audible prayers were heard amidst screams. I just wanted to land, and until we did, I gripped the armrest with both hands and rode the ride, terrified but keeping it masked as much as I could.

When we were promised by the pilot that the roughest part was over, I sat and daydreamed my funeral, imagining Luke's face hearing the news—then Shawn's, my brother's, and my mom's. It all became so real, I had to snap out of it. So, I started a conversation with Kayla about college.

Being stateside inspired her desire to enroll. Kayla began asking about how difficult the workload could be. She had taken the GED while in Italy and had been reviewing ACT questions online.

"Have you ever been on a date?" I asked, picturing her in college.

She shook her head with a *Why do you ask?* look on her face. I didn't think she had, with Luke around, or her grandmother before that. She was different, not just from me, but from everyone, in a good way.

She became bold with the new line of questioning. "You ever been alone with a boy? I mean, naked?"

I didn't see that coming. There were just some things you thought people knew. What I loved about her was that she never assumed.

She continued before I could respond. "I think I'm going to wait until I'm married. I want it to be right. You know?"

I took a deep breath. "Yeah. I do." I thought of Andy.

"So?"

"I wanted to wait, too. I just didn't have the choice."

"Sure you do. We all do."

"No, I mean he ... It was an ex-boyfriend. I told him no, but ..." I always hated how that sounded.

"Maggie, I'm so sorry."

There it was. The part I hated.

"You could still just start over, like that never happened."

"That's hard to do, but it's not just that. I have other memories, too." I rolled my eyes, picturing Luke above me. "Moments where ... You'll know what I mean when you get alone with one sometime." I felt too ashamed even to say it. I wanted it. What did that mean? Was I coming to terms with what Andy had done? Was I healing? I shook the thought from my mind. I didn't want to think about it.

"Are you talking about my brother?"

"Let's just not go there. I don't think we should talk about your brother's sex life."

"I've lived with him for two years, Maggie. I think I know my brother very well. We had talks. He taught me about men. He encouraged me to wait ...till I'm married. I know you think I'm naïve and all, but I will. I have help. I trust God to help me."

"Well, what he wants for his baby sister may not be what he wants from the women in his life."

Kayla squinted her eyes at me. "You should get to know him better."

"I doubt that will happen."

"Oh, Maggie—"

The pilot's voice came overhead and interrupted our conversation with descent instructions. I welcomed the silence between us to think about Luke telling his baby sister to wait, warning her about men. Was that part of the reason he didn't make a move on me that night in his bed? Why were my thoughts of Luke so conflicting? On one end, he seemed too good to be true, and on the other, a liar. Which one was he?

We both went to baggage claim distracted. When Luke erupted through the doors, he still made me stare. His broad shoulders stretched his t-shirt tight, and he smelled freshly showered, so good in fact, my mind wandered back to the Villa. As with all memories, I took a deep breath while it unfolded in my mind's eye. I wished things could have been different between us. Would he always invoke that inside me? Would I ever be able to live life without regrets?

I had plenty of nights to wrestle with the conclusion of us. I'd decided I would never let him know he had any power over me, nor would I let on I had anything more than a crush. This wasn't the first time in history a girl fell for a guy more than he did her. If he really cared, he would have told me his plans, he wouldn't have run off, he wouldn't try to get himself killed. I chalked it up to a lesson learned. Exactly what was still being fleshed out.

Luke walked toward us and hugged Kayla first but never took his eyes off me. His bright smile glimmered with the light in his eye. I had to turn away, fearing he would discover all that swirled inside of me. I noticed my bag on the conveyer belt. Looking over my shoulder, I nodded a *hello* to Luke as he stood behind me with two people between us. I grabbed my bag, and he came to help before it got away from me. I had packed everything I brought from Italy and many things from my closet at Mom's house in a suitcase Mark had loaned me.

The weight of the bag was winning the fight when Luke came and snatched it up. He rolled it back to where Kayla stood. I followed him.

"It's great to see you, Maggie. You look really good." He reached with his arms and then hesitated.

I leaned in and patted his shoulder for Kayla, or out of pity. I didn't know why I didn't feel anger now that he was standing in front of me. His energy was contagious, and the weight he seemed to carry around in Italy was gone. He appeared light and free, beaming with joy. In this moment, I could see brother and sister similarities.

"The car's right out here," Luke said and took off toward the doors.

We both followed Luke, who rolled the two suitcases, one in each hand, and loaded them into a silver Toyota 4runner. Kayla bounced into the front passenger seat, and I was relieved the seat arrangement wasn't awkward or discussed. It began to rain as Luke pulled out, and turned on the windshield wipers.

"Are you hungry?"

"Absolutely," Kayla answered for the both of us. I nodded but was less animated.

We drove toward Columbia's downtown, and Luke pulled into a Mexican chain restaurant. "Is this okay?"

"Perfect," I said. Mexican was the one food I truly missed in Italy.

"Can never get too much Mexican," Kayla added. Dodging raindrops, we ran into the restaurant with a slight dampness to our hair and dark spots covering our jeans.

The lunch went by as if we'd all been friends for a long time. The events in Italy did something between us that would supersede any other type of disagreement Luke and I had. It was the three of us again, as if Primo had never happened.

After lunch, Luke drove me to Christina's, but no one was home. Luke didn't mention staying in town again, but I sensed he wanted to talk. He asked Kayla to stay in the car. After saying goodbye to Kayla with all our normal hugs and promises to see each other soon, Luke took my suitcase to the front door and waited on the stoop. I went around back and retrieved a hidden key. With wet hair, I hurried, unlocking the front door.

Luke rushed in behind me, carrying my bag. "Where's your room?"

We stood in the foyer. Water fell from his wet, spiky hair onto his shirt. A chill came through me and raised the hair on my arms. "You don't have to do that."

"I don't mind. You'd have to unload it here if I didn't take it to your room."

He had a point, and I had a bum shoulder I'd been trying to play down, so I agreed. He followed me down the narrow hallway to the first door on the right.

Luke turned the corner, carrying the luggage with a slight drag across the carpet. He smiled when he saw my room. "This is you? It fits."

I watched him take it all in, then I scanned the room it as if through his eyes. The periwinkle afghan at the end of my bed matched the baby flowers in the bedspread. An Ansel Adams black and white picture of a snowy tree on one wall contradicted the girl and boy laughing in a field of flowers on the opposite wall. Two books—*Wuthering Heights* and *Jane Eyre*—sat on the nightstand next to the lamp. A small basket of dirty clothes in the corner beside the dresser still had my pajamas, underwear, and towel sitting on top. I grabbed the towel and dried my hair as we walked down the hall.

"Thanks," I said and followed Luke to the living room. I offered him the towel. The silence was awkward, making me talk too much. "Y'all be careful driving up there." There was my nervous southern accent again.

He took the towel. "Maggie, it's not that far." He wiped his head and neck. The right side of his shirt was soaked worse than the left, and his nipple was visible through his shirt. I turned away.

"Yep. That's great." I didn't know what to say.

"Why are you so cold?" He cleared his throat. "To me?"

"I haven't been cold. We just had a great lunch," I snapped.

"What are you doing? Do you even know?" His brows pinched together.

My face revealed shock at his directness. "*Doing*? What are you talking about?" I'd hoped he would just leave.

"You act like nothing happened between us in Italy. I mean, before the warehouse."

"Oh, something happened." I shook my head. "Summer fun, that's all. It's fine."

"That's what you think?"

"That's what I know."

"I thought you were smarter than that."

"Hey, I'm not stupid," I snarled.

He snuffed a laugh.

"Fine. You want to hear it? You weren't honest with me. And look what happened."

He sighed. "I couldn't." He ran his fingers through his wet hair. "I should have never let you get as close as you did. That was a mistake." Something protruded on his side, but his hand came down too fast for me to see it.

"Don't worry. The stiff arm you hold out to everyone is plenty strong."

"I mean to Primo. I should have never let you get near him."

"You could have told me your plans. I know you knew him before I arrived."

He shook his head and stared at one spot with a wrinkled forehead. "Neither you nor Kayla should have been anywhere near him."

I dropped my eyes. Like a bull, I exhaled through my nose, waiting for the words. "She knew you weren't dead. She ..."

"*She, she, she*. What about you, Maggie?"

"I thought you were dead." I couldn't prevent my eyes filling with tears. "That ... wasn't fair of you." My voice quivered.

He reached for me, but I stepped backward. He shook his head at the floor, searching. "No, it wasn't. I sent word to Paul, but the email was cut short." His eyes closed with regret. "I was going to meet up with you, but then you were both kidnapped."

"Why couldn't you tell me about him?" I pleaded.

"I didn't want you involved. I didn't want him to hurt you."

"Not telling me the truth didn't protect me," I yelled. "What about following him to his dad's office?"

"Oh, Maggie. You have to believe me. I didn't know he was involved with Arman at that point. I thought he was just a punk kid. Once I looked into it and found out his connections, I couldn't pass up the perfect chance. It all happened so quickly, and I never dreamed it would involve you. I looked at your mom coming as the best way to get you free and far away from it all."

"I understand Kayla's safety is the most important thing to you, and that's why you had to go after Arman." I flailed my hands at him. "And, you will do anything for her. So, I don't hate you, Luke. I get that kind of love. My dad had that for me." I swallowed my tears. "She is very lucky to have you."

He turned his head to the side and stepped forward. "Maggie?"

Fear popped out from the coat closet. I shook my head.

Luke sat on the edge of the couch table and spoke softer. He stared into his hands. "I'm sorry about Primo. I was scared shitless to find you in the warehouse that day. What followed was my attempt to keep us all alive. I regret putting those I love at risk."

Yes, there were so many things we both regretted. I wanted to cry, throw up, or scream.

Luke walked to the window and pulled the curtain aside to set his eyes on Kayla. "I'm not going to apologize for going after Arman. Kayla has a chance to live a normal life now." He paused.

I waited, letting him continue while I tried to control the anger, pain, and resolve swirling inside me.

"I'm going to teach officer's training at Quantico Marine Base for a year. When my new assignment comes up, I will make sure Kayla stays here —in college." He turned and looked at me. "I'm not perfect, Maggie, but I'm a quick learner."

He walked to the door and paused as he opened it. "By the way, I think you're a strong, incredible woman but … too afraid to love. I have a heart, too, and it can only take so much."

The door neither slammed nor closed quietly.

I stood there and watched him walk away. Not one clear word came to mind, only emotions I couldn't control. I walked over to the window and watched the 4runner leave. I replaced my silence with an angry roar and hit the window with the outside of my fist. But, he didn't come back. He didn't come back. My tears fell with the rain.

Chapter 28
The Beginning

That night, before Christina left for her waitress job, she checked on me. I hugged her without getting out of bed, thanking her for being such a great best friend. I faintly relieved her concerns with an excuse of fatigue. Later, after hours of sleep, when she returned, I put on some kind of an appearance, consisting of a ponytail and brushed teeth. I promised we would talk soon, but I had to run errands first. She probably knew I was stalling, but she gave me my space.

For days, I had shut down my mind, my senses, and just slept. I forced myself not to think, but in the end, all I could do was think about the last few weeks in Italy, and what I learned about myself.

I went to the park and watched it empty for the night. I sat alone on the swing set without energy to lift my feet off the ground. Then, I spread out flat on the slide and watched the coming night. Strokes of smokey-grey pushed the washed-out blue aside. The sparkles of light stood out against the deep, dark air, so motionless compared to the ocean. I imagined my hand running through space, trying to hold on to something, but there was nothing there. Even the streaks of clouds fading into the dark would be nothing in my hand. I was chasing something, an unreachable letter to an untouchable word.

The truth kept flying away from my view, like the lone plane in the sky. My thoughts drifted back to Italy when I'd first landed. All the control I felt before had disappeared. The ground beneath me, where my views, beliefs, and values stood as pillars, began to shake.

I had become comfortable with Fear. So many moments, I could have shot Fear in the face with a silencer, but I chose to save him. This wasn't working. This same Fear caused me to walk away from Shawn, and even now, it clouded my view of Luke. Fear wouldn't protect me from pain. I saw that now, returning home with some understanding.

I went into my bedroom, opened my closet, and took off my shirt to throw into the hamper. The long mirror inside the closet door, reflected the pearl necklace hanging around my neck. I was afraid to fail my father, afraid I wouldn't measure up to what he wanted of me, afraid I wasn't good enough. I was afraid to love someone and then lose him to death.

My nose stung as my eyes watered. My head dropped like a stone. I fell back into the closet and landed on shoes and half-dirty clothes.

Motionless, I lay and wondered how one got out of such a mess. I sat there so long, I couldn't tell if I was breathing. It was as if something was on my chest, pushing me down deeper. I could go to sleep forever. *Help.* Was all I could utter.

I sat up and opened my eyes, gasping for air. As if an angel had kicked something off my chest, I took another deep breath and I felt more alive. I stood, and again, I took the deepest breaths I could.

"Get out!" It came from deep inside me. "I don't need you anymore. Fear, *leave!*" I hung my head and began to pray. I surrendered my heart, my desires, and my fear.

It wasn't too late to change. Why did I expect myself to have life all figured out at nineteen? Maybe it took a lot longer than that to become a pearl. For the first time in my life, I could see that being an adult was just the beginning of the journey, not the end. The only thing I had to do now was decide to start. And, that's what I did. I read into the night, remembering Kayla's words.

The next day, when Christina arrived home, she told me Shawn had called earlier. I returned the call, and discovered he was home, not even in the hospital. He wanted to see me, and as our conversation was long overdue, I went to his house.

The all-brick basement ranch house had a driveway on the right forming a half wall. He was there, waiting for me. I assumed he didn't want his mom to hear our conversation, and I didn't want to go inside, so I sat beside him. A bandage peeked out from below his cap. He loved his Dallas Cowboys hat. He looked so normal, but when he pulled his cap up to show me how his hair was growing in, I was reminded of the traumatic event he had gone through.

I tried to find out how bad it was. Other than anti-seizure medication for a year, he said he was lucky.

"Thanks again for getting me to the hospital so fast."

I couldn't believe he thanked me for anything. He should be blaming me. It didn't feel right. "It wasn't me. That was all Paul."

"Tell him for me, okay."

I nodded. The strain between us was obvious. Something had happened to change us forever—our relationship, maybe even our friendship.

He cut to the point. "I take it this isn't going to go the way I'd hoped."

I confirmed no. I stopped to see if he had anything he wanted to say.

He stood and leaned against the wall. I continued. "I accused you of not opening up when I didn't even do it myself."

He unfolded his arms and dropped his hands, palms up. "Like what?"

I shook my head. "It doesn't matter now."

"You came over here to tell me I don't matter anymore?"

"No, I just mean things from my past. I'm putting them all behind me now. Starting over with a brand new beginning." I remembered Kayla's words, and I knew I wanted to try.

"I see. Cut out the old dross—"

I sighed. "You're not dross. You will meet a girl one day who has dealt with all her baggage or doesn't have any, but ... you deserve better."

"Do you think you're selling this? You don't just talk someone out of love. I understand you're going through a hard time right now. If all you can handle is friends, then that's what we'll be."

"I didn't know you were this stubborn."

"You didn't?" He smiled.

"Okay, maybe I've seen it a time or two." We both smiled.

"Come here." He held me longer than normal. When we stood there facing one another in an awkward stare of sadness, he changed the subject. "When do you start school?" He was unable to hear what I couldn't say or unwilling to let it be final. We finished with small talk, another hug goodbye, and I drove away.

I dialed Paul's number when I pulled out of the driveway. One emotional pond into another, that was how I avoided feelings. We talked around the job he couldn't tell me about.

"I got a call from Eleana and another from Mom. A Christmas baby, huh? That's going to be great. Will you be moving here, then?"

"I need to be working on that, yes," Paul said with a laugh.

"At least, it's not twins. Talk about a double load. That would have been crazy."

"Twins? Why do you say that?"

"Eleana never tell you about losing the other baby?"

"I don't know anything about another baby."

"She lost one. That is why she told you she miscarried, she wasn't lying."

"Stop. How far along is the baby?"

"Eleven weeks. Why?" I heard him beeping around on his phone. "Paul? Are you still there?" Did he just cut me off? "Hello?"

"Maggie?"

"Yeah?"

"Eleana told me she was pregnant eleven weeks ago. I haven't had sex with her since way before that."

"Then the dates are off. That happens." I popped my pearl into my mouth while sitting at a red light.

"I have to go. I have to call Mom."

He promised to call back later. He had to be wrong. I jumped out of the car once I pulled into Christina's driveway.

"This is bullshit."

I scrambled to the computer and began searching everything I could about multiple pregnancies. My head spun after two hours. I didn't have enough information to figure this out. I walked away from the frustration of the unknown. After everything that had happened, here we were.

The next morning, I woke to the doorbell and laughed at the mess in my room. It was scattered with piles to throw out, pictures to put in albums, and clothes to give to Goodwill. I had stayed up late with Christina, telling her everything as we cleaned the house while we ate chocolate chip cookies until three in the morning. She had been thrilled about my revelations.

I stepped over the laptop on the floor to answer the doorbell. "It's probably UPS," I called to Christina as I threw a green sundress over my head, not bothering with a bra or brushing my hair for that matter. The UPS guy is like forty.

I opened the door. Staring back at me was Luke, bent over laughing. I went to shut the door out of morbid embarrassment, but he blocked its closing with his hand against the door. We knew who would win that fight, so I let go.

Luke looked me, up and down. "Rough night?"

I turned around and walked into the living room, leaving the door open, and he followed me in.

"No. Yes."

"Were you drinking?" Luke grinned.

"No, I—" I glanced down the hall.

"I'm sorry. I should have call …" His smiled dropped as his eyes followed in the direction of my bedroom. "I– will just call you later. I didn't know you had someone here." Luke turned toward the door to leave.

"No, There isn't."

He faced me. "Oh, well that's good." His face lit up. "Umm, could I talk to you?"

I folded my arms to hide my breasts. "Maybe I should change—"

"Don't."

His interruption startled me. I dropped my head to the floor, not knowing how to respond.

"I would love to just take a walk. We could go to the backyard."

"Okay." I slipped on some flip-flops and walked back to the front door where Luke waited for me. I shut the door behind me and walked along the sidewalk with the pearl in my mouth, the chain draping out of each corner. We opened the backyard gate. I looked around for a place to sit other than on the deck.

Luke led the way to the end of the yard and stared past the short fence into the woods. "Thanks for seeing me. You been okay?"

I pulled the pearl out of my mouth like a piece of chewing gum. "Sure. I thought you went back?"

"No, I told you I had a few days off. Kayla and I went to Finley Park to hike yesterday. It helped clear my head. I didn't want to leave again without seeing you."

"Really?" I couldn't suppress a smile. I wasn't afraid today. There was even something I hadn't had much of lately, hope.

"Listen, Maggie. I know when you met me, our start was probably the weirdest in history. You thought I was married, then—"

"You are."

"Okay. I'm married. Then, you found out I was married to my sister. Who does that?" He threw his hands up and ran his fingers through his hair. Walking back and forth, he smoothed a four foot path into the dirt.

There it was again. What was that under his shirt?

"Then, you thought I was dead, but found out I'm working for a mob boss, only to kill a Russian who killed my parents. You blame me for your kidnapping, and now you hate me. 'Cause it's all too much. Did I miss anything?"

"Is this supposed to be helping?" I tilted my head, squinting at him.

"I get it. I say it, and it sounds crazy. I wouldn't blame you if you want nothing to do with me, but I can't ..."

"You forgot that I thought I helped get you killed."

"What?"

I nodded. "The lone bottle from the roof. I wanted to make sure you and Paul were okay and nothing blew up, but then ... I screwed up and ..."

"That was you?"

"Worrying about you has been exhausting. By the way, what is this?" I lifted his shirt, and his rib was padded, it crinkled to my touch.

"Oh, that. It was Yak's bullet. I was lucky. Scratched the rib is all."

"The bullet intended for me?"

He pressed his lips together and nodded. He swallowed, and for the first time, his eyes said everything. He was exposed.

I shook my head in disbelief. I knew he was giving us a chance to get away, but I didn't know he *tried* to save me. No, he *did* save me. I thought when he took off in the boat he was saving his own skin, but he didn't get in the boat until Yak and Thick-Neck were on the ground with bullets in them. Did he dive to meet the bullet? It was all too incredible.

I took a deep breath as I looked at him. Our eyes talking, he leaned into mine. I closed them and felt his lips fire up my whole body. How could he do this to me? I even felt lightheaded and knew I had to pull away, clear my head. I remembered why it wouldn't work.

"But, you will live seven hours away."

"Well—"

I couldn't let him talk. I shook my head. "So much has happened. Too much drama. My head is spinning. I need time to process it all."

He nodded. "I get that."

I rubbed my face. "I'm sorry, I—"

"No, it's okay, Maggie. Time will do us both some good. I just didn't want to leave things the way we did yesterday."

I shook my head. "No, me neither. No matter what Luke, I ... I want the best for you." I couldn't hide the pain in my eyes, thinking of not being with him.

He reached to hold me, and I knew we were saying goodbye. It hurt like hell. Had I really thought I could fix this? In my dreams at night, there were no more doubts, no more obstacles, and no more miles between us. However, with my eyes open, they were still there, even though I had fought Fear and finally felt ready to love. Maybe Luke helped me get ready for someone new. I closed my eyes at the absurdity of the thought and squeezed him tighter. I didn't want to let go, but I didn't trust we could make it work either, and my heart just couldn't take watching him slowly slip away. That, I was sure, would kill me.

He released me as I eased up my grip on him. With a tender smile, he said, "Keep in touch. It would mean so much to Kayla." His voice was weak.

I hoped it would mean something to him, too, but I pressed my lips together and nodded. He backed away and pursed his lips with a pensive look, but this time his eyes didn't tell.

He walked away, and I didn't slam my fist. My throat tightened, and a burn in my stomach rose to my nose, as my eyes filled with tears. He was already in the SUV when I blinked, and the tears fell down my face. I stood motionless like the Italian statues. Could you really fall in love with someone in so little time? I had to know if this was real, and only time would tell.

Four Months Later

"Okay, sure. I'll be home after this test, and we can change and go then." I told Christina over my cell phone.

After hanging up, Shawn asked, "Got plans?"

He sat at the desk next to me in our Western Civilization class. He had stuck to his promise to be my friend, but he was too attentive at times, and I knew he still had feelings for me. We had settled into a nice routine and planned to take Western Civ II next semester. He was nice to me. He was there for me. Whenever I needed anything, I could count on him. Not to mention, he was pretty dang smart. He made history class sound like we were talking about people we knew.

I nodded as I pulled out my spiral to take notes and then faced him. "I've not been to an Italian restaurant since I got back, afraid I'd be disappointed. But we're going to Delucca's tonight."

"That's nice."

"You ready for the test?" I asked.

"Of course, no problem."

"How has that bump on your head made you smarter? That's so not fair."

He glared at me saying, "Really?"

"I know, I know." I sighed. "I am glad you're doing so well."

"I'm fine, Maggie. I'm not going to break." I thought he probably hoped the Florence Nightingale effect had happened, but since it didn't, he was trying to be tough. It was so easy to read Shawn. Not that I ever told him. There was something nice and simplistic in being able to.

"What is Paul going to do now?"

"He's going to take Eleana to Chicago, where her mother's family is located. After that, I guess he's done."

"It's not his?"

"No. It's Primo's," I said.

"He doesn't want to try to help her with it?"

I squinted, thinking of the possibility. "I don't think he's anywhere near ready to be a father, but no, too much has happened between them." I paused.

"I hope you don't feel that way about us."

"Shawn, no. You're my friend. I care about you. I always will."

"But ..."

"No. No, but."

"Okay. I'll take that. For now." He grinned.

"Give me another minute."

"I'll give you five, but we may lose our reservation," Christina yelled back down the hall to me.

I came out with one shoe on and carrying the other. "You know this whole reservation thing is so the opposite of Italy. They don't rush over there, and we are just going to the closest one, not the fancy one downtown."

"There is probably Italian food on every corner over there, but not so much here."

I rolled my eyes, slipped on my other heel, and stood up. "Okay, all ready. I'm so excited to be out and about. I haven't been dressed up since ..." Melancholy came over me, dropping my smile as I remembered—the yellow dress with my headband on. The dress I wore for three days. It had hung in my closet too bright with memories, so it was now folded in a drawer.

Christina interrupted my thoughts. "Don't go there, Maggie. Not tonight. Tonight is about new beginnings."

I nodded. "You're right." I plastered a fake smile across my face. "Do I look okay?" I smoothed out the deep green dress from Anthropologie.

"You look incredible. This is about not avoiding Italian memories but making new ones."

"It's a good idea."

Christina had convinced me that instead of avoiding everything that reminded me of the past summer, I needed new memories to go over them. She suggested I eat Italian, buy yellow clothes, go to the Irish pub downtown, and even take a taxi. These were things on our list, and she promised it would help.

I bought a pair of yellow pumps. I took a taxi to the Irish pub last weekend with her and two friends from school. I even pulled out my pink pearl to wear tonight. It had already had so many memories of my dad; after the summer, it held the entire journey of Italy and all my feelings for Luke. But, with my new-found life without Fear guiding every step, this too was something I could no longer avoid. So, with courage, I clasped it as Christina drove.

"I haven't seen that in a while. Any reason?"

I shook my head. "Just taking your advice to face everything and make new memories and not be afraid of the old ones."

"Now we're talking," she said.

We huddled together as we walked into Delucca's Italian restaurant, despite wearing coats. Giggling and talking, we made it inside, arriving for our reservation one minute late. The lady eyed us, and we stood straight, giving our names. She took two menus and walked away without a word. We followed like we were in trouble. As we passed the hostess stand and turned right into the main restaurant, I stopped.

Feeling as if I had been punched in the stomach, and pretty sure I was about to hurl, I didn't know if I was even breathing.

Christina stood to my side watching where my eyes had landed, immovable.

Luke sat at a table, it appeared, alone, with a huge smile. "Hello."

I walked up slowly. Realizing my mouth had turned dry, I swallowed. "What ... what are you doing here?"

"Well, there was this girl I had to check on. I just couldn't get her out of my mind."

I looked over at Christina. She put her hands out and shrugged as she turned and left, following the waitress to the table.

I walked up to his table and grabbed the chair, afraid if I didn't sit down, I would pass out. "I don't understand. How are you here?"

"This time, I took a plane." He smiled, appearing as if this was enjoyable.

I was about to lose it. "You know what I mean."

He laughed. "Are you okay? You look a little pale."

"Luke! Why are you here, in this restaurant, in this city, right now?"

After another small laugh, his face became serious. "I live here. Ever heard of Fort Jackson? And, I rather like Italian. In fact, I've liked it so much, I've eaten here almost every night for the past few weeks."

My breathing quickened. I thought about his words and what they meant. Had he been trying to run into me?

He interrupted my processing. "Have you had enough time to think? This is my ninth fettuccine alfredo, waiting for you."

Tears welled up in my eyes. I never thought this was possible. I never thought he would or could live here, that he would do that for me. I sniffed back my tears. "So how is your friend you came to check on doing?" My breathing was still so choppy.

He smiled. "Oh, she is more beautiful than my memory reminded me. And, I think she's happy to see me."

I laughed with more tears welling up. He stood up and came around the table. He grabbed me as I let the tears run down my face, smearing them into his chest. He pulled me away and kissed my cheek, kissing where the tears flowed, then I tasted the tears when his lips touched mine, and I laughed in between his gentle kisses.

"I love you, Maggie," he whispered.

I reached up to touch his face. "I was pretty sure when you walked away I loved you. Now—I know emphatically."

He kissed my lips again as we both inhaled.

We hugged, and that was when I noticed the patrons of the restaurant in awe of the romantic moment between us. I wiped my face. "We better sit down before we become the main show."

He looked around. "I think we already are."

"Oh, my gosh. I have to introduce you to someone." I got up and went to grab Christina, telling her to bring her drink and purse. We stopped by the podium and told the lady we would not be needing our table.

"This is my best friend, Christina," I told Luke. I turned to her and said, "And. this is Luke."

She reached across the table and shook his hand. "The infamous Luke." She nodded. "Very nice to finally meet you in person."

"You, too, and thanks for everything."

I sat down, looking at them both and their huge smiles. Luke grabbed my hand and rested his over it on the table. We both had inerasable smiles as Luke began telling her our story.

Time, I had learned could be my friend. I had processed the whirlwind of Rome, the hurricane in my heart, and the calm after it all had settled. Maybe we grew the most through the storms. I can only *try* to explain it. I sat and listened to Luke's story of us roll across my memories.

Why do the wrong choices make the right ones stand out? No one would understand. I wasn't sure I did myself. I went to the other side of the world, and messed up my life, only for it to make sense in the end.

1 John 4:18.

"There is no fear in love; but perfect love casts out all fear, because fear involves torment. But he who fears has not been made perfect in love."

Your opinion is important to the success of this book, consider leaving a review.

Don't miss out on Michelle's newest releases! Join her mailing list:
Michellegilliamauthor@gmail.com

Michelle would love you to connect on:

Twitter: twitter.com/gilliammichelle

Facebook: https://m.facebook.com/authormichellegilliam

Website: michellegilliam-writer.com

Pinterest: www.pinterest.com/Michellegillia

Acknowledgments

The journey to be a writer is not an easy one, certainly not one arbitrarily chosen. It chooses you. So many times you try to ignore the call that speaks to you late at night, first thing in the morning, or when you are driving in a car. Thus, it is with conviction, unable to escape what has become a part of me, I write—

I would like you to know Jesus saves us from ourselves, the desires within us, and the evil that tries to invade and consume. Choose love. First of all, I thank God for helping me, even when I didn't realize it was grace at work, and for all the times the creative spark leapt into my fingers and into my dreams at night. I love Him with my whole heart.

Thank you: David Gilliam—my wonderful husband—for everything; Mom and Dad, for giving me what I needed and helping me believe I could do it; Edward Francisco (English teacher and two-time Pulitzer nominee), I will never forget *Tour de force* on my paper. You gave me the confidence to keep learning. There are so many other teachers who encouraged me along the way–thank you with my whole heart. To my longest and best friend, Kelly Floyd, thank you for speaking into my life and for that birthday card! You dared me to dream, do it, and live it.

For all the ones that led the way and taught me about commas, plot, voice, translations, and so much more. Here, I acknowledge all you have done for me and tell you all: I cherish every moment. To my critique partners and editors: Alison Miller, Chris Connor, David Hicks, Sara Vose, Betty Southworth, Paul Garty, Susan Daugherty (Thanks for writing the back jacket!), and Jo Gilliam, thank you for being honest and for all your time. You made me better with your keen eyes and sharp minds. And, to my editor, Liv Radue, I hope we get to do many more of these. Thank you. I've learned so much.

<<<<>>>>

Made in the USA
Charleston, SC
22 October 2016